RIBBONS

J R Evans

Published and designed by Invasive Designs.

Please send inquiries to: invasivedesigns@gmail.com

Editing by Double Vision Editorial.

ISBN: 0692518126
ISBN-13: 978-0692518120

FOR BRANDON

Who keeps me on my toes by occasionally elbowing me
in the junk.

AND MELISSA

Who tries to stop him . . . sometimes.

1

Bethel's cart pulled to the right. She gave it a shove to get it back on course and continued shuffling down the hall. The cart had tormented her for months when she'd first started working here, but now she barely noticed it. Her shoves and shuffles were on autopilot, much like the rest of her job. The hotel was new, one of the newest in Las Vegas, which didn't make it the best but did make it popular. The cart, on the other hand, had been around awhile. Bethel suspected it was older than any of the hotels on the Strip. She and the cart had that in common. At least she didn't look her age.

Bethel's cleaning cart shuffle was accompanied by an incessant bass rhythm coming from the other side of the door marked Vista View Suite. It was hard not to fall into step.

Whump! Whump! Wha. Wha.
Shove. Shuffle. Shuffle. Shuffle.
Whump! Whump! Wha. Wha.
Shove. Shuffle. Shuffle. Shuffle.

She wasn't dressed for dancing. Her uniform fit well, of course—she had tailored it herself—but the prim style, matched with Bethel's full figure, made her feel more matronly than elegant. However—

Whump! Whump! Wha. Wha.

—wasn't a very elegant tune anyway.

One final shove put the cart in front of the door. She gave three sharp knocks and raised her voice in a way that might be heard above the music but still sounded polite. "Housekeeping!"

She waited. Bethel knew the room was registered to a Mr. Darin Dunn, and apparently that was a big deal, especially if your major source of news was found on a rack next to Kit Kats and Life Savers in the grocery store check-out line. With high-profile guests like Mr. Dunn, she was instructed not to barge right in after a quick knock on the door.

Whump! Whump! Wha. Wha.

She sighed and rested one elbow on the handle of her cart. "You called guest services? Can you please come to the door, sir?"

Whump! Whump!

She could just barely hear, "I really can't," between beats. It sounded distant, maybe from some other room off the entrance.

Wha. Wha.

She used her polite shout again. "I'm going to use my key and come in now."

"Looking forward to it." The reply didn't sound too sincere.

Bethel muttered under her breath as she slid her key card through the slot. "Here we go . . ."

Bethel had found that when people described a disaster as being "of biblical proportions," they were usually just trying to sound witty, or maybe trying to scare people by buddying up with the Bible. In Bethel's case, she had personally witnessed nine disasters of biblical proportions.

She could say that because those disasters were actually retold in one of the books of the Bible. She had seen one other, just outside the city of Arrapha in what was then called the Guti Kingdom. But the guy—the prophet, or survivor, or whatever—who had recorded it hadn't been a very good writer, and his book hadn't made it into the Old Testament. So technically, that one didn't count.

The VISTA VIEW SUITE wasn't a disaster of biblical proportions, but it was trying to be.

She noticed the bras first. They were spinning like festive streamers from the blades of the rotating ceiling fan. All the rooms in the hotel had air-conditioning, of course, but a ceiling fan added a touch of class. Clearly that wasn't being appreciated here. The bras didn't even match, and Bethel assumed they had probably been contributed by party guests who had, thankfully, passed out somewhere else. From the looks of it, the bras didn't really match the theme of the party, either.

No less than five ice sculptures decorated the room. Each was in a similar state of decay. The one nearest to Bethel must have started out as a triumphant-looking Viking, wearing nothing but his helmet, having sex with a winged Valkyrie. Doggy-style. Now, after hours of wasting away one drop at a time, it looked more like a garden gnome tackling a startled pigeon.

A banner strung above the wet bar proclaimed, IT'S A SNOW DAY!!! Skis leaned in one corner of the room next to a pair of crisscrossed snowshoes nailed to the wall. An inflatable snowman gave a lopsided smile behind a glass coffee table covered in white streaks and smudges. Next to one streak was a rolled up dollar bill that looked like it had been dipped in powdered sugar.

The whole thing seemed vaguely disappointing, like

decorations at a bad prom.

Whump! Whump! Wha. Wha.

Movement caught her eye, but it was just the wall-sized TV across the room. It was hard to make out which of the On Demand titles was playing due to the spiderweb crack in the screen. Bodies collided in a scramble of tan lines and razor burns. If she had to guess, it was probably *Porn Wives of LA 3*.

That's when she saw somebody lying facedown on the couch in front of the broken porn screen. Somebody naked.

Whump! Whump!

Bethel jabbed a button on a wall panel without looking. The music cut off mid-*wha*.

"Hello?" said Bethel.

The woman raised her head off the couch. It looked like it took tremendous effort. She appeared both dazed and pouty. Even bleary-eyed, she was pulling off "sexy", except for the drop of dried blood peeking out of one nostril.

She managed a "Mmm-uh?"

Bethel realized then that the woman wasn't completely naked. She was wearing big fluffy white earmuffs. The kind that looked warm but were more for show during a day on the slopes. The only powder this woman had seen last night was still on her upper lip.

"Don't mind her. She's useless," a voice called out from behind a closed door across the room.

Bethel had been in there plenty of times. It was the master bedroom. She picked her way across the living area toward the door. On her way, she nudged bottles and glasses aside with her feet, noting which ones were broken and where to spray extra carpet cleaner.

She opened the door. Dimmed lights just barely illuminated the master bedroom. Even so, she could tell that this room had been spared the brunt of the damage from the night before. Satin lumps crowded the bed, and she could make out the shape of somebody sitting up against the headboard.

She jabbed a finger at another wall panel. This time, the Strip appeared, as if by magic, as the curtain slats twisted and then retracted on their own. The man in the bed tried to cover his eyes with his hands when the bright light hit him. He couldn't, though. They were handcuffed to the headboard. Instead, he squeezed his eyes shut with a wince and then slowly pried them open. When he smiled, Bethel finally recognized him.

"Uh, hello. Thanks for—" was all he got out.

"Mr. Dunn, I am not cleaning up your drugs!" Bethel's polite shout was gone. It was replaced by something more scolding.

"There's . . . leftovers?" he asked.

One of the lumps under the satin sheet mumbled something that sounded like, "Mmaphetic!"

"I know, right?" agreed Mr. Dunn.

He was good-looking, she supposed. The sheet covered him from the waist down, but it was clear he was naked. He didn't seem embarrassed at all. His smile was more confident than apologetic. Like, *Look what I got myself into this time*. The other lump under the sheet was most likely a woman if the feet sticking out at the end of the bed were any indication. Thanks to the harsh light from the window, Bethel could tell that the woman's head was buried in Mr. Dunn's crotch. Apparently, she was not coming up for air.

Bethel pointed sharply down at the woman-lump. "What the hell is that?"

Mr. Dunn raised an eyebrow dramatically, making up for the fact that he couldn't gesture with his hands. "Um . . .

Melanie?"

"Muhlina," the lump corrected him.

"Oh right. Melinda," he said.

Bethel crossed her arms and raised her own eyebrow. "And how come Melinda couldn't come to the door? Is she handcuffed, too?"

"Oh no. Thank God, no." Mr. Dunn pointed his chin down toward the edge of the sheet where Melinda was holding out a cell phone. "She was actually able to reach her cell phone and call the front desk. She's flexible."

"So her business was too pressing to unlock you?" Bethel asked.

"No, no," he said. "You may find this a bit shocking but . . . Melinda's a hooker."

"Ephcort," stated Melinda.

Mr. Dunn shook his head. His expression made it seem like he was trying to be a better person, but kept failing. "Sorry. Escort."

Bethel rolled her eyes. She didn't even try to stop herself. "Shocking."

"So, anyway, she was doing her . . . thing. And she has this tongue ring," he began.

Bethel's eyes narrowed.

Mr. Dunn pointed down toward his crotch from his restraints. "It turns out I had also put a ring on . . ." He obviously wanted her to make the mental leap on her own, but when she didn't react, he added, "They got caught."

She knew what was next. She knew what was expected of her. But, dammit, she just wasn't in the mood. She lost her shit. "Oh! Hell! No!"

"Yeah. She tried to feel around to unhook us but—"

"Um oo cloph oo it," Melinda tried to explain.

Mr. Dunn translated. "She's too close to it."

Bethel pressed her palms against her eyes. She backed off when she started seeing white starbursts. She made a sound that, she knew, sounded very much like a death rattle.

Mr. Dunn flashed a winning smile. It was lost on her. "What's your name?"

"Bethel."

"Bethel, don't worry." He gave a reassuring nod. "It's limp."

"I wasn't worried," Bethel assured him.

"Good. Just don't do anything sexy."

She didn't.

■ ■ ■

And she didn't start cleaning the room right away, either. She figured she deserved a break. She would have taken a cigarette break, but these days smoking made her stand out more than blend in. Her job, her *real* job, was all about blending in. Or more precisely, it was all about being ignored. She was so good at being ignored that she had to clear her throat twice before people noticed her enough to move out of the way to let her on the elevator. At least she didn't have to fight her way forward to push a button; everyone was already heading down to the casino.

Bethel's real job was simply to *watch and be wakeful*. It was usually up to her to decide what that meant. When she had first been sent down to walk among the sons of God, it had been easier to know what to do and what not to. That was back when people lived in mudbrick huts and used giant standing stones to track the seasons. She had helped people see the divine truth all around them—sometimes with a hug, sometimes with a fist. Now things were always so complex. Everything seemed to have a justification. It was like there was no good or evil anymore. She hated that. Instead of feeling righteous, she usually just felt confused and a little useless. The Assyrians had a name for those who did what she did, *Iyrin*. She preferred the Slavic word, *Grigori*. It was a thankless job.

She didn't get lonely exactly—familiarity bred contempt, and she was familiar with everybody—but she did feel the need to vent from time to time. This was one of those times, so she was happy she had a coworker to talk shop with. She wound her way through the slot machines and tables until she found Sam.

He was dealing cards at a blackjack table. It wasn't his only job. When you didn't sleep, you had to find something to pass the time. Sam also managed a club, drove a taxi, and, when he was feeling particularly bored, handed out stripper cards on the street corner down by the Tropicana. He liked dealing with people face-to-face. Bethel was content cleaning up after them and going through their dirty laundry.

Sam pulled off his company vest well. Hair slicked back and white at the temples, he was a compromise somewhere between smarmy and sophisticated. His mustache hid most of his sarcastic grin that never quite made it to a real smile. The crowd at the table leaned in closer as he flipped over his facedown card. Bethel knew this was his favorite part.

He had a three and a king.

"Winner," he started, his voice low.

The crowd held its breath. There were a lot of chips on the table. He flipped over a two.

"Winner," a little louder now, though everyone was silent.

He tapped the card at the top of the deck and snapped it down onto the felt. A six.

"Chicken dinner!" he finished, the mock surprise in his

voice barely contained.

The crowd made lots of angry sounds. Most of them left, gulping down their free booze first. He didn't get any tips. At least it freed up a stool for Bethel. She plopped down and eyed Sam, arms crossed over her apron.

"What?" he asked, not really trying to sound innocent.

"I didn't say anything," she said.

"Let me guess, then." Sam's hands seemed to sort the scattered chips in front of him on their own. "Somebody left you a big tip because they were so impressed with the great job you did cleaning up the hooker juice in the shower, and you were feeling so good about yourself that you decided to come down here to have a drink and maybe double your money?"

"No . . . Ass." She wasn't in the mood for his shit, but then again, what did she expect from Sam? "Okay, kinda close to that. And yes, I will be drinking."

The couple still sitting at the table was obviously a *couple*. They leaned in close to each other, mourning their lack of chips. The man's arm was casually draped across the woman's shoulders as he tipped back his beer. She rested her head on his chest and stirred her cocktail with the world's tiniest straw. And, of course, they were ignoring Bethel. So she decided to unload on Sam.

"Sam, I have *had* it with this place."

"So go next door. I'm sure they could use somebody with your particular blend of class and charm." He started to shuffle the deck. "And cleaning skills."

Bethel gestured around the glaring lights and chirping slot machines. "I mean Vegas. I'm done with it."

"Bad day, I take it?" he asked.

"Not particularly," she said. "That's the problem. They all seem to be equally crap."

Sam finished shuffling. "So you're just gonna pack up shop?"

The couple was, apparently, ready to lose the rest of their chips and were looking at Sam expectantly. The guy tried to flip a chip along the back of his knuckles to emphasize the point. It made it past one knuckle and then dropped onto the table with a muffled *thunk*. Bethel gave him a sideways glance.

"I don't think I'm doing much good here," Bethel said. "It's the same story over and over again. There was a time when people came here to flirt with sin. Now they want to jump straight into bed with it. No foreplay."

"It's no Sodom or Gomorrah," said Sam.

The couple seemed confused now.

"I don't know. I think they're lost before they even arrive." Bethel pointed at the couple. "Like these two."

The couple finally noticed her.

Bethel stared at them and tilted her head from side to side as if she were trying to decide what flavor milkshake she wanted. She pointed at the guy and leaned toward him. He gave her a half smile as he looked sideways at the woman next to him, then he decided to play along and leaned forward himself. Bethel whispered something to him in a language that was made up more of tremors and heartbeats than of syllables and words. It was a language that existed before there was much to talk about. A time before things had names. Most things, anyway.

The rough translation was, *Tell me true*.

Bethel's gaze froze the man in place like a bug stuck to board with a straight pin. If you were close enough, you might have seen Bethel's eyes jittering in their sockets and her pupils turning the faintest bit blue. Those eyes could see his heart and the things hidden deep inside.

She spoke again, this time using real words. They came out in short, jagged bursts. "They're here on their honeymoon . . . He's been cheating on her . . . typical . . . boring . . . it's with a guy . . . so that's something . . . Didn't want to marry her . . . She said she was pregnant . . . He thinks she lied about that, though . . . stuck with her anyway . . . Her family has money . . . He lost his job over a month ago."

Sam snorted. "Whoa! Honeymoon's over, I guess." It was like he couldn't *not* be a smart-ass.

Bethel squeezed her eyes shut and then blinked several times, as if she were trying to get rid of a stray eyelash. "I bet it's not just him."

"What? She's got a deep dark secret, too?" Sam shrugged. "So what? Everybody does."

The man still had not blinked. He looked like he was about to say something and then just went back to staring at Bethel. The woman took a long sip from her drink while her eyes slowly rolled from her husband over to Bethel.

"If there's a flicker of love in her . . . *love*, not lust, not desperation . . . If that flicker is there, I'll stop my rant and go back to cleaning toilets."

Sam turned to the woman. "All right, let's see."

The woman dropped her straw. "Is this, like, a magic trick or something? Are we part of a show?"

Sam gently took her chin. He turned her face to look her in the eyes. Her cocktail started to tip forward, threatening to cover the blackjack table with ice and paper umbrellas. Instead of jittery eyes and magic words, he simply leaned forward and kissed her lightly on the lips. This had a similar effect, however. The woman froze in place. Her eyes rolled back a little, and her lips parted slightly as if they were still locked with Sam's.

He leaned away from her, his eyes closed. He spoke as if trying to remember the details of something he hadn't thought about in a long time. "She really was pregnant. She stopped taking her pills. She told him she lost the baby after they announced their engagement. But . . ." Sam's brow furrowed, and he turned his head slightly. "That was a lie. She didn't cry at the clinic. She went to look at wedding invitations that same day. She thinks she can do better, but he's easy to control."

The man's eyes started to drift away from Bethel. "Baby?"

When Sam opened his eyes, his half grin returned almost immediately. "Looks like those toilets will have to wait."

Bethel shook her head. "This is bullshit! Wars used to be fought over love, Sam. Epic. Fucking. Battles!"

Sam didn't seem sure how to respond. "I'm . . . sorry?"

The couple was consciously not looking at each other. Instead, they both stared at the pathetic pile of chips in front of them. Sam's grin faltered.

"Hey, dumb-asses! You won!" Sam shoved a pile of chips their way. "Go to a buffet, catch a show, enjoy each other's . . . sex parts. Continue the circle of life." Then Sam took pity on them. He touched each of their hands. "You don't need to think about this." It wasn't a suggestion. It was a command. The couple instantly cheered up.

"Yeah, that's how you do it!" The guy did an honest to God fist pump. Then he added, "Boom!"

The woman clapped her hands. "Yay! Chips!"

Bethel bowed her head and looked down at her hands. The couple was ignoring her again. She glanced at Sam without raising her head. "I'm done watching, Sam."

"The Grigori *watch*," said Sam. "That's what we do."

"What good has it done?"

"That's not for us to say."

"Nobody has said anything lately," she said. "The things I've seen should have pissed off *somebody*. We should have seen some kind of apocalyptic wrist-slap by now. But there haven't been any plagues. No pillars of fire. No wives turned into salt. Just silence."

"True," said Sam. "But that's not really in our job description. At least not anymore."

"Neither is cleaning toilets."

"Okay. So what do you want to do about it? Retire?"

Bethel considered this for a few seconds. But then she sighed. "No. I wouldn't know how."

"So have that drink," said Sam. "Hell, have two."

"Oh, you can bet I'll do that," said Bethel.

■ ■ ■

She was on her third drink when she had an idea. It was a pretty bad idea, but one that wouldn't be ignored.

2

Quentin Bradley James didn't like his last name. Or rather, he didn't like the history it represented. He asked most people to call him Quentin, but his friends and employees called him Uncle Quent. It started off as one of those ironic nicknames that people used to make something seem less intimidating—like calling a big guy Tiny or naming your assault rifle Vera. Most days he felt like the person he used to be was just underneath his skin, and if he didn't keep it in check, it might come bursting out in fits and jerks. He had to work hard to relax around people.   His nickname stuck, but it didn't help much.

Uncle Quent's place of business wasn't far from the Strip. He ran it out of an old Victorian. Actually, there were no real "old Victorians" in Las Vegas. He knew that this one was actually built in the thirties, long before he'd taken over. It hadn't been built out of some sense of nostalgia. No, it had started out as a business. A funeral home, in fact.

Back then, the Hoover Dam had been called the Boulder Dam, and building it had brought a lot of people to the area. It had also killed a lot of people. The work had been dangerous and the living conditions just as lethal. But jobs were scarce and the company store was always fully stocked. It had seemed better than starving in the Dust Bowl. It wasn't really, but at least it *seemed* that way. A classy funeral home added to the illusion.

Uncle Quent's business was a little different. He wouldn't call it classy, but it still had a *sense* of class. As did his employees.

Erica sat across from him in his office. She wore an innocent-looking polka-dot dress complete with an overly large bow at the waist. A black ribbon choker accented her long neck. Uncle Quent noticed that the polka dots were actually skulls.

"You know you have to ask," he said. He hated that he sounded so condescending.

Erica smiled but didn't meet his eyes. "I don't like asking."

"That's why you have to," he said.

She sighed. "Fine. Can—" She stopped and then started again. "Can I please have two?"

"Good. Last week it was three. Now two. Maybe soon it will be down to one."

"Yeah, maybe."

He slid the lid off a cardboard box. Inside were fifty individual paper compartments. Each held a large brass bullet. He plucked out two and stood them up on their flat ends. They looked right at home on his antique desk, like something out of an old Western. Erica reached forward and picked them up.

"I'm not a professional, you know," Uncle Quent told her. "A clinic could help you better."

"You're the only one I trust," she said. "The only one who gives a fuck. Even when I don't." She dropped the bullets into her clutch. "Plus, you don't offer health insurance."

Uncle Quent grunted. "You're hard to insure."

"It's my clients who need the insurance."

Uncle Quent liked Erica. Most people who met her liked her . . . for about half an hour. That was how long it usually took for her to find a flaw in you that she could expose. It came naturally to her, and she probably wasn't even aware that she was doing it half the time. It was like finding a hairline crack in a shell and then picking at it until it broke and she could get at the nut beneath. He couldn't blame her. It *was* part of her job. Uncle Quent was made of flaws, though, and nobody picked at them as much as he did himself.

Erica stood. "Are you coming down? Christy was looking for you. I think she left you some dinner in the fridge."

"Is it green?" he asked. "I'm not going down if it's green."

"Next time, I'll smuggle you in a cheeseburger. Everybody has their supplier, right?"

"Yeah. I guess so."

Erica turned to go but then paused at the door. "Thanks."

She meant well, he supposed, but it made him feel like an asshole.

"No need," he said. But she was already gone.

Uncle Quent rubbed his palms against his forehead. Blue ink decorated each arm. His tattoos had faded enough so that they all kind of blended together if you didn't look too closely. If you did take the time to focus on them, they told a tale of punishment and excess, punctuated by demons both real and imaginary. To Uncle Quent they were more like battle scars than artwork.

One of his tattoos was a heart pierced through by three spears. In the center of that heart was a symbol branded into his skin. The symbol was made up of a sun, a moon, a cross, and fire. The tattoo was the beginning of his story. It was when he'd taken control of his life. The brand had been there first, though. He hadn't put it there. The same symbol was burned into one of the beams in the ceiling above. He hadn't put that one there, either. It had already been there when he'd moved in.

He didn't want to think about that right now. It made him think about his family, and his family made him think about drinking. Instead, he spun the chair around to face the window and closed his eyes. He let them rest for a couple of minutes before he figured he'd better head downstairs and start checking on things. Customers would be arriving soon, and he still had to figure out a way to discreetly get rid of the green stuff waiting for him in the fridge.

When he opened his eyes, he saw Bethel reflected in the glass, sitting behind him. He wasn't happy to see her. He spun the chair back around to face the desk. "Bethel."

She looked like she'd come straight from work. She always looked like that. He knew her outfit hadn't changed in years, except for the hotel logo on the nametag. He also knew that cleaning hotel rooms wasn't her real job.

Bethel tried to break the ice. "That was Erica, right? How's she doing?"

"Better." He bent over to put the cardboard box into one of the desk drawers. "Still wants to be famous. And she practices at it too damn much."

"Yeah," she said. "We're friends online. Though I'm sure she doesn't know it."

"I didn't know you went in for that sort of thing."

"Are you kidding? It makes my job a whole lot easier."

Uncle Quent straightened and then leaned back into his chair. "You're here. Why?"

She gestured to the room around them. "It's time for it to change hands."

His stomach dropped, and he wished he had gone downstairs with Erica.

"When?" he asked.

"Now."

"*Now* now?"

Bethel reached forward and gently touched one of his clenched fists. "It's better if it's now."

To his surprise, Uncle Quent didn't want to fly into a rage. Instead, he felt sad. Sad and tired and old. "But they need me."

"We'll send help." She leaned in closer to him. "And we'll keep it in the family."

Uncle Quent stiffened. "Who?"

"Matt."

He was confused. And then kind of amused. "Matt? Are you sure he's up for this? He's kinda soft."

Bethel gave a tiny smile. "Were you up for it when I came to you?"

Uncle Quent sighed and then reached down to another desk drawer. His hand came up with a bottle of whiskey and some glasses. "No."

Bethel watched him fill the glasses. "We have a trial for him . . . and others."

Uncle Quent touched his glass to his lips. "Mm-hmm."

"This house will bring them together. With you here, we already know the outcome."

Bethel took her glass but didn't drink. She stared into the amber liquid and then back up at Quent.

His empty glass tapped the table, and he poured again. "I had a good run. The past ten years, anyway. I owe those to you."

"Nine. But who's counting?" She swirled her drink. "You did a lot of good."

"I had to. Had to make up for old times." He reached forward and grabbed a picture frame from the corner of his desk.

Bethel stood and walked around to stand next to Uncle Quent. He kept his eyes focused on the picture.

"Not my heart, okay? I don't want people to say I had a weak heart." He finished his drink and carefully placed his glass back on the desk. His hand barely shook.

"Sure," Bethel whispered into his ear. "It was strong."

Then she whispered something else, this time in a language older than words. It seemed familiar, but it made no sense. Fragments of memories tumbled through his mind. Sensations from his youth. Things he forgot he *could* feel. Invincibility as he ran through a grassy field. Wonder pouring into his mind as he stared up at a sky full of stars. Laughter beyond his control bubbling up from his belly. The certain knowledge that he could be anything he wanted if only he walked down the right path.

There was a moment of vague disappointment.

Then nothing.

3

Matt was tied to a chair. The chair had come with the apartment like most of the other furniture. He was young and didn't have anybody to impress yet, so he hadn't really thought about the chairs at all. Now he thought the chairs in his dining nook were ugly and uncomfortable. And the apartment wasn't quaint or charming. It was a dump. Most of the time Matt felt right at home. Not today. Today was special. Today, he had a guest.

"Uh, Thug Guy?" Matt's guest hadn't offered his name yet.

There was no answer.

Matt twisted his neck to try to see what Thug Guy was doing. So far he had been all business. Five minutes ago Matt had been enjoying lunch. Then he'd made the mistake of answering a knock at the door. There hadn't been any small talk, just a quick jab to the gut. That had been all it took to make Matt forget how to breathe. By the time he had figured it out again, Thug Guy had him zip-tied to one of those ugly, uncomfortable chairs. Now he could see Thug Guy rummaging through the cupboards in his kitchen.

Thug Guy was big but not particularly fit. His family

probably came from Eastern Europe or maybe Russia—Matt wasn't too good with geography. He wore a collarless dress shirt with the sleeves rolled up, and his suspenders looked like they were straining against his shoulders. He turned to look at Matt with a triumphant grin.

"You're not gonna get all freaky are you?" Matt asked. "Like, sex-freaky?"

He looked over at Thug Guy and had time to notice the black newsboy cap pulled low on his head. It was oddly accented with some kind of bird skull. Then Thug Guy was right next to him, and all Matt could focus on was the blender that dropped onto the table in front of him. *Thunk.*

Matt instinctively pulled away from the blender. "So that's a *no* then?"

Thug Guy finally spoke. He had a thick accent. "This is good one. Do you make the smoothies?"

Matt didn't want to answer that.

"Hmm . . ." Thug Guy frowned. He looked from the blender cord to the wall socket. "Do you have extension cord?"

"No?" Matt tried.

Thug Guy tilted his head and arched an eyebrow. Then he nodded to himself as if he finally remembered where he'd left his car keys. He went into the living room just a few steps away. He talked over his shoulder as he eyed Matt's entertainment center.

"You know, you stole much money. You should have better place to live."

"Borrowed," Matt corrected. "I borrowed much money. And I intend on paying it back. Soon . . . ish."

"Well, until then, is stolen."

Matt was actually relieved. A little, anyway. At least now he knew who had sent today's houseguest. Matt was relatively new to Reno, but to get an apartment of your own there, even a crappy one, you needed a few basics: identification of some sort, relatively good credit, and money. Matt hadn't had any of those things when he'd arrived.

He could have tried to rent a room somewhere. Then he would have just needed money and a convincing lie. But privacy was important to Matt. He wanted a fresh start. Mainly because he was being hunted. Well, he was *pretty* sure he was being hunted anyway. His family wasn't going to give up on him that easily.

Thug Guy swept aside a couple of movie cases and a little pyramid made out of diet cola cans. He did this with two quick flicks of his hand like he was dusting away crumbs or lint. He made enough room to peek behind the TV.

"Oh! Here we go. It is . . . uh . . . rat's nest . . . back here." English may not have been Thug Guy's first language. "Too many cables. Is fire hazard."

He reached behind the TV and came up with a power strip. Every plug was filled. Matt didn't even think he had that many things to plug in. Thug Guy gave it a hard yank. The power strip came free. Then the TV hit the floor with an unmistakable *crack*.

"Dude! I just got that!" Matt blurted it out before he could stop himself.

"Maybe is not best thing to tell me right now?"

When Matt had moved into the apartment, he had unpacked in about fifteen minutes. He'd only had a duffel bag and a tiny suitcase with wheels, the kind that can fit above your seat on an airplane. One bag held his clothes; the other held everything he wanted to remember from his past. The TV *was* a new purchase but not one of many. He had actually bought it using a credit plan through the electronics store. His new identity had *great* credit. But after paying for that identity and a few months' rent, his loan money was pretty much gone.

Matt clenched his teeth when the blender blades started spinning. He never liked that whizzing sound. It reminded him of the dentist. He tried to avoid the dentist, and he had only ever used the blender once.

"What's going in there? Not my hands, right? I need my hands or I can't get your money back." Matt couldn't stop talking. "I need my feet, too."

"You don't need . . . uh . . . junk?" Thug Guy said.

Matt looked down at his crotch. "I need my junk." He reconsidered. "Okay, take a foot. Or my hand."

Thug Guy had zip-tied Matt at the elbows so his forearms were still free. Matt thought to himself and made a fist with his left hand. He pumped it back and forth a few times. He was right-handed for most things, but late at night in front of his laptop, he needed his left hand free. He nodded and clarified. "Wait, take my *right* hand."

Thug Guy responded by dropping two objects onto the table, one on either side of the blender. The first was a comic book. It had been on display next to the TV. *Sandman*, issue one. The cover was in perfect condition except for the silver pen mark where the author scribbled his name. The author had also put a strange little doodle underneath his signature that looked like some kind of ancient symbol. The second object was a tiny alien encased in plastic. Boba Fett looked up at him from a slightly yellowed blister pack. This was the proud Boba Fett from *The Empire Strikes Back*, not the comic relief version from *Return of the Jedi*.

"Choose."

Matt stiffened. "Oh! Hardball!"

Thug Guy picked up the blister pack and read the package carefully. He was mouthing the words to himself. Then he asked, "What is Bo . . . ba . . . Fett?"

Matt didn't realize he was holding his breath until he let it out to answer. "Well, he's a bounty hunter. Technically he's a clone from—"

Then Thug Guy peeled open the pack to get a closer look.

Matt gave a high-pitched screech and almost tipped himself over. "That was mint!" He let out a sigh and hung his head in despair. "Fine, do that one. Worthless *now*."

Sandman issue one disappeared amid frantic whirring sounds and a poof of confetti.

Matt lifted his head. His world didn't make sense anymore. "But . . . but Neil Gaiman signed that. I had a fauxhawk back then. He said he liked it."

"I don't know what that means, but this is torture." Thug Guy spoke slowly like he was talking to a child. "I am torturing you."

The doorbell rang. Matt knew this must be a dream. Nobody *actually* got saved by the bell.

Thug Guy stood up and then stopped to point a deadly looking finger at Matt. "Quiet please. Or I make another smoothie."

He continued toward the door. As he walked, he reached around to the small of his back and pulled out a knife that had been clipped to the inside of his belt. The knife was small, almost stubby, and it had a hook at the tip. He held it hidden behind the door as he pulled it open. He only opened the door a few inches, so Matt couldn't see who was there, but the voice he heard was chipper and confident.

"Good afternoon. I'm looking for Matt?"

"Busy," said Thug Guy.

"I just need him to sign for this real quick."

"I can sign. Is no problem." Thug Guy's grip tightened on the knife.

A hand reached out and touched Thug Guy's shoulder. Thug Guy turned his head a fraction of an inch to look at it, and his whole body coiled. Matt was pretty sure that was going to be the end of that hand. Then Matt's ears popped, and he couldn't quite make out what the owner of the hand said next, but Thug Guy's body relaxed almost at once. Thug Guy took a pen that was offered to him and signed something on a clipboard.

"Make sure Matt gets that letter." The voice sounded very serious, and Matt thought about screaming for help. Then Matt looked at the knife again.

"I will."

"Okeydokey! Have a good day!"

The door closed, and Thug Guy turned toward Matt. He looked a little confused as he stared at the envelope in his hand. He shook his head and blinked his eyes like he was trying to wake himself up. Matt noticed how blue his eyes were—too blue.

"Registered mail. Must be urgent. I will read for you." His voice sounded quieter than before. "It is from your Uncle Quentin."

"Really?" Matt's hands were tingling. The zip ties were starting to cut into his arms.

"Really."

Thug Guy took a seat next to Matt, knife still in hand. He slid the blade under the flap of the envelope and gave a gentle pull. The paper cut without a sound. He looked at the knife, blew on it, and put it away. Then he pulled a single folded piece of paper out of the envelope. Matt couldn't quite read it, but he could tell it was printed or typed rather than handwritten.

Thug Guy started to read slowly and carefully. "*Matt . . .* that is you," Thug Guy clarified. "*You know I am not one for . . .* uh *. . . verse? But read this and take it to heart. He who brings trouble on his family will inherit only wind, and the fool will be servant to the wise.* That is quote. *Proverbs, eleven twenty-nine.*" Thug Guy looked up at Matt briefly and then back down at the letter. "Then he says, *Come to my place in Las Vegas. We need to discuss your future. Our fate and fortune are . . .* uh *. . . intertwined.*"

Thug Guy set down the letter. It didn't look like it was signed but he saw his uncle's name and address at the bottom.

Thug Guy pursed his lips. "What does this mean?"

"I don't know. He doesn't talk like that." Matt thought for a second. "I don't *think* he does anyway. It's been awhile."

Thug Guy peered into the envelope while he absently traced a finger over the skull on his cap. Empty.

"In fact, I'm not sure how he even got this address." Matt was speaking more to himself now.

"Fortune?"

Matt grinned. "Well I guess I'll have to go find out."

Matt was starting to feel like himself again so he added, "Unless you want to pull out my salad shooter and play with that for a while?"

"Ha-ha. Funny guy." Thug Guy didn't laugh, though. Instead, his fist shot out.

Matt's head snapped back, and a little arc of blood splattered onto the letter.

4

Foster adjusted his glasses and watched Candice work. The glasses always seemed to sit at an odd angle on his nose. He wasn't sure if the nose pads needed adjusting or if his ears were just crooked. The glasses were the same ones they issued him in prison, and he was kind of embarrassed to go in to ask for an adjustment at the local Lens Hut. They might ask him where he'd gotten them.

Candice looked like an angel. Meaning she was actually wearing angel wings. They were the kind you might find at a Halloween costume shop. She wasn't wearing much else. Her white lace bra was puddled on the ground at the back of the stage, lost in the darkness now. She had shot it back there like a rubber band. Green bills had fluttered onto that stage like falling leaves. Now she was working up to her big finale. She turned her back to the audience and slowly bent over. Just as slowly, she pulled her thong over her hips, down her thighs, and around her ankles. Then she straightened and grabbed the pole, one arm low, one high. With a kick, she flipped herself upside down so that she faced the crowd. She paused, letting the crowd wonder what came next. Then her legs spread apart to match her wings.

To Foster's surprise, he wasn't hard. Not even a little. He had seen the act many times before. He was more into watching the crowd. There was a rhythm to it, aside from the driving beat coming through the sound system. When Candice bent over, the crowd leaned in. When she kicked, they all leaned back. When she slid off the pole, hands flew out and more bills fluttered down. She was a conductor.

The lights dimmed and Candice wrapped a white satin robe around herself. The next dancer was already heading to the stage. A couple of guys noticed Foster in his janitor's jumpsuit. They were obviously drunk, but it probably didn't matter. They were cruel and horny and needed some kind of release.

One of them had a goatee that was dyed blond. "Oh man, look at this guy. I bet he has to polish the pole every night."

The second guy covered his mouth, but it didn't do much to hide his snorting laugh. Between grunts, he managed to add, "All three inches of it."

It was the obvious joke to make. Foster pretended not to notice and pushed his cart forward. Stuff like that really bothered him. He knew it shouldn't, but it always did. Trying not to think about it just made him think about it more. Sometimes, a rage built up in him out of nowhere. Sometimes he got so depressed that he took sleeping pills just to make the day end earlier. He was floundering between the two when Candice stopped in front of him.

"Hey, Foster." Her smile made him feel like he was part of something. Not much, but something.

"Oh, hey, Candice. Nice show." He meant it. He knew she practiced to get it right.

She must have seen Mr. Goatee and Mr. Snort watching. They were in the back row, which meant they didn't tip much. She touched Foster's arm and leaned in to give him a kiss on the cheek. He supposed she meant well, but that only made him feel more uncomfortable. She slowly and deliberately gave the two in the back row the middle finger. Which probably only made them more excited. Then she turned to head backstage.

As she left she added, "Watch out for the boss."

Foster pushed his cart forward again, but his eyes followed Candice as she disappeared behind the stage. Then a hand grabbed his cart.

"Yeah, watch out for the boss!" It was the boss.

Foster stopped short. His boss always looked overdressed for the Tail Spin. His suits were too formal, and the white at his temples made him look more distinguished than lecherous. He might look right at home dealing cards at a casino. He'd told his employees to call him Sam, but Foster always called him sir.

"Sorry, sir!"

Sam gave him an intent look, as though he was considering something. Then he raised his eyebrows and tilted his head with a smile. "Foster, I have an important task for you. It's going to require all your limited concentration. I know you've been working on your mopping skills?"

"Yes, sir."

Sam held out two hands and rotated them one after another like he was scrubbing something. "Wax on, wax off?"

"Huh?" The reference was lost on Foster.

"Somebody just waxed off all over one of the stalls in the bathroom."

"Men's room?"

"Nope, you're in luck. Women's room. But cum's still cum." Sam pulled Foster in close, as if he was about to trust him with a secret. "Don't forget to check the ceiling."

While Foster was still processing that, Sam left him to his work and followed Candice to the dressing room.

Foster didn't *love* this job, but he did love not being in jail. Minimum security wasn't really violent, but it was dehumanizing. When you were bad at fitting in in the real world, it was worse in prison. You never had any privacy. He couldn't remember sleeping for more than two hours at a stretch during his two years, eight months, and five days of incarceration. And when he had finally gotten out, nobody had been waiting for him.

Finding a job was crucial to his parole. It meant he could stay in his own apartment instead of the halfway house. That time alone let him right himself when he felt off-balance. He still didn't get out much, and he didn't have any friends. He remembered having friends at the orphanage, but he also remembered feeling like he was always losing them as they made their way through the system. Eventually, he stopped trying. By the time he'd turned eighteen he'd stopped caring.

Foster propped the door to the women's room open with his cart. It was empty. It usually was. The employees had their own bathroom next to the dressing room, and while some strip clubs in Vegas got their fair share of female customers, the Tail Spin was generally not one of them. He found the right stall on the first try. He'd had a fifty-fifty shot.

Foster wondered if people carried Sharpies in their purses or pockets for the sole purpose of defiling bathroom stalls. Did it give them a thrill knowing that they had a pen ready to help express whatever twisted thought happened to wander through their minds while they popped a squat? It implied some kind of forethought. They would call it "premeditation" on one of those crime shows. The contributions on the stall door didn't seem to support that theory, though.

Instead, there was poetry:

Twitter me this, Twitter me that,
No Wi-Fi so here I shat.

And there was religion:

Jesus is Lord

Which apparently struck a cord with another customer who added:

of the Rings

And another:

Spoiler alert!

At least it was bringing people together.

The artistic mood had struck somebody who'd decided to draw a nice, calming beach scene. Two driftwood logs with a clamshell in the middle. Foster was disappointed when he realized those weren't logs. And the thing in the middle wasn't a shell. He became disturbed when he realized the thing that wasn't a shell had *teeth*.

Surrounded by such masterpieces, it was hard to tell how somebody had mustered up the willpower and imagination to keep an erection long enough to add his own, more *biological* contribution to the walls. And yes, the ceiling.

Foster went to work, thick rubber gloves pulled tight over his hands like industrial strength condoms. He dipped his sponge into his bucket. He didn't squeeze it to wring out the excess water. He figured he needed all the help he could get. He held his breath and pressed the sponge against one of the metal walls. It was more of a reflex than a precaution. Like holding your breath right before you rip off a Band-Aid. Soapy water reluctantly bubbled out of the sponge and sloshed down the wall toward the snot-like streaks. That's when Candice came in.

Foster was startled and pressed the sponge a bit harder than he intended. A wave of soapy water cascaded down the wall and splattered on the ground. Well, not *just* water. Foster did a little hop backward and ran into the toilet. He was going to have to mop the whole floor now.

Candice didn't seem to notice. In fact, she stared straight ahead, looking at herself in the mirror above the sink. Her eyes were wide, and she didn't blink. Foster had never noticed how blue they were. They almost looked unnatural. She muttered something that Foster couldn't quite make out. He was just about to ask her if she was all right when she turned on him with a snarl.

"What are you doing in there, you little perv?" It was like she'd just suddenly remembered that she hated him. Which was strange, because she had always been so nice to him before.

He didn't know what to say. Maybe she thought he was a customer hiding in the stall to spy on her. He tried to explain. "Candice, it's just me. Foster."

She took two steps over to the stall door. It had started to close a bit on its own. She pushed it back open. Foster still hadn't seen her blink.

"I know who it is." Her eyes scanned the walls, then the floor, and then Foster's crotch. "That's fucking disgusting."

Foster looked down at his own crotch. He was the exact

opposite of horny.

"I don't—" he started.

"Is this what you do when nobody's looking? Hide in here and stroke that pathetic cock?"

"No, the boss said—"

She leaned in close to his face. She had a doll's eyes, unfocused and too wide. "Did you run in here right after I touched you, to do your nasty little business?"

Foster cringed and tried to step back, but he was right up against the toilet. He lost his balance and had to sit down. Candice continued.

"Fuckin' sad. I bet I remind you of your sister, or your mom or something."

She paused to cross her arms and sneer. Foster took a breath and tried to rally. He was cut off by somebody else this time.

"What the fuck's going on in here?" It was Sam.

Foster remembered having nightmares where he knew he was going to be grabbed at any moment by the thing in the dark without eyes. The thing that would tickle his ribs with savage jabs while sniffing him with its tongue. All he had to do was scream. To cry out for help. In his dream he would open his mouth, but all that came out was a breathy squeak. He felt like that now. It was a good thing he was already sitting down. And it was probably a good thing that he was sitting on a toilet.

"I found this little prick jerking off to me!" Candice said.

Candice backed up as Sam came to stand in the stall doorway. Sam's foot made a little splash and then slid on something in the water. He put out a hand to steady himself, but his hand slipped on something too. He didn't fall, though. He saved himself by grabbing Foster's shoulder. The sudden jolt shook something loose in Foster. That *something* was gas.

"That's it, Foster. Get the fuck out!" Sam hooked a thumb toward the bathroom door behind him. "You're done here."

Foster finally found his voice. He had to work to push the words out, one deep breath for each syllable or two. "You. Said. To clean. This. Up."

"Yeah, clean it up. Not make more," said Sam.

Foster felt the jabbing at his ribs. "No," he pleaded. "No. This is all I got."

"Take it up with your parole officer."

Foster looked past Sam to Candice. She finally blinked. She couldn't stop blinking now. She also kept turning her head from side to side, like she was trying to figure something out. She didn't look angry anymore. In fact, she didn't seem to notice Foster at all.

Sam put a hand on Foster's shoulder. He spoke as he helped Foster to his feet. It seemed like he was saying a lot more, but all Foster could make out was the last part.

"Go home, Foster."

5

Matt loosened his tie. Then he tightened it again. He hadn't planned on wearing a tie at all, but he was glad he had. Apparently there was a party going on or something. A couple passed him on the sidewalk and climbed the steps up to the large double doors. The man wore a black suit. The woman on his arm was half his age and wore about half as much clothing. Matt chalked that up to being in Las Vegas, but this place wasn't really near the Strip.

The Victorian looked out of place, like a forgotten Hollywood set. It contrasted nicely with the barren landscape off in the distance behind it. The double doors were open, and Matt could hear the droning chatter of party guests, punctuated occasionally with bursts of laughter. He started to pull off his sunglasses as he climbed up to the entry, but when his hand brushed his cheek, he winced and remembered the bruise still decorating his eye. Better to leave the glasses in place, but he did make the snap decision to pull the bandage off his nose. The swelling was mostly gone now, and there was hardly any blood when he sneezed.

There was a kid at the door. He wore a suit, too, and was

currently holding up his jacket pocket to get a closer look. He tried to poke a finger inside but frowned when he could only get about half his fingertip in.

Matt saw the problem. "They sew them closed," he explained.

The kid replied without looking up. "Why would they do that?"

"To keep them looking nice, I guess."

"Why bother adding pockets if you can't use them?"

"Beats me. They make up for it by adding a secret pocket inside." Matt patted his chest to show him where.

"Oh." The kid looked inside his jacket with renewed interest. "Cool."

"Yeah, perfect for your smokes." Matt winked but forgot he was wearing sunglasses.

The kid looked Matt over and seemed to make up his mind about something. "We're closed. There should have been a sign out front."

Matt didn't remember seeing a sign. "What's going on?"

The kid was distracted before he could answer. He had a small stack of pamphlets in his hand and stepped forward to offer one to the couple coming up behind Matt.

He turned back to Matt. "I don't know if we're reopening."

Matt offered his hand. "I'm Matt."

The kid looked at Matt's hand but didn't shake it.

Matt continued to hold it out awkwardly. "Do you know Quentin? I need to talk to him."

"Uncle Quent? Sure."

The kid put a folded paper in Matt's outstretched hand. It wasn't a pamphlet. It was a program.

In Loving Memory of Quentin Bradley James
Please join us as we celebrate and honor his life.

The flowery script didn't match the gruff portrait of Uncle Quent, who looked like he was doing his best not to be in the picture.

Matt pulled his sunglasses down and took a better look around. Past the entrance was a small foyer with a staircase to one side. It was full of people wearing black, drinking cocktails, and snacking from little plates of food. By the staircase was a wreath of lilies.

"Huh, this must be really weird for you," said the kid. "It's weird for me, too."

"He's dead?" Matt sounded dubious. "That doesn't sound like him. Who are all these people?"

"Mainly people he worked with," said the kid. "It's a wake. He didn't pray much. But he did drink."

"Okay, that does sound like him." Matt turned back to the kid. "Did you know him well?"

He was handing out another program. "Sure, I had Cheerios with him every day."

The kid started walking through the foyer. Matt fell in behind him.

"You said he was your uncle?" asked Matt.

"Yeah. But not really. He said I could call him Uncle Quent if I wanted to. It seemed to make him happy."

"He was my uncle, too. But for real, I guess." Matt paused to take a tiny quiche from a silver tray. Then he had to catch up. "We never had Cheerios, though."

"He didn't mention you."

"So were he and your Mom . . . lovers?"

"I'm nine." The kid stopped suddenly. "You're talking to me like I'm old."

"Oh. How do you talk to a nine-year-old?"

"Usually people just treat me like I'm really dumb. Or like I don't know about sex. But I can do math better than most of them."

Matt didn't know how to respond to that. Thankfully, he didn't have to.

"My mom's over there," said the kid. "She worked for Uncle Quent."

The boy pointed into a large room that connected to the foyer through a set of open doors. Rows of chairs had been set up facing a small raised stage. On the stage was an open casket. Matt almost didn't recognize the man inside. The Uncle Quent he remembered had always looked like he desperately needed to be somewhere else. This man just looked at peace. Most of the guests were still milling around and eating bite-sized food, but a few were waiting in line to pay their respects. The boy's mother was at the front of the line. As Matt watched, she kissed her fingertips and then touched them to Uncle Quent's forehead.

She seemed too young to be the boy's mother. She looked like she was in her mid twenties, and if the boy was nine, that meant somebody hadn't taken her Sex Ed class very seriously in high school. Her blond hair was tied back with a black ribbon, the bow drooping in wide loops. Her skirt was black, too, offset by her white blouse. She held a tissue in one hand. It was stained black at the corner where she must have been wiping away tears mixed with mascara.

Matt started to head down the aisle between the chairs. Before he could introduce himself, there was a high-pitched squawk from the PA system as somebody turned on a mike. The man testing it seemed to be a preacher of some sort, but Matt was pretty sure he had gotten ordained online. He had a peace symbol around his neck next to his cross. Both were framed by his unbuttoned jean jacket.

"Hey, guys, could you please find your seats? I promise I won't keep you long. Just have a few words to say about Uncle Quent."

People started wandering in. Uncle Quent knew some good-looking people. Matt caught himself staring at a woman in a black A-line dress. The bottom trim was black lace that acted as a veil for the tattoo on her thigh. It was hard to tell what it was because the lace kept sliding back and forth as she walked down the aisle toward him. When she stopped he made a silent *Aha* as he realized it was a skull. He was pleased with himself until he looked up and saw her eyes narrow at him. He quickly took a seat.

He wasn't able to sit next to the boy's mother, but there was a seat opened behind her. He leaned forward and tapped her on the shoulder. When she turned to look at him, her eyes were glassy, a tear trembling at each corner. She held up her tissue and blew her nose. She was stunning.

Matt just stared for a second. Her eyebrows arched in a question, and he finally introduced himself. "Hey, I'm Matt. The, uh, small gentleman by the door said you knew Quentin."

"His name's Adam." Her voice sounded low and sultry, but that was probably just the snot.

"He said you were living with my uncle?" Matt said.

"I'm Christy." After another blow into her tissue her voice cleared up a bit. "I live here. In my *own* room." She emphasized that last part with another raised eyebrow.

"Did he mention me at all?" Matt asked.

"You said your name is Matt?"

"Yeah."

"No."

"What?" Matt was confused.

"No, he didn't mention you," she said.

Matt pulled his uncle's letter out of his back pocket and unfolded it. Christy must have thought the conversation was over because she turned back around toward the stage. Matt was about to offer her the letter when Preacher.com started speaking again.

"Thank you all for coming. I'm sure Uncle Quent would have been both surprised and amused by the turnout today." This was met with a few chuckles and a couple of snorts.

"Quentin Bradley James was a son of a bitch." The preacher paused for dramatic effect. "He told me so himself. He told me about the sins he committed and the people he hurt. He told me about the drugs and then the drinking. He told me about his regrets."

Matt looked around. All the seats were filled now, and there were a few people standing at the back of the room. He saw Adam over by the doorway.

The sermon continued. "And he told me how thankful he was to have God slap him in the face about ten years ago. That slap landed him in a hospital bed surrounded by tubes and machines rather than family and friends."

The woman with the skull on her thigh was sitting in Matt's row. She sat at the aisle, legs crossed. She was facing forward, but her chin was tilted slightly toward Matt. He caught her smirking and watching him out of the corner of her eye. Something spun around between her fingers. It looked like . . . a bullet?

"He saw both God's wrath and God's love, and it changed him. These past ten years he devoted himself to running a business that makes people feel good about themselves, and to treating his employees like family. We can't say he started living without sin, but we can say that at least he sinned in the right direction."

Matt felt uncomfortable for the rest of the sermon. Thankfully it was short. He was probably Uncle Quent's only blood relative at the service, but he felt like an outsider. The preacher didn't offer any prayers, and he didn't ask anybody to come up and speak. Instead, he placed a quarter over each of Uncle Quent's eyes and ended with, "All right, that's enough out of me. Let's go get drunk and let Uncle Quent dine in Valhalla."

Everybody else continued to dine on hors d'oeuvres. As Matt grabbed a plate, he saw Christy head to the bar. He tried his hardest not to look like a stalker as he caught up to her.

"Uncle Quent sure has a lot of friends here." Matt thought that was a safe opening line. He was wrong.

"You sound surprised." Christy's tears were gone now, and she was rehydrating with a beer. "Like you never visited."

"Well, Uncle Quent and I both shared a desire to be far removed from our family. But obviously that didn't bring us any closer."

"Obviously."

Matt set down his plate on the bar and wiped his mouth with a napkin. The napkin was decorated with a silhouette of a naked woman eating an apple. It would look right at home on a trucker's mud flap. Matt fished out his letter again.

"Maybe you can tell me why he would have sent me this letter?"

Christy took a long drink, set down her bottle, and then finally took the letter. "He was a good man. And a good man to work for."

"What did he do?" he asked.

She was frowning at the letter and eyeing it suspiciously. "He ran this place."

"What is it? Is it like a funeral home or something?"

She was reading the letter and didn't respond.

"Crappy part of town for a funeral home." Matt looked around. He saw the preacher sitting on a red plush couch talking to the woman with the skull on her thigh. She was laughing and touching his knee. Another woman stood behind the preacher. Her hand reached around and stroked his chest underneath his jean jacket.

Matt had another aha moment. He turned back to Christy. "Wait, what did you do for Uncle Quent?"

6

Foster was trying to remember the words to the song. Everybody knew the tune. Any time a TV show or movie needed an old-timey barbershop quartet, that song would play. But it usually only went on for a couple of lines before the scene changed and the story continued.

Foster whispered to himself, unsure if he was getting it right. "All 'round the little farm I wandered." He hesitated, then nodded and continued. "When I was young."

Then the music box stopped, and he had to wind the key. It was an antique, or maybe it was made to look like an antique. Foster couldn't tell. With the lid up, you could see the mechanism inside that plunked out the tune. A cylinder with spiky bumps flicked the metal fingers over the tiny sounding board. The cheery notes it played seemed out of place coming from the tarnished clockwork. The wood was stained dark, and there were very few decorations or embellishments on it, but if you turned it upside down there was a brass plate etched with the title of the song and its composer: OLD FOLKS AT HOME BY STEPHEN FOSTER.

There was also something scratched into the wood next to the plate. Foster had wondered about it many times. It seemed like a doodle, but the scratches were deep and precise. Meant to last. Two parallel lines were joined by an arch, with a third line between them ending in a diamond shape under the apex. Above the arch was a kind of lopsided cross or X. The pattern reminded Foster of a logo or a symbol. He thought it might be a manufacturer's mark of some kind, but he had never found any reference to it. That's also where the tiny key stuck out.

He closed the lid and gave the key a few turns.

He was standing in the front of a condemned building. If he were twelve again, he would have been sure it was haunted. Now, in his thirties, he was more mature, and he only *suspected* it was haunted. Of course, he *had been* here when he was twelve. The weathered sign near the entry proclaimed that it used to be the TULE SPRINGS GROUP HOME. From the look of it, the building hadn't been anyone's home for several years. Foster hadn't seen it in at least fifteen. Before the windows had been broken and the roof had started to sag; before the paint had started flaking and the birds came to roost; before the lawn died and the graffiti tags; this was his home.

He lifted the lid on the music box, and the tune started plunking out again. Foster tried to keep up with the lyrics.

"Something . . . something . . . days I squandered," he whispered. "Many the songs I sung."

The name of the building actually made no sense to Foster. A group home could be anything. It sounded like a place people went when they were waiting to die. Instead, it was a place you went when you were waiting to start your life. And if there was a Tule Springs, it was nowhere near here. Like it did everywhere in Las Vegas, if you didn't water your lawn every day it would turn to dust and clumps of weeds. Even when the orphanage was full of kids, the playground lawn never saw a shade of green that wasn't half-yellow.

"When I was playing with my brother," he sang. The words were coming to him faster now. "Happy was I."

The playground looked worse than the building. The teeter-totter looked cancerous with rust. He was afraid of the sound it might make if it actually teetered. He remembered busting a tooth on one of those little horses mounted on a big spring. That horse wobbled to one side now, and some of the paint had flaked off its face, making its eyes look wide and panicked. It seemed like it was trying to run away from a fire or something but got stuck on that damn spring instead. The swing set still had one seat intact, so he sat down and whispered his song.

"Oh, take me to my kind old mother. There let me live and die."

He let it play on a little longer before clicking the lid closed. They had told him that when he'd come to the Tule Springs Group Home, the music box came with him. He was too young to remember, but he liked to think that his mother had left it with him. Some last act of love and desperation. Foster imagined her telling herself that she would come back for him someday. When things were better. He guessed things had never gotten better.

The double doors in front were chained and padlocked together by the handles. He gave them a tug, but they seemed pretty solid. He walked around the side of the building. It stood on the outskirts of a residential area, but nobody saw him. That or nobody cared. A fence followed the property line on three sides—one of those chain-link fences with the green plastic slats weaving through the wire. The plastic was starting to crack, and several slats were missing. Foster wasn't sure why anybody would've taken them. It's not like you would want to see *more* of this place if you lived next to it.

Some of the windows were boarded up, but not all of them. One window had a sheet of plywood lying next to it, covered in shattered glass. Maybe somebody else got nostalgic for the closest thing they had to a home. Or maybe they were just looking for a place to get high and have sex. The graffiti suggested the latter. The broken window was low so Foster didn't have to pull himself up to get inside. He just had to hike one leg up, and hop high enough to avoid smashing his nuts on windowsill. He surprised himself by making it in with a full complement of nuts.

He landed in a TV room . . . from the eighties or close to it. In fact, when he landed he stumbled a bit and almost fell down on a beanbag chair. Instead, he ended up kicking it and sent beans spilling out all over the floor. The floor had a sticky feel to it. Foster might have blamed the stickiness on the water damage he saw in one corner, but then he remembered the floor had been that way back when he used to watch *He-Man* in here after school. There had always been more kids than seats, so you were lucky to get a beanbag or even one of those miniature plastic chairs that always seemed ready to collapse. The place hadn't changed much since he'd left, and he wondered if it had closed down right away, or if it had just never gotten any new stuff.

There were toys here, too. Or things that used to be toys. Foster picked through the remains until he found something recognizable. He put the View-Master up to his eyes and looked toward the window. He found himself between slide frames and gave the lever a pull. There was a cracking sound, but the lever didn't break. The cardboard slide-wheel turned, and a frame locked into place. It was an undersea picture. A puffer fish was all ballooned out, its spikes acting as a warning to whoever had taken the picture. Half the frame was coated in mold, and it took Foster a few seconds to realize what he was looking at. When he figured it out, he quickly dropped the toy back where he found it and wiped his hands on his pants. Being a janitor, he knew what caused mold like that to grow.

He let his hands drift over stuffed animals with missing eyes, a Lite-Brite with a handful of discolored pegs, and a snow globe that was so hazy he had a hard time seeing the faces on Mount Rushmore. They finally landed on a book. He didn't remember reading this one: *The Woman in the Garden*. The cover was plastic and strangely thick. He opened it to find a cutout that held a cassette tape. The book seemed mostly intact, and he flicked through a few pages. It looked like one of those storybooks that read itself to you when the adult in charge needed a break. On the same bookshelf was a cassette player.

There was no way that thing was going to work, but Foster slid in the cassette and pushed "play". Nothing. He turned the player over and popped open the lid to the battery compartment. Inside were the mummified remains of two D batteries. They had corroded and burst long ago, coating the compartment with whitish-green sludge. The batteries made grating sounds as he pried them out. He blew into the compartment and then immediately coughed as he inhaled a cloud of ancient battery dust. His throat burned. He leaned over and spit to get the metallic taste out of his mouth. It seemed like a lot of trouble to go through, but Foster could use a story right now. A calming voice to tell him everybody would live happily ever after.

He had brought a flashlight in case the lights didn't work, which, of course, they didn't. He unscrewed the bulb and let the two D batteries slide out into his hand. He slotted them into place in the cassette player and snapped the lid closed. He pushed "play." Nothing happened. He gave it a whack, because that's what you did to technology from the eighties that was being stubborn. The pins started to turn. They caught the teeth of the cassette tape and hesitated. Then with a warbling lurch, the story began. The woman's voice started out distorted but had smoothed out by the end of the title page.

"*This is the story of* The Woman in the Garden. *Please read along with me and turn the page when you hear the owl say,* Hoo hoo-hoo."

Foster left the tape deck playing on the shelf. He took the book over to the beanbag chair a flopped down into it. The chair gave a hiss as it settled under his weight, and a couple of squeaks as he shifted around to get comfortable. Then he opened the book on his lap.

"*Once upon a time, in a forest that time had forgotten, there lived a beautiful woman who tended a garden.* Hoo hoo-hoo."

The illustrations were interesting. They looked pre-Disney. Realistic depictions of a fantastic world. No gigantic eyes, no gigantic breasts. Foster fumbled around in his pocket. The way the beanbag chair folded him up, it was impossible to get his hand all the way in. He arched his back so that he could straighten his legs and finally managed to grab what he'd been looking for. Then he relaxed and had to make himself comfortable all over again.

"*The woman planted her garden in a nice, quiet clearing by a stream and an old oak tree.* Hoo hoo-hoo."

He held the box cutter up in from of his face and slid the blade open with his thumb. It was new, gleaming and sharp. The blade had a wet looking sheen to it from the light coat of machine oil keeping it rust free.

"*In the oak tree perched Mr. Owl who helped her look over the garden to make sure none of the creatures of the forest defiled it. Hoo hoo-hoo."*

Foster's eyes filled with tears. He stifled a sob as the blade slid across his wrist. It burned a bit, but he barely noticed the pain once he was done. He sniffed back his tears and held the book up in front of him. It turned out to be a pop-up book, and that made him smile.

"One day a scaly old snake slithered into the garden, whispering lies and secrets. Hoo hoo-hoo."

Beads of blood started to trace a line down his forearm to his elbow. From there, they dripped a steady rhythm onto the floor next to his music box.

"The snake said a man was coming to help tend the garden and to give the woman a child. Hoo hoo-hoo."

Foster thought he should be trying to think of something important. Trying to answer some last question he had, or maybe relive a good memory. Nothing came to him, though, and he was happy to let the storybook fill his mind with images.

"Mr. Owl said, 'This snake tells nothing but lies. This man doesn't come for you. He'll ruin the garden.' Hoo hoo-hoo."

Foster tried to pull the tab to make the owl's wings flap, but his hands were starting to get very cold. His eyelids drooped, and he thought he heard a distant buzzing sound. He wanted to look and see what was making the sound, but his eyes weren't cooperating.

"The woman said, 'Now, now, Mr. Owl. We mustn't judge somebody we haven't met yet. Besides, I've never met a man before. Tell me, Mr. Snake, what is this man's name?" Hoo hoo-hoo."

Foster couldn't turn the page. He was missing the story.

Turn the page when you hear the owl say, "Hoo hoo-hoo."

The buzzing sounded closer.

Foster, turn the page.

Buzz.

Turn the fucking page.

Foster's eyes snapped open.

The buzzing had stopped and was now replaced by a pounding in his head. He lifted a hand to rub his forehead and the pain in his wrist made him suck in his breath. His mouth was dry, and the room smelled like pennies. The storybook that Foster had been reading was on the floor next to his music box. Both were stained red by the small pool of blood forming around the beanbag chair. The book was on the ground, but the Woman in the Garden stood in front of him.

She stood in her garden, but that garden was now in the TV room. The oak tree looked real. Its roots dug into the cracked linoleum, and its branches pushed up into the ceiling. As Foster tried to take this in, a leaf fell off one of the branches and fluttered lazily to the ground. Something shifted in the branches, and Foster saw an owl rotate its head from the Woman in the Garden to him and back again. The bird looked flat and empty, like a poster of an owl tacked up in the tree. Except that it moved and hoo'ed.

There were plants in the room, as well. Foster recognized some but not many. Vines or maybe some kind of ivy looked like it had been painted on the wall. Where the wall ended, the vines leaped out and started creeping along the ceiling. Bushes hid the bookshelves. Some leaves looked vivid and waxy, some looked dull and spotty, as though they had been hastily colored in with crayon. As he watched, a rose unfolded from the ground, like origami being formed by invisible hands.

The woman stood under the tree. Her white sundress was modestly cut, but there was nothing else about her that suggested innocence. Certainly not the long green snake coiled around her arm. It probed and flicked with its tongue, starting at her shoulder, then moving to her exposed neck. She didn't seem to notice. Her long dark hair was pulled back and tied with a ribbon. Her arched eyebrows were severe and seemed to be asking an unspoken question that Foster didn't know the answer to. In fact, he had a hard time looking at anything other than her eyes. They held him in place, and he couldn't decide if she was beautiful or terrifying.

He realized he was holding his breath.

Then the Woman in the Garden spoke. "I was just getting to the good part."

7

"A whorehouse?" Matt might have said that a little too loudly.

"The legal term is *brothel*." This guy had introduced himself as Mr. Fitch. He was the lawyer who'd been hired to read Uncle Quent's last will and testament. "It's called the Golden Delicious. I hope you don't mind me pointing out the irony that it used to be a funeral home. In fact, Mr. James wanted me to point out the irony."

They were in the office upstairs, and the lawyer had taken over Uncle Quent's desk. That had seemed fair when he'd started pulling out all the forms and documents that had come with him. Several stacks of paper now covered the desk, each with its own rainbow of colored sticky tabs pointing out things that needed to be signed or initialed. Dying seemed to involve a lot of paperwork.

Matt sat in one of the two cushy chairs in front of the desk. Christy sat next to him in the other, Adam on her lap. Several other employees were in the room, too, either standing or sitting in the old beat-up couch against one of the walls. The woman with the skull tattoo sat on the low windowsill next to the desk, staring at Matt and generally making him feel uncomfortable. He had heard somebody call her Erica. They had all been asked to come up after the memorial was winding down and guests were either starting to leave or passing out.

"He left me a brothel? Can he do that?" Before the lawyer had a chance to answer, Matt added, "Are you a real lawyer?"

Mr. Fitch was mostly hidden behind a piece of paper he had held up to read. Matt could see his eyes though and the angle of his eyebrows suggested strongly that he was not amused. Adam apparently thought it was funny though, and snorted a half laugh before he caught himself.

"He left you the *property*." Mr. Fitch sounded out each syllable of the word to emphasize the point. "While a brothel is a legal establishment in *some* counties in Nevada, this is not one of them. But I'm not here to enforce any municipal codes or laws. I'm just here to read the will." He squinted at the paper he was holding up in front of him. He hmmm'ed. Then he shuffled back and forth among the papers in one of his stacks, checking pages with colored tabs. He hmmm'ed some more.

Christy leaned around Adam and started to ask the lawyer a question. "Does it say anything about—"

Mr. Fitch cut her off. "Seems the will was updated the day he died. He must have known he'd be leaving us soon." He set down his papers and looked at Matt. "Probably wanted to reach out to a family member at the end."

Matt turned to Adam and whispered, "Yeah, like at the end of a zombie movie when a hand reaches out from a grave."

This time Adam couldn't hold it in and let out a loud "Ha!"

"Mr. James!" The lawyer apparently didn't have a sense

of humor at all, which Matt found strange considering who had hired him.

Matt was getting a lot of glares now from all over the room, so he went on the defensive. "Well, it's a bit of a shock, especially if you knew the rest of the family."

Christy leaned the other way around Adam to have a clear shot at staring down Matt. "*We* were his family! Believe me, we're just as shocked as you are."

Matt held his hands up in front of him. "Okay, okay, I agree. It's probably a mistake." Then he put down his hands and reached inside his jacket pocket. "But he did send me this the day he . . . you know."

Matt held up the letter that had saved him from torture a few days before. Erica slid off her perch and snatched it from him.

"Let me see that," she snapped. "Who writes a letter anymore?"

"Lost art really," Matt said.

All eyes were on Erica as she read to herself. Finally, she looked up from the letter. She seemed confused.

Matt shrugged. "He wanted me here for some reason."

Erica passed the letter over to the lawyer and returned to the sill. The lawyer read it, too, and took notes, even snapped a picture of the letter with his phone.

Matt asked a question to nobody in particular. "The real question is, how did he find me? I never told him where I was living. And I'm pretty good at losing myself in a crowd."

Erica narrowed her eyes at him. "We'd be happy to help you get lost again."

Matt turned to face all the Golden Delicious employees. None of them looked very friendly. "Look, we'll figure something out."

Christy stood and led Adam toward the door. She stopped and spun around to glare at Matt. "We work here. For some of us, it's also our home. Don't just *figure something out*." She walked out of the room. The other women followed suit.

Erica was the last to leave. She stopped next to the desk, and Matt prepared himself for a parting blow, verbal or physical—he wasn't ruling out either. Instead, she reached down and picked up a small picture frame. He couldn't see the picture itself, but whatever it was, it made her glare relax for a second. Then it returned and she quickly left, taking the picture with her.

After that, Matt filled out most of the paperwork in awkward silence with Mr. Fitch. The lawyer told him to return the following afternoon. Once the papers were filed, he would deliver the keys and deed to Matt. That was Matt's cue to leave.

As he walked down the hall toward the stairs, he passed by a closed door. There was a faint sobbing coming from the other side. There had been tears at the memorial, but it had seemed like more of a bittersweet celebration—tears mixed with laughter. Now there was nobody to laugh with, so that just left the tears. Matt hurried out.

It was late by the time his cab dropped him off at his motel. He thought briefly about going out, but he wasn't sure where exactly to go. He was in Las Vegas, so it seemed like he should go check out the Strip. *That's what people did here, right?* Matt had been in Nevada for a while, but for most of that time—okay, the whole time—he had been broke and trying to keep a low profile. The Strip didn't seem like it would help with either of those things. Tomorrow he would be less broke, though, at least on paper.

Maybe he'd go out tomorrow night.

■ ■ ■

The next morning, Matt had waffles for breakfast, but by the time he'd eaten them, they'd actually been lunch. He didn't have a car so his dining choices were limited to what he could see from the parking lot of the motel. He hadn't felt like tacos.

The rest of the day dragged by. Matt was too cheap to pay for another night at the motel and the lawyer wasn't going to meet him until four, so he packed his things and started walking. He felt like he was on the run again, duffel bag slung over one shoulder, wandering from coffee shop to bar to coffee shop. Being on the run wasn't as fun as it sounded, especially if you were doing it right. There was no adrenaline rush, just a nagging voice telling him, *You really should be moving on*, and *No, you shouldn't have that third beer*.

When four o'clock finally rolled around, Matt had already walked all the way back to Uncle Quent's place and had been waiting outside for half an hour. The lawyer was another half an hour late. Matt felt too uncomfortable to knock on the door to see if anybody would let him in. And if anybody inside had seen him waiting, they hadn't offered on their own.

Then Matt's life changed in the matter of minutes. The lawyer finally pulled up to the curb out front. When Matt went to the car to meet him, Mr. Fitch got out and greeted him with a nod and a snort.

"Sign here," was all the lawyer said as he held out an official-looking document.

Matt signed, and the lawyer handed him a manila envelope. Matt unfolded the metal brad and tipped the contents into his hand. Two keys slid out—one big, one small.

"What's this—" Matt started to say, but the lawyer was already closing the door to his car.

Matt turned to look at his new . . . house? Business? The keys were still in his hand as he knocked on the door. He waited. No answer. He knocked again. Nothing.

He'd slid the big key halfway into the lock when the door opened. It was Christy.

She looked at the key with a raised eyebrow and crossed arms. "It's unlocked."

Matt put the key in his pocket. "I figured I'd knock first."

"Yeah, I heard. Eventually. I was upstairs." She pointed to the wall beside the door. "We also have a doorbell. Which is way easier to hear, especially when you're in the bathroom *upstairs*."

"I'll use that next time," Matt said.

Christy just stared at him. "Why? You have a key."

"This isn't going well," he said.

Matt could see that Christy was about to snap at him, but she caught herself. Her voice changed, and she uncrossed her arms.

"Look, why don't you tell me what you want?" she asked.

"I'm not sure. A tour, I guess." He shrugged.

Christy took a step back to let him inside. "Welcome to the Golden Delicious." She didn't sound very enthusiastic, but she didn't sound too bitter, either.

Matt stepped into the foyer. A vase of fresh flowers was the only remnant of last night's wake. It sat on a small ornamental table by the stairs. The staircase was blocked off by a short, red velvet rope, suggesting anything upstairs was off-limits, or at least exclusive. It looked like more of a reminder than a barrier. The podium the preacher had used last night was now set up a few paces from the door. It had a sign attached to its front. The brothel's name circled the silhouette of a golden apple with a big bite taken out of it.

Christy saw him looking at the podium and explained, "That's where the hostess greats guests. The door stays unlocked during business hours."

"Aren't you worried about . . . I don't know, weirdos walking in off the street?" Matt asked.

"That's never happened. At least not while I've been here. Uncle Quent didn't seem too concerned about it. And he always took care of anybody who got . . . out of hand. Anyway, we don't get a lot of foot traffic. Most of our guests are either return customers or part of organized parties."

She led him across the foyer to the same doorway Adam had shown him to the night before. The room looked entirely different. It seemed like it should be called a parlor or something. The stage was clear, and the coffin was gone. Now that it was empty, Matt could see that it wasn't really much of a stage. There was a step up to a raised wooden floor that was maybe a dozen feet wide and just deep enough to hold, well, a coffin. It was backed with red velvet curtains, but Matt didn't think there was anything behind them.

Matching curtains covered the windows, as well, and recessed lighting was dimmed down to a seductive level. Bright enough to see but dark enough to hide any flaws. The rows of folding chairs were gone, replaced by a few clusters of plush sofas, love seats, and chairs. They all went nicely with the red curtains. The bar was cleaned up and ready for business, though there was no bartender in sight.

"Let me guess. This is the Red Room or wait, no, the Crimson Cove!" Matt was proud of himself.

"We're not pirates," Christy clarified. "It's the parlor."

Matt was a little disappointed.

"After guests check in, they take a seat here and wait for the lineup." Christy spoke over her shoulder as she reached down to pick up a crumpled napkin hiding under a chair. "Maybe have a drink."

"Lineup?" Matt was thinking it must be a sports analogy, but he wasn't very good with those.

"Yeah," Christy said. "The girls who are available line up onstage."

"And?"

"And you pick one you like."

She started to leave the room, but Matt was still looking at the stage.

"That's not offensive?" he asked. Then he realized he was getting left behind and had to do a little jog to catch up. "That seems like it should be offensive."

Christy kept walking. "Would you rather draw a name out of a hat?"

"I was thinking more like a big wheel that you could spin." He had his smart-ass grin on, but Christy couldn't see it. "Like on *Wheel of Fortune*."

She stopped abruptly and turned to face him. "Sure. That's way less offensive."

He had to stop short to avoid running into her. By the time he'd recovered, she was already walking again. This time down a hallway off the foyer. He caught up again. "Equal opportunity, though."

Instead of replying, she pointed through an open door. "The kitchen and break room are through there."

Matt glanced in and saw a room that seemed out of place. Not that it was messy or crappy looking or anything. In fact, it was nice. Not elegant, not fancy, but simple and . . . lived in, Matt supposed. It had small dining nook to one side, just big enough for a breakfast table and four chairs. On the other side was a worn couch facing a tiny TV. Beyond that was a small kitchen with a sit-in counter. It all seemed very homey.

"Moving right along." Christy had stopped halfway down the hall to wait for him. Behind her was a vintage portrait of a fan dancer. They both looked at Matt expectantly as he caught up *again*.

Before Christy could continue the tour, Matt had a question. "So how does the money work?"

"People pay us," Christy's expression was deadpan, "to have sex."

"Yeah, but there are lots of different types of sex. I've read books on it," he assured her. "Picture books. Is there a menu or something?"

She cocked her head slightly, as though she didn't quite know what she was looking at. Then she shook her head and continued down the hall. "Our clients know what they want. Part of our job is to make them feel comfortable enough to ask for it. We're not concubines. We don't do tea ceremonies. We know what our clients like because they ask for it over and over again." She opened the door to another room. "It can be intimidating. Usually we just start with a drink and then discuss business on a little tour."

He leaned in to take a look. The room was dominated by a large king-size bed with a silky-looking comforter. The comforter was partially folded down, revealing matching satin sheets beneath. One small end table displayed both a Tiffany lamp and a bowl full of condoms. On the other end table was a bottle of champagne and a couple of glasses. Mounted on the wall opposite the bed was a large flat screen TV with a small collection of pornographic DVDs fanned out beneath it.

"Oooh . . . Uh, Champagne room?" Matt guessed.

"Close," Christy conceded. "Party room."

"Really? Seems a bit . . . dull."

"Most clients don't think so."

Christy continued down the hallway to a door at the end. She stopped and gestured at it with a thumb.

"And if you wanted something a little more adventurous, we'd take you here," she said.

"VIP room?" Matt asked halfheartedly.

"Yes, actually." She finally grinned.

He returned the smile and opened the door. Christy didn't stop him in time.

"Whoa!" Matt actually jumped back. But he couldn't take his eyes off the man in the black vinyl gimp suit. He was standing spread-eagle in the center of the room, his wrists and ankles chained to a large wooden X-shaped cross. His back was to Matt, but he was trying to turn around in his chains to see what was going on. His suit had a matching mask with zippers over the eyes and some kind of ring holding his mouth open. Only one eye was unzipped, and it made him look like he was frozen in an exaggerated wink. His ass was exposed through a zippered flap, the pale moon recently decorated with red welts. Matt couldn't have said for sure he was a man, except that there was a clamp currently forcing him into an impossible erection.

"Occupied! Didn't you see the light?" It wasn't the gimp. Someone else was in the room—a woman—but Matt's eyes were still stuck in place.

"I was just about to point out the light." Christy was reaching for the door.

A muffled voice came from the Gimp's mask. "Who's that?"

"Did I say you could speak?"

Matt moved his head to see who was talking, his eyeballs forced to follow. It was Erica. She looked furious, but half of that could have just been her outfit. It was vinyl, too, accented with pointy chrome bits, and ending in potentially deadly heeled boots. And there was that skull tattoo again, this time on full display. She wore a half jacket over her body suit, but somehow neither of them covered her breasts.

Matt was trying to take it all in when his attention was suddenly focused on the riding crop pointing at his nose.

"Out!" Erica seemed pretty insistent.

Christy quickly pulled him back into the hallway and closed the door behind them, leaning against it as if she expected Erica to come bursting out.

Matt looked up and saw a small, glowing, red lightbulb above the door. He had seen those in movies. Whenever a radio station was broadcasting live or on the air they had a red light turned on above the studio door. It seemed pretty obvious now.

"I—" Matt started. There was a meaty slap from the room, followed by a muffled grunt. "I thought we were closed," Matt managed.

"We are." Christy took a step away from the door, still keeping an eye on it. "Until you open up again, that is. But he's a regular. And Erica doesn't always follow the rules." She turned toward the closed door and raised her voice. "Or lock the door." She was answered by a metallic click—a bolt sliding into place.

Christy started leading him down the hall again.

"That seems kind of crazy. Locking yourself in with total strangers," Matt said.

"Trust me," said Christy. "She's in charge when that door closes. Besides, Uncle Quent had a master key in case he had to rescue anybody . . . from her."

Christy led him back to the foyer and stopped by the stairs. "You've already seen your office upstairs. That's also where the *real* bedrooms are."

"So now I'm officially a madam? Madame?" Matt asked, then quickly added, "No, wait, a pimp."

"Manager," she clarified.

He rubbed his chin in thought. "I need to get a new hat."

"You really don't," she assured him.

"So now what?" Matt asked, genuinely wondering.

Christy took a couple of steps over to a window near the front door. She opened the blinds. Hanging against the glass was a neon sign. It was facing out toward the street, but Matt could tell that it was the same logo displayed on the receptionist's podium.

"Turn on the sign and wait . . ."

8

Dani rang the doorbell. She and her partner were still in their police uniforms. She pulled out her shirt collar and gave it a quick test sniff. Not good. Normally they would have changed out of their police blues before heading to the Golden Delicious, but today her partner was anxious. As anxious as he was, though, he still let her ring the bell. She knew the door was usually unlocked, but it felt weird just walking in unannounced. So they waited.

When Dani had been assigned as Sergeant Dwayne Murdock's partner, the first thing he'd done was buy her lunch and explain a few things about himself: his last partner hated him; his last partner was a racist, sexist asshole who now worked as a bouncer at a casino on the Strip; the sergeant hated casinos; he was generally left-handed but shot with his right; and he was a crap shot anyway so she should stay behind him if "shit got real." The second thing he'd done was bring her to the brothel.

They had been visiting regularly for the better part of a year. It had been a couple of weeks since their last visit. Normally, Dwayne liked to stop by about once a week, but with Quent suddenly dropping dead and then the funeral, it seemed like a good idea to let things cool down a bit.

The truth was, she looked forward to the visits now. It was the highlight of her week. Most of her days were filled with people looking the other way when she got near, not wanting to meet her eyes. That or they would openly resent her for ruining their God given right to self-destruct. Nobody was happy to see her. Except here at the Golden Delicious. Here all that bullshit was checked at the door. It was illegal, of course. They knew that and she knew that, but the sergeant let it stay open and didn't ask for anything in return. Not that she knew of anyway. So there was a mutual respect, and no reason to hide who they were anymore.

"The sign's turned on," Dwayne pointed out.

It was a pretty obvious statement, but Dani had been working with Dwayne long enough to know that he often pointed out the obvious. The sergeant looked like a blunt weapon in his uniform, square jawed and well muscled, and statements like that didn't help inspire confidence. People who didn't know him often dismissed him as a stereotypical *beat down first, interrogate later* cop. She did know him, though, and she knew that when he started pointing out glowing neon signs, it usually meant he was just taking in his surroundings and noting things that seemed out of place.

When he was calm, Dwayne still cataloged everything he saw. He just didn't talk to himself as much. That's not to say he was some kind of supersleuth. Just because he was observant didn't mean he made all the connections. They worked well together because Dani could draw details out of him and then use him as a sounding board to try to piece things together.

The guy who opened the door looked guilty . . . *of everything*. His cocky grin melted away when he saw the two of them. It was replaced with an *Oh shit* look that Dani had seen hundreds of times, right before she had to say something like, "Hold it right there" or "Put down the bong." Usually the next thing they said was . . .

"Uh," said the guy at the door.

"Your sign's turned on," said Dwayne.

"You're cops," he replied.

It was like reading a picture book. *See Jane. See Jane run. See Jane pull out her service pistol and* —

Dani pushed past him into the foyer before she could finish the story. As she did, she said, "You must be the new guy." Now she was doing it, too—pointing out the obvious.

It took him a second to reply. "I'm not . . . a pimp."

She ignored him and looked around. The place seemed the same, but then why should anything be different?

Dwayne got in the guy's face and gave him *the stare*. "Christy here?"

"What do you mean by 'here'?" asked the guy.

Dwayne's stare narrowed into a scowl. That was never a good sign, and the guy must have picked up on it, because he took a step back.

"Don't you need a warrant or something? Because I can explain." The guy seemed confident for about one second, then he caved. "No, I can't."

Luckily for him, Christy came out into the foyer from the parlor. She was dressed for work. She looked nice—elegant, seductive, and confident. She pulled that off in an evening gown, while the other girls who worked here usually went straight for the skimpy lingerie. She made them all look cheap by comparison. Well, except for one.

"Dwayne. What do you want?" Christy didn't sound like she was going to waste any of that charm on the sergeant.

Dwayne ignored the new guy now. "We need to talk. Where's Adam?"

"Kitchen. Doing his homework."

"Can we go upstairs?"

Christy looked at the new guy, then back at the parlor, then at Dwayne again. "Fine," she said and led the way up the stairs.

The new guy started to follow them, but Dani put herself in front of him.

Her mouth said, "Private conversation." Her tone said, *Fuck off.*

He seemed confused. "Should I be bribing you or something?"

"What's your name?" she asked.

"Matt."

"Matt, you got something I want?"

"He doesn't." This time it was Erica coming to the rescue.

She was dressed for work, too. Erica called that particular outfit Madam Lovefist. She had a couple dozen work getups, each with its own name. So far, Dani had been introduced to about ten of them. Normally Madam Lovefist's boobs were on display, but she must have zipped up the half jacket to come out to the foyer. Maybe she was on a break.

"Who is he?" Dani asked.

"New owner. He's a bit of a douche," Erica explained.

Matt turned to look at Erica. "Which means, technically, I'm your boss."

Erica stared him down. "I'm not gonna change my answer."

Matt seemed to take it personally. He deflated a bit and turned back to Dani. She guessed it was his first day. She had heard that ownership of the GD had changed hands, but she wasn't expecting *this*. Especially after dealing with Quent. She'd never really gotten attached to Quent. He'd tolerated cops, but he hadn't like them. At least he had seemed to know what he was doing and had generally been respected by the girls who worked here.

This new guy had a long way to go before he was going to be respected. Erica wasn't helping any. She pretty much treated everybody like that. Sometimes it was hard to know when she was being serious or just toying with somebody. Matt was obviously a toy, though. At least for now. Until she got bored.

She and Dani had started out the same way. To Erica, Dani must have seemed like the sergeant's faithful sidekick when they'd first met, complete with wide-eyed wonder and "Golly-gee" questions. Which *was* how she'd felt when she'd started working as the sergeant's partner. It had taken a few months for the newbie stink to wear off. And a couple more before Erica had kissed her.

Dani pointed a finger at Erica and used her cop voice, even but stern. "Ma'am, I'm gonna need you to answer a few questions. Is there someplace we can talk?"

Erica responded by bowing her head slightly and biting her lower lip. She normally reserved that move for when she was wearing Miss Priss. It looked out of place on Madam Lovefist.

Erica started walking down the hallway, Dani close behind, and they left Matt foundering in the foyer.

Maybe Erica was still toying with her, too. Dani wasn't sure, but there were times when she thought she was seeing the real Erica. When the flirting paid off and costumes were piled on the floor, the woman who remained was far more interesting than any of her personas. She was clever, challenging, and above all, honest. Dani had a feeling that Erica wouldn't let that side of her show unless there was something real between them. She would see it as a weakness, and the Erica who worked here couldn't afford to be weak.

But today wasn't about breaking down walls or sharing intimate secrets. Today was about forgetting the crappy week she'd had and reminding herself that sometimes people were actually happy to see her. Even if they just wanted to play.

Erica led Dani to the VIP room. The red light was on, but that didn't seem to concern Erica, who barely broke her stride to open the door. Before Dani could join her inside, a man covered in zippers and vinyl was shoved out of the room. She stepped aside to avoid him, and a hand grabbed her wrist to pull her in.

The door closed, and Dani heard the gimp's muffled voice on the other side. "So . . . we're done?"

Dani wrenched her hand free while using the other to push Erica up against a workbench. Mounted on the wall behind it was a pegboard covered with hooks and clamps, each holding a tool of the trade. Something medieval looking tumbled down from its place on the board as Dani spun Erica around and pressed her up against the edge of the table. She might have pushed a little too hard, and she heard Erica grunt as the table thumped into the wall. Erica didn't seem to mind; she didn't fight back at all. That would probably come later. She held Erica in place by jamming her hips against Erica's ass, freeing up her hands to grab the handcuffs off her belt. There were cuffs on the pegboard, of course, but she like to go for authenticity.

As the first cuff clicked into place around Erica's wrist, she threw her head back to look at Dani. "Why don't I ever get to be the cop?"

Dani used the empty cuff as a handle to yank Erica's arm behind her back. Then she secured her other wrist. "You make a better bad guy."

Erica started to stand, but Dani pulled the chain on the handcuffs straight up, forcing Erica to bend over again. Then her other hand reached out and held Erica's head firmly down on the table. Her fingers threaded through Erica's hair, and then she made a fist, pulling the hair tight. With Erica pinned in place, Dani turned her hip so the flashlight on her belt pressed against Erica's tailbone. Then she rocked her hips, letting the bulge follow the natural lines of Erica's body.

"What did I do this time?" asked Erica with an exaggerated gasp.

"Smuggling," Dani said. Then she used one booted foot to kick Erica's legs apart.

Erica pushed back, grinding into Dani's thighs. "Smuggling what?"

Dani's hand slowly slid along the small of Erica's back down between her legs. The vinyl was warm and tight and hid nothing. She reached down to the snaps holding Erica's bodysuit in place. There were two straining at her crotch. Dani hooked a finger between the snaps and pulled. The bodysuit sprung up toward Erica's waist like a rubber band. Smooth black curves were replaced instantly by soft pink skin. Dani's hand came away wet.

"I'll know it when I find it."

9

There was yelling coming from Christy's bedroom upstairs. It had started out as a loud, muffled conversation, but Matt missed most of that, thanks to the cop *questioning* Erica. He was pretty sure he was going to jail soon and didn't know why he wasn't heading out the door right now. He was working up the courage to leave when the muffles turned into shouts.

"Look, I just need you to sit down and stay calm for a couple minutes!" It was a guy's voice. Didn't Christy call him Dwayne?

"I don't need this. Can't you tell we're going through a lot right now? He just died!" That was definitely Christy's voice.

Matt looked at the front door. All his stuff was upstairs. He hadn't settled in yet, but he had thrown his duffel bag into Uncle Quent's old bedroom. His laptop was in there, too, along with some of his "improvised" IDs. On top of that, he only had about twenty bucks in his pocket. That wasn't much to start over with, and he would be on the run again. He needed that bag.

Maybe he could just claim that he was a customer. They

could book him if they wanted to, but they seemed more interested in the employees at the moment. No, that wouldn't work. They'd probably point him out as the new owner if they thought it would help. He hadn't exactly made any friends here yet.

He started heading up the hardwood stairs. They weren't quiet at all, despite his careful steps. Every other one seemed to squeak. He decided to go for it and sprinted to the top, hoping no one would notice over the shouting.

"Isn't this over?" The cop yelled the question, trying to force it into a statement.

Christy held her own. "Well nobody told the hospital that the whorehouse was closed. Adam's still sick, and they keep sending bills. So no. It ain't over!"

Christy's room was to the right. Luckily Matt needed to go left where Uncle Quent's old bedroom stood next to his office. In fact, Matt wasn't sure how much his uncle had actually used that bedroom. The office looked more lived-in. It had pictures of his travels and misadventures, as well as some knickknacks that he must have picked up along the way. Food crumbs hid in the love seat cushions, and the throw rug had a threadbare path worn through the middle. Plus, it smelled like biker.

The bedroom, by comparison, seemed empty. The bed was lumpy and covered with a plain comforter so faded Matt couldn't tell what its original color might have been. There was a thick layer of dust on the dresser, and he had to rock the drawers back and forth if he wanted to open them. The chair in the corner was missing a pad on one leg that made the whole thing wobbly. He would bet that Uncle Quent slept on the love seat in his office most nights. Matt was tempted to do the same. He grabbed his bag off the wobbly chair and headed back out into the hallway.

He stopped two steps away from the stairs when he saw the boy. Adam must have come up right after him. He didn't look at Matt. He was standing at the top of the stairs with a notebook in one hand and a pencil in the other. Matt thought he saw math equations on the page it was open to, but the symbols didn't look like anything he could remember from school. Adam took a step toward his mother's door but then stopped when the shouting started again.

"I thought we could make another run of it. He's my son. I can help." The cop was loud but sounded like he was trying not to be.

Christy, on the other hand, wasn't trying to quiet down at all. "He's not your son as far as I'm concerned. You wrote him off years ago."

Adam took another step forward. He was right in front of the door now.

"I was eighteen!" shouted the cop.

"I was seventeen!" Christy shot back. "Just because you have a badge now doesn't make you a good father!"

Matt watched Adam as the boy stared at the frame around Christy's door. It had pencil marks going up one side with Adam's name next to them. Based on the ages next to the names, Adam and Christy had been here awhile. Adam dropped his notebook, and he reached out a hand toward the doorframe. He slowly slumped down the wall next to it until he was on his knees. He started to shake.

"This isn't a good life for him." The cop was almost using an indoor voice now, and Matt barely heard him.

He didn't have any trouble hearing Christy. "We do fine! Together. Just like we have for nine years."

Adam's eyes were closed. He sat on the floor with his back to the wall and his knees drawn up to his chest. He shook harder now. Matt remembered sitting like that when he'd been a boy, trying to cry as quietly as possible. He dropped his bag and went to sit next to Adam.

"Quent's gone. This place is done," said the cop.

"We'll find a new place," said Christy.

When Matt was nervous, his knee-jerk reaction was to crack a joke or make a smart-ass comment. Things couldn't be that bad if he could make somebody smile. Even if they were trying to hurt him. Where there was a smile, there could be hope. He didn't even have to try anymore; the comments came out on their own.

"Lying down on the job?" he asked Adam. He gave him a shoulder bump as he said it.

Through the door, Matt could hear the cop getting louder again. "Well, you're not leaving Vegas."

Christy matched his volume. "We'll go wherever we need to!"

"I can't just pick up and leave!"

"Nobody's asking you to!"

Adam didn't react to the bump at first. Then he started to slowly slide away from Matt down the wall. As he did, his head turned, and Matt could see his eyes. They were squeezed shut but Adam wasn't crying. Instead, his eyeballs visibly vibrated under his lids and his head nodded to some unheard rhythm. Blood started to trickle from one corner of his mouth as he opened it. There was a long draw of breath and then Adam started speaking? Ranting? Babbling? Whatever it was, it came out in a torrent, and it was in no language Matt had ever heard.

Matt quickly reached for the boy. "Dude! Fuck!" The boy's whole body was starting to shake now, and Matt had no idea what to do. "Adam!"

Adam's babbling stopped suddenly, and all at once he was speaking English. It was fast and jammed together, hard to follow, but it sounded like, "Do-not-think-that-I-have-come-to-bring-peace-on-Earth-I-have-not-come-to-bring-peace-but-a-sword."

Matt leaned down on Adam and tried to hold him still. He reached one hand back and banged on the door. "Hey! Something's wrong! He's bleeding!"

"For-I-have-come-to-set-man-against-man."

Christy yanked the door open. The cop was standing behind her wide-eyed.

"And-a-man's-foes-will-be-those-of-his-own-household."

Christy shoved Matt aside and grabbed her son. She sat down and started cradling him in her lap. "His pills! The bathroom!"

The cop ran down the hall and ducked into a room as Christy forced the flat of her hand into Adam's mouth and rocked him back and forth. Adam's jaw clamped down hard and his babbling was muffled. "It'll be okay, baby," she whispered. "Shh. Shh. Shh."

The cop hurried back toward them a moment later with a small plastic bottle in his hand. He knelt down beside them. Water sloshed onto the floor as he set down a chipped mug. He was shaking as he poured the pills into his palm. Some of them fell and clattered across the floor. He managed to hold on to a few. "Open his mouth!"

Christy pulled her hand out of Adam's mouth, and Matt saw a semicircle where teeth had broken skin. She didn't seem to notice. The cop dropped the pills in Adam's mouth and then forced it closed. The blood at the corner of the boy's lips was bubbling as his throat struggled to make sounds. Christy grabbed the mug, and the cop took his hand away from Adam's jaw. She held up Adam's head and pressed the mug to his lips. His mouth filled with water, and he was forced to swallow.

"What's wrong?" Matt asked. "Should I call 9-1-1?"

"He gets these seizures. They were getting better but . . ." Christy held Adam to her chest and started rocking him again.

The cop yelled down the stairs. "Where the fuck is Dani?" Then he turned to Matt. "Go! Call!"

Matt dug through his bag and pulled out his phone. He got to his feet and dialed.

■ ■ ■

It was past midnight by the time Matt sat down again. When he did, it was in Uncle Quent's office. Or his office, he supposed.

He still hadn't unpacked his duffel bag, but the house was quiet. Christy and Adam were staying the night at St. Jude Children's Hospital. So was the cop—no, the *police sergeant*. That was a fun fact. Matt didn't want to think about what that might mean for him. Nothing good. Potentially a special kind of *bad*

Matt rubbed his forehead. At least Adam seemed to be doing all right now. The seizures had almost stopped by the time the ambulance had arrived. The blood had looked worse than it was. It turned out that Adam had bit the inside of his cheek rather than his tongue. The paramedics didn't seem too concerned about that. They did flash a light in his eyes and jab an IV into his arm. He must have taken an ambulance ride before, because Christy seemed to know all the right things to say when the paramedics asked. She even had a card ready listing all the medications he was taking.

Matt had been able to talk to her briefly on the phone to see how Adam was doing. It sounded like they were coming back early the next morning unless there was another episode during the night. Matt hadn't mentioned the rambling string of words that had come out of Adam's mouth. He couldn't really remember exactly what the kid had said anyway. It sounded a bit fire-and-brimstone, but beyond that, it was gibberish. Probably something he had read somewhere.

Needless to say, Matt had turned off the neon sign after the sirens had faded away. None of the girls seemed to mind. Not even Erica. Matt was glad he didn't have to deal with her again tonight, though he would likely see her tomorrow.

He took a deep breath and looked around the office. He remembered that Erica had taken a picture from the desk right after the reading of Uncle Quent's will. There were several other pictures on the desk, too. Some of girls he recognized, some he didn't. He picked up one of the pictures. It was of his uncle wearing an apron in the little kitchen downstairs. He was making pancakes. The apron said KISS THE COOK, and Christy was pointing to it while she kissed him on the cheek. It looked like Uncle Quent was tolerating it the way an eight-year-old might tolerate a kiss from a grandparent.

Matt spoke to the man in the picture. "What the hell were you thinking? Did you think this would be funny?" Matt put down the picture. "It probably is. If you're not me."

Next to the picture was a wooden cigar box. Matt didn't smoke, but he was curious. He couldn't remember ever actually holding a cigar. Maybe he would just put one in his mouth and chew on it. He flipped open the lid. "Whoa."

Matt reached into the box, and his hand came out holding a pistol. It was pretty for a gun, though he hadn't seen too many before, and certainly not long enough to take in all the detail. Uncle Quent's pistol was a revolver. He wasn't sure if it was considered a big gun, but it seemed like it was somewhere between *Maverick* and *Dirty Harry*. It was shiny. Maybe this was what they meant by nickel-plated. The handle was made of some kind of wood—light, with a fine grain. There was scrollwork engraving on the handle and along the barrel, too. Some of the scrollwork suggested writing, but if it was text, Matt couldn't make it out. Its design didn't really seem to reflect its previous owner at all.

He pointed it high and looked along the barrel at the sight. He felt pretty badass. He was tempted to cock the hammer and was wondering if a gun like this had a safety, when he noticed something on the ceiling.

He lowered the gun and squinted up at the exposed rafters.

"What . . ."

He took a step closer. Then rubbed his eyes and tried to blink the image away.

"The . . ."

The image remained. Burned into one of the rafter beams was a symbol—an arrow connected to a cross, connected to a circle, connected to a crescent. The lines were thick like a cattle brand, and some sort of old coin had been nailed to the center of the circle.

"Fuck . . ."

F-bombs were pretty rare for Matt. He usually found it more funny or more clever to come up with some other expletive. But this was the second one he had dropped today.

The marking on the ceiling itself wasn't that shocking; it was pretty simple, really. The F-bomb had dropped when Matt realize that same symbol was burned into his own wrist.

10

Foster had a habit of mouth-breathing when he was trying to concentrate. The more he focused, the wider his mouth opened. His hand started to shake as he inched it closer to the prostitute's breast, and his lips parted a little more. She said her name was something like Vicky. Normally he was pretty good at remembering people's names, but he had been really nervous when they'd first met. His mouth had dropped open almost immediately. He must have looked like a bit of a dork. It hadn't scared her away, though. Which was a shame. She seemed pretty nice.

"You're sure this washes off?" asked the prostitute who was probably Vicky.

Foster kept his eyes on his hand when he answered. "Oh yeah. They're for kids. You could eat them if you wanted to."

He was straddling Vicky. She was naked, but he was still dressed. His hand held a felt-tip marker, and he was using it to draw a line along her skin. It started at Vicky's left ankle and then curved, and swirled, and looped, as it made its way up her thigh and over her hip. Then it dipped back down toward her crotch before circling around her labia. From there it traced up her abdomen and spiraled around her belly button. Sometimes the line crossed itself, and Foster drew a more detailed pattern when it did, sometimes it arched in wide, lazy loops like cursive handwriting. It was all one line, though; the pen never left her skin. The Woman in the Garden had him practice several times to make sure he could finish the line without lifting the pen.

He was just about to start a pretty complex flourish on her right breast. His mouth almost made a perfect *O*. It was going to be tricky.

He paused, started, and then stopped abruptly when she said, "Well, they smell tasty. What is that? Strawberries?"

Foster took a breath. "I thought so, too, but the pen says it's something called Fluffleberry. I don't think that's a real berry, though." He continued his line.

"Smells like it should be real," said Vicky.

"Mmm. Sorry, this is the hard part." Foster drew slowly and deliberately. If Vicky was ticklish, she was keeping it under control.

They were in a cheap motel room. It was nowhere near the Strip, but it did have a faded print of all the casinos lit up at night above the headboard. Most of them, anyway. The pyramid was missing, so it was a bit dated. Still, it was a step up from sleeping on the beanbag chair in the orphanage.

The garden was no longer bleeding into the orphanage TV room, but the Woman in the Garden still spoke to him. She had finished the storybook for him while he wrapped up his wrist and sucked down a couple of juice boxes. He was pretty sure he was going insane.

She told the story of how she had given her heart to the first man she'd ever met. How they'd made a life for themselves tending the garden. She made the guy sound like a real tool. The way she described him, he had almost no personality. They hadn't had a "meet cute" or anything like that. He just kinda shown up and they started farming together.

Foster had still been a bit fuzzy from the blood loss, but it sounded like this guy had just wandered off into the woods one day and had gotten lost. The next day he'd shown up at the garden with another woman, only this one had a name— Eve. And then he started calling himself Adam. He said they were in love and that God wanted them to be together.

The Woman in the Garden had gotten pretty pissed off when she'd been telling that part of the story. She'd gone off on this rant about how *they* had changed the story and how *they* couldn't stand seeing the man and the woman as equals. Foster wasn't sure who *they* were, and he was too frightened to ask. And then this new woman had given Adam children. Children! The Woman in the Garden lost her shit then, yelling about how those should have been her children.

While she had been telling her story, a snake slowly wound its way around her body and up her outstretched arm. It started climbing one of the branches of the oak tree the woman was standing under. When it approached the owl, it flicked out its tongue a few times to smell the bird's talons. The owl had stared at it for a second with its huge unblinking eyes. And then it grabbed the snake with its beak and ripped the serpent's head off.

Foster had gone to Sunday school when he was a kid, of course. It had been mandatory at the orphanage. The woman's story sounded kind of familiar, but he didn't remember Adam choosing between two women, or being such a tool, or that crazy screech owl in the oak tree. That's when he'd figured out he was losing it and wondered why he'd bandaged up his wrist at all.

Then the Woman in the Garden had said something that made him have another juice box. "You feel like trash. Me too. Maybe we can help each other."

And now Foster was in a cheap motel room straddling a naked hooker.

"Is this from, like, a movie or something?" asked Vicky.

Foster had moved on from her breast and was working the swirls on her cheek. She was trying to follow the pen with her eye, but he could tell she was having trouble focusing because she stopped and squeezed her eyes shut for a second.

"Huh?" said Foster.

"Like *Avatar*? Do you want me to wear a tail or, like, cat eyes? That would be cool." Vicky sounded genuinely interested. It might have been Vicki with an *i* actually. He thought that's what her business card said. It had been surprisingly easy to find a prostitute. There had been people literally handing out her card on a street corner—hers and dozens of others. The card said she was an "exotic dancer," but when Foster called the number, the person on the line had been pretty accommodating after asking a few questions. No, Foster wasn't a cop. No, he wasn't working for the cops. And yes, he had money. Tips were encouraged.

"No thanks." Foster clicked the cap back on the pen. "That's it. Done."

Foster leaned back and looked down at her. Vicki was beautiful. Or at least young and cute. She was covered with Fluffleberry-colored lines, and Foster was quite proud of his work. Seeing it on an actual woman rather than the orphanage wall made it look exotic and elegant. She didn't look nervous at all. Her bright, wide eyes and tiny smile made it seem like she was having fun. Foster, on the other hand, was shaking.

"Okay. Ready to go?" Vicki asked. "Don't be nervous, baby. They're always bigger than you guys think."

Foster carefully lifted himself off her and stood next to the bed. He took a step back. "I'm just gonna . . . be in the bathroom."

Vicki lifted her head slightly and looked at him. She seemed a little concerned. "Okay. Take your time. It's okay to be nervous."

Foster took another step back and held out his hands. "Don't move. I got it just right."

Vicki gave him that tiny smile. "Okay." Then she laid her head back down.

Foster cupped his hands under the faucet in the bathroom. The water bubbled up in his fists and then spilled over into the sink. He watched the motion of it for a second before splashing it on his face. Then he looked at himself in the mirror. There was nobody standing behind him, but he still heard her voice. His Adam's apple bobbed as he swallowed.

"You're nervous. Why?" the Woman in the Garden whispered. "You're doing a good thing."

"It doesn't feel good," Foster whispered back. The water filled up in his hands again.

"Everybody wants to open the gates of Paradise. And you have the key."

"Do they? Maybe she's happy. Maybe she just wants to go home and watch TV."

The storybook was open on the counter next to the sink. He remembered putting it there, but he didn't remember opening it. A paper woman stood beneath a pop-up tree. A tiny bunny jiggled on a metal spring in a field of flowers, hopping toward her outstretched hand.

"Pathetic," she said. "She's tainted. She doesn't know

what she wants. But I do. She wants what you want. What we all want. She wants to come home."

"Did you say something?" Vicki raised her voice a little to be heard from the bedroom. "All this ink is making me kinda dizzy."

The voice in Foster's ear whispered, "Play her some music and take her home."

Foster looked over at the storybook. Next to it was his music box. He picked up the box and stared at the lid. Then his eyes flicked toward the bathroom door. He pushed it open but didn't walk through. Instead, he sank down to the floor and sat on the linoleum. Then he lifted his butt up a little and pulled something out of his back pocket. The blade slid out as his thumb pushed the button on the box cutter.

Three clicks. Full length.

He poked the blade into the carpet just outside the bathroom door.

Then he flipped open the music box. He kept his eyes focused on the clockwork inside as the tune started to play. He pushed the palms of his hands against his ears and mumbled the lyrics to himself.

"Way down upon the Swanee River, far, far away. That's where my heart is burning ever, that's where I want to stay."

The blade moved on its own. It cut through carpet. Then it cut through sheets. Then it cut through flesh. It followed Foster's line perfectly.

11

Matt was trying to figure out how to cook breakfast. He had cracked a bunch of eggs into a pan and swirled them around, hoping they would turn into scrambled eggs. Instead, they stuck to the pan like glue. The bottom layer started turning black while the top remained a runny mess. He tried to scrape up the bottom layer in an attempt to flip the whole thing over. Maybe he was actually making an omelet? But the eggs wouldn't come off the pan, and he started to wonder if eggs could actually catch fire. He wasn't sure whose eggs these were, but they were going to be disappointed.

Adam and Christy were sitting at the little round table. Matt could see them from where he stood in the kitchen. The TV was on, but none of them were really watching it. Adam was rooting around in a cereal box with a look of disappointment on his face as Christy opened a fresh carton of milk and poured some in his bowl.

"Are you digging for buried treasure?" Christy asked him. She seemed mostly recovered from the night before.

The boy set down his cereal box, the toy inside eluding him for the moment. "What's a brain embolism?" he asked.

It took Christy a second to reply. "It's when somebody's brain doesn't work the way it should." She folded the milk carton closed and then added, "You don't need to worry about that."

"But sometimes my brain doesn't work right." Adam patted the cereal in his bowl with his spoon.

"That's different. The doctors said it's because your brain is working extra hard. Plus, they gave us new medicine for that." Christy used a finger to turn Adam's face toward hers. "Did you take your pill?"

Adam dug a pill bottle out of his pocket and set it on the table. Then he turned back to his bowl and took a bite. Mouth still full, he pointed his spoon at the bottle and said, "It says, 'Take with food.'"

"Then eat up."

"Why would Uncle Quent's brain just stop working?" Adam asked. "That doesn't make sense."

"I don't know, honey." Christy sipped her coffee.

Matt turned off the stove. He looked at the contents of the pan and then immediately started scraping it into the garbage disposal. He decided he would blame the pan. Damn stainless steel.

He flicked a glance up at Adam again, who was kicking his legs back and forth under the table as he ate. "Are we going to have to move out of Uncle Quent's place now that he's dead?"

Christy didn't look at Matt. She kept her eyes on her coffee. "I don't know, honey."

"What about your job?"

"I don't know." It came out a little harsh, and Christy turned away with her hand on her forehead.

Adam stopped eating. "Mom? Are you mad?"

"Yes," she said. "But not at you."

Matt had heard them come back to the house a couple of hours before. Adam might have slept a bit at the hospital, but Christy looked strained and worn thin. It was a weekday, but clearly Adam wasn't going to school today. And they were opting for breakfast instead of collapsing into bed. Breakfast for Adam, anyway. Christy hadn't made anything for herself other than a cup of coffee. He really wished his eggs had turned out better.

Matt pretended that he hadn't been listening to their conversation as he walked toward the table. "Mmm. What's for breakfast?"

Adam frowned at his bowl. "Not quite Cheerios."

Matt sat down at the table and opened the box. He grabbed a hand full of O's and popped a few into his mouth. "Oh, come on. You can't taste the difference."

"I can." Adam gave him a matter-of-fact nod.

"So can I," Matt admitted.

Christy rubbed her forehead a couple of times and sniffed. Then she turned to Adam. "They're organic," she said, her voice a little more cheerful.

Matt leaned over to Adam and gave him a stage whisper, "You know, there was no organic food when I was growing up. It was all fake."

Matt looked at Christy out of the corner of his eye in a way that was obvious he was sneaking a look at her. He gave her a little smile. Christy stared at him over the top of her coffee cup before shaking her head and taking a sip.

Matt turned to look at her for real. "So how many people live here?"

Christy set her mug on the table but left her hands wrapped around it. "Full time? Just me and Adam. And you apparently. Some of the other girls stay from time to time but not for more than a couple of days. Uncle Quent was kinda looking out for Adam and me."

Matt tossed a couple more organic O's into his mouth. "Seems kinda weird, doesn't it? How does that work?" Matt pointed a thumb at Adam. "With him here, I mean."

Christy started to glare. It probably wasn't the right time to ask that question, but it had just kinda popped out of his mouth.

"Weird?" she said. "Aren't you the one who just inherited a brothel? *That's* weird."

Adam spoke up. "It's okay, Mom. It is kinda weird living here."

Matt started to open his mouth to reply, but Christy went on the defensive. "People live above bars and casinos all the time. That's probably way more dangerous for a kid."

Matt started again. "I was just—"

Christy was still going, though. "When he's not at school, he mainly stays up in his room. Nobody's allowed up there. You saw the velvet rope, right? Besides, we didn't have too many options when Quent took us in." Christy took a sip of coffee, then turned to Adam. "Which reminds me . . . You still need to take your pill."

Adam made a zombie face. "They make me feel funny."

"Hospital bills make me feel funny," Christy countered.

Adam rolled his eyes but popped the pill into his mouth. He used his cereal milk to wash it down, tipping the bowl up to his face. When he lowered it, he had an epic milk mustache.

"What's that?" Matt asked Christy. He gave a nod toward the bottle of pills.

"I never get the name right," she said. "It's supposed to help with his episodes."

"Seizures?"

"Something like that. The specialists aren't even sure."

Christy started clearing the table. "They say the pills can help suppress the shaking. But they don't know what causes it."

Matt looked at Adam. "Must be hard."

Adam wiped his face with the back of his sleeve. "It's all right. I think it's getting better."

Matt looked past Adam to Christy, who was putting dishes in the sink. He caught her eye, but then she looked down and gave a slight shake of her head.

"Should I, uh—" Matt hesitated and almost didn't continue "—ask about the sergeant?"

"I'm tired. I don't really feel like yelling right now," she said.

Matt held up his hands in defense. "No problem. Didn't know if there was anything I should be doing."

"No." Christy kept her eyes on the bowl she was scrubbing. "It's fine. He won't do anything about this place. He comes by every week or so to check in on Adam. He knows better than to come during business hours. *Usually.*"

Adam twisted in his chair to watch TV. "Dad said he could pick me up from school sometime."

"He doesn't really know our routine," Christy said. "He hasn't been around long enough."

"I could tell him when I usually do my homework and when I need to take my pills," Adam suggested.

Christy seemed to ignore that. "Plus, he could get called away for work at any time."

Adam turned to look at her. "But he's been trying," he pleaded.

"What did I say about not wanting to yell?" It was kind of a half yell anyway.

Adam gave in and turned back to his show. He looked like he had tried to start this conversation a dozen times before and knew what the final result would be. Better to cut his losses before yelling turned into being grounded with no TV.

Matt didn't know what to do with himself in the awkward silence that followed. He decided to watch TV, too.

When Christy came back to the table, she had a cup of coffee and a cereal bar in her hands. She set them both on the table in front of Matt. "So how long do we have?"

Matt raised an eyebrow at the cereal bar but then went ahead and opened it up. "Before?"

"Don't you want us out of here?" Christy asked.

"Not particularly," Matt said. "Truth is, I don't know what to do with this place."

Christy sat down next to Adam and ruffled his hair as a peace offering. "And until you do?"

Matt took a bite of his bar. "Business as usual."

12

Dani's breakfast had consisted of a slice of pizza straight out of the fridge, a lonely cup of coffee from her single-cup brewer, three Tic Tacs to get rid of the coffee breath, and the last of the chocolate chip cookies from a batch she made over the weekend. She justified the last by telling herself that they were going stale. Which, unfortunately, was true.

She was regretting all those choices now.

She leaned up against the wall outside the motel room. The smell alone had been enough to make her break a sweat. She knew that if she got to the point where her stomach started turning on her, she would probably pass out before she vomited. So at least there wouldn't be a mess to clean up. At least not *her* mess. She wasn't a lightweight, either. Blood didn't usually bother her. She even donated whenever the hospital made its rounds with the mobile clinic. That was different, though. Then, she knew what she was signing up for. Today, she was going to have to pace herself.

She had gotten the call about an hour ago and had almost ignored it. She wasn't supposed to be on duty until noon. She and Dwayne had the swing shift this week, and that always screwed her up. She never had any idea what to do with herself in the morning. She was used to rolling out of bed, getting straight into the shower, and then picking up breakfast on the way to work. She'd forgotten how to sleep in long ago, though, so she had been awake and showered when they called her in. Dwayne still wasn't here, but then, last night had been pretty rough for him.

The motel was small. It was right off the freeway near the air force base, and Dani wasn't sure how it stayed in business. If she had to guess, the rooms were either rented by the week or by the hour. The dated sign pointing to the check-in office might have been considered nostalgic fifteen years ago, but now it had decayed to creepy. All the room doors faced a small parking lot, so at least she was outside. A couple of doors down, a police officer was questioning a cleaning lady. Dani was pretty sure they were speaking Spanish, and she tried to translate to give her mind something to do.

The officer probably said, "One more time. A bit slower please."

The cleaning lady's reply wasn't slow, and Dani only got bits and pieces. ". . . about eight in the morning . . . going to get the laundry . . . bad smell . . . bloody hell . . ."

No, not *hell*, *huella*. Dani thought for a moment, then remembered the translation. *Footprint.* She focused again on the woman.

". . . told the boss . . . he said clean . . . knocked on the door . . . used key . . . blood on the . . ." Dani guessed *pomo* meant *doorknob* because there was now an evidence bag taped around the knob to room 105.

The sergeant's car pulled into the parking lot then, so she wasn't able to hear the rest of the conversation. Dwayne didn't bother using one of the regular parking spaces. Instead, he parked his car right in the middle of the lot, a clear indicator that people might want to reconsider staying there tonight.

Dani met him as he was stepping out of his car. He looked like he hadn't slept, and he certainly hadn't showered. She took the coffee cup out of his hand and put it on the hood of his car.

He didn't stop her, but he did say, "Uh, what the fuck?"

"It's bad, sir," she said.

"It must be real bad if you're calling me sir." He looked at his cup like he wanted to take another sip but then left it where it was.

They started walking toward the yellow tape blocking off room 105.

"Sorry, I know your night was shit," Dani said. "How's Adam?"

"He's fine." Dwayne didn't sound convinced. "They say he's fine, anyway. He should be home by now."

"What else did they say?"

"Nothing new. Make sure he takes his pills. Reduce his activities. Be careful of overstimulation. Watch his diet. Basically, avoid being a nine-year-old boy."

The officer who had been questioning the cleaning lady looked up from his notes as they ducked under the tape. He was done with his questions, and the cleaning lady was pushing her cart back toward a door marked STAFF ONLY. He held out something to Dani.

"What's that?" she asked.

"Got it from the cleaning lady," the officer said.

"Evidence?" Dwayne asked.

"No. Toothpaste." The officer unscrewed the cap. He offered it to them. "Put a dab under your nose. It might help with the smell."

"Really?" Dani asked. "That's not something they taught

at the academy."

"Maybe," he said. "I read it online."

A minute later they were standing at the foot of the bed in room 105 with toothpaste mustaches. Dwayne stayed quiet for a long time, taking it all in. He didn't point out the obvious like, *There's blood everywhere* or *She didn't put up a fight*. That was good. It meant he wasn't nervous. Dani needed him firing on all cylinders for this one.

Dwayne finally spoke. "There was an evidence marker on the ground outside. Number two, I think? Was that a blood stain?"

Dani didn't have to look at her notes; she knew what he was talking about. "Yeah, partial footprint."

"What about fingerprints?" he asked, still looking at the bed.

"The guys are coming in after you're done, but yeah, I've already seen some on the doorknob."

"So he was either sloppy, or high, or he just didn't care."

"He?" Dani asked, though that's what she was thinking, too.

"There's a condom on the nightstand. It's still in the wrapper but . . ." Dwayne shrugged.

"Yeah," she said. She didn't like to assume anything, but the simplest explanation usually led to your dirt bag.

Her eyes flicked involuntarily to the bed and then intentionally away. They landed on a glass of water sitting on a small table that served as the room's desk. There was lipstick on the rim of the glass and a swirl of blood floating in the water. As she watched, another red drop plunked into the glass, making the swirl of blood dance. The drop came from the lamp above it. The lampshade had been splattered with two stripes of blood that merged together before drooping toward the glass.

Dwayne took a few steps forward to stand at the head of the bed.

"The room was paid for with cash," Dani said. "And the motel doesn't have any security cameras, which is probably one of its selling points. There's an ATM across the street, though. We're working on getting the video from that."

Dwayne snapped on a pair of latex gloves and started working the fingers into place.

"And there's this." Dani stepped forward carefully. It was almost impossible not to walk in blood. She handed Dwayne a small plastic evidence bag. Inside there was a glossy card with a picture of someone who could have been the girl. In the picture she was wearing a tight white T-shirt that had LAS VEGAS spelled out in a flashy font across the chest. She was pulling the hem of the shirt down to just barely cover her crotch. Underneath that, it said, *Vicki wants to show you the REAL Las Vegas.* The phone number underneath was partially obscured by blood, but she was sure they could figure it out.

"She must have had a driver," Dani said.

Dwayne sighed. "I guess he wasn't paying attention."

"We'll track him down."

"Did you see her eyes?" he asked. He was looking at the Vicki in the room, not the Vicki on the card.

That forced Dani to look down at the bed again. If she just looked at the girl's eyes, Dani was fine. They stared straight up, frozen in a look of wonder rather than pain or fear. On the card they were a brilliant blue and her eyelids were closed just enough to be seductive. In the room, her eyes were opened as wide as they could be, and the blue was clouded with a translucent white. Her lips were parted like she had just oohed and ahhed after a fireworks display.

But nothing from the girl's neck down looked like a

person anymore. Just one glance made Dani start sweating again. She imagined it might look like what was left over on the floor of a slaughterhouse after a hard day's work. Muscle tangled with viscera, and bone gleamed through congealed blood. Nothing seemed to connect or fit together the way it should, and skin spiraled off in ribbons.

Somehow, Dani managed to keep her shit together this time. Maybe the toothpaste was helping.

Dwayne knelt down to look at the girl's arm dangling off the side of the bed. It was mostly intact and hung limp over a pool of blood on the carpet. He grabbed a flashlight off his belt and clicked it on. Then he bent down a little farther.

"Looks like we need another Baggie," he said. He straightened up again, holding something with the tips of his gloved fingers. It looked like a pen of some sort, the big felt-tip kind that they use in preschools. This one was covered in blood, but Dani could make out the cartoony picture of some kind of berry on the side.

Over the next several hours there were a lot more things placed into Baggies. Pictures were taken, and things were covered in fingerprint powder. When the ambulance came, Vicki was also placed into a bag. Dani and Dwayne followed her out.

As the EMTs loaded the body into the back of their ambulance, Dani glanced across the street and saw the vultures starting to circle. The news vans were blocked from coming into the motel parking lot so they were lining the curb across the street. Cameras were zooming in, and reporters were getting their money shots.

Nobody was near them, but the sergeant still spoke in a low voice. "We're in the shit. And I'm not just talking about some hooker—" He caught himself. "Some girl getting killed. I'm talking about news vans parked outside my office, shining a spotlight on everything we do. If somebody did this for attention and we *give it* to them, we'll be cleaning up another body by the end of the week."

One of the police officers intercepted a paparazzo who rushed forward to try to get a closer shot. A couple of other officers were standing by the police cars blocking the entrance, keeping the gawkers at bay.

"So what's our play?" Dani asked.

"Move quick," Dwayne said. "Keep quiet for as long as possible. This guy's already screwed up pretty big."

The ambulance driver got behind the wheel and then looked at them expectantly. The woman nodded her head toward the roadblock to emphasize the point.

Dani nodded back at her and held up a finger, the universal sign for *Just a sec*. She turned back to Dwayne and motioned at the news vans with her thumb. "What do I tell these guys?"

"No comment, on-going investigation, fuck off, I don't care." Dwayne seemed half-serious. "Just no details."

13

Matt was hoping for something a bit more risqué. The track lighting in the parlor was turned all the way up. It wasn't even this bright during the funeral. The girls were milling around, chatting in small groups and generally getting ready for the workday to start. Some were reading, some were snacking, and some were putting final touches on their makeup. None of them were having pillow fights in their lingerie.

He expected the TV by the bar to be looping through porn the same way a sports bar might have the game on in the background, but right now, it was tuned in to a cooking show of some sort. A studio audience clapped and laughed at all the right places as a host made fun of a celebrity chef. The chef was making something with chicken. She mixed some kind of glaze up in a glass bowl and then spooned it over a chicken breast. Then she stared rubbing the glaze all over the chicken with her fingers. The closed captioning read, *Don't be afraid to dig in with your hands and get sticky.*

Matt realized he was a little bit turned on by the show.

That was quickly remedied by the snore-snort coming from a love seat in front of the stage. One of the girls was napping. A line of drool had crept out of the corner of her mouth and formed a wet stain on one of the cushions. Her own snoring woke her up when the quiet but rhythmic breathing turned into a gargling snort. One eye popped open, and her hand instinctively went to her mouth. The back of her wrist came away covered with saliva, and she looked down at it, confused. Not quite awake yet but obviously embarrassed, she looked around to see if anybody had noticed. Matt pretended not to by quickly turning back to the food porn.

"This is super sexy," Matt said under his breath.

Matt was startled when somebody responded. "Well, it is a bit early," said Erica. She was checking her makeup in a compact and scrapping off a bit of stray lipstick with a fingernail.

"It reminds me of the military. Hurry up and wait," Matt said. He pulled himself up to sit on one of the barstools.

Erica closed her compact to look at him. "You were in the military?"

Something was on the chair Matt sat on. He lifted up his butt to see what it was. "No, but I saw some movies."

"Oh, well, I guess you *are* qualified to run this place, then," Erica said.

Matt held a bra up in front of him. "No."

Erica snatched the bra out of his hand. "No?"

"I haven't seen any movies about brothels," Matt said.

Erica rolled her eyes. The look she gave him was like an older sister who had just found her younger brother going through her underwear drawer. Her gross, sticky younger brother. She jammed her bra into the back pocket of her jeans by one of the cups. Then she looked at him deliberately before grabbing the hem of her T-shirt and pulling it off in one fluid motion. Suddenly, he was staring at her breasts.

"Better get used to it," she said, snatching the bra out of her pocket again. She pulled a strap over one shoulder. "This happens in the movies all the time." The bra fastened between her breasts, and she flicked back her hair to make sure none of it was caught in the straps. Next, she shrugged on a tight leather vest. She was going for a different look today—more straps, fewer spikes. With that shade of red lipstick and her cuffed jeans, she could have stepped right out of a 1950s biker bar. He might have actually seen a movie like that.

The doorbell rang.

The girl who had been drooling on the love seat sat up straight, shook her head, and got to her feet. She shoved the fuzzy slippers she was wearing under the couch and stepped into some heels. Another girl pointed the remote at the TV. The studio audience clapped and the cooking show was over. It was replaced by something called *Game of Bones: Winter is Cumming*, which looked both ridiculous and awesome. Magazines were hidden, outfits were straightened, and snacks were swept away. Erica filed a fingernail.

Matt looked toward the foyer. "What's that?"

"You remember?" said Erica. "The doorbell? We have a gentleman caller. Don't freak out like last time. It's not good for business."

Christy came in from the foyer. She was taking the last of the rollers out of her hair. Matt ducked as she tossed it behind the bar. Then she reached over to the wall and dimmed the lights. She gave the rest of the room a quick glance and must have thought it looked good enough. Then she was gone again.

"Okay, everybody, act cool," said Matt. Nobody was listening to him. He turned to Erica, who was putting away her file. "What do I do?"

She stepped past him and went behind the bar. She flicked a switch and soft rhythmic music started playing through hidden speakers. Then she poured herself a glass of something clear. "You let him in. We take care of the rest." She threw back her shot. "Unless you want to start offering services?"

"I'll let you guys take this one," Matt said. He walked to the doorway leading to the foyer but then stopped and turned back to the girls. He thought he should say something, show them he was here for them. He tried to think of something inspiring and relevant. He froze up and somehow he landed on, "Smiles, everyone, smiles."

The man at the front door looked confused when Matt opened it.

"Hi there! Welcome to the Golden Delicious." Matt hoped his smile didn't seem too forced. "Please, make yourself . . . comfortable?"

The man didn't seem any less confused. He wore a puffy vest over a flannel shirt, and he pushed up the brim of his baseball cap with the hairiest finger Matt had ever seen. He raised his eyebrows at Matt, like he was expecting something more.

Then Matt realized he was still blocking the doorway. He stepped aside.

Christy came out from behind the reception podium when she saw the man come inside. She reached forward and put a hand on the man's arm. "Hi, Hank! Sorry about that. He's new. Good to see you again. How's the road treating you?"

The man—Hank apparently—seemed to relax almost at once. "Well enough. Good to be back, though. Sorry to hear about Quent."

Christy started leading Hank toward the foyer. "It's been rough, but friendly faces always cheer us up."

She sat Hank down in one of the love seats facing the stage. "Take your coat?"

"Sure," he said and pulled off his vest.

Christy folded the vest over one arm. "Stayin' in town a while?"

"Well," he said, "no offense, but it's not a town I like to stay in too long. All the lights start messin' with my Zen."

Christy smiled. She hung the vest on a coat rack by the bar and then reached behind the counter. She came up with beer and a bottle opener. When she popped the cap, a little beer foamed out and ran over her thumb. She licked the beer off her finger as she brought it over to Hank. To Matt, it seemed more like reflex than seduction.

"Thanks, hon," he said. "You know me better than I know myself."

Christy sat on the arm of the love seat. She motioned toward the stage. "So whatcha feelin' like today? You want the girls to give you a little spin?"

Hank gave a sideways nod as he took a pull from his beer. "Mm-hmm. That'd be great."

Christy didn't have to say anything more. The girls had been watching them getting comfortable. Five girls stepped onto the stage, each telling a different story by the way she walked or glanced over her shoulder.

Erica strode up with confidence. She gave Hank a look out of the corner of her eye before turning sharply to face him. She cocked her hips to one side and threw back her head with a hint of defiance. Her story seemed to promise a no-nonsense encounter that would start off fast with clothes being torn off and bodies crashing into each other, but then end with her slowing things down and taking control. Matt might have been projecting a bit on that story.

One girl played the shy schoolgirl, complete with fake modesty and a finger dangling strategically from her mouth. Another took the opposite approach, showcasing skin and rubbing herself while licking her lips. Each was trying to read Hank and present a different style of sexy.

Christy didn't go onstage. Instead, she watched with Hank. She joked with him without saying anything. She caught him staring at the schoolgirl and jabbed him lightly in the ribs and gave him knowing smile. He nodded at Erica and tipped his ball cap; Christy ruffled his hair. He seemed undecided. Finally, she rested an arm on his shoulder as though they were watching a movie together. Her index finger traced a casual line on the back of his neck.

Hank turned to Christy. "Well, I wouldn't mind spending some time with you," he said. "You available?"

Christy gave him an exaggerated, bashful smile. "As it turns out, I'm all freed up."

She stood and held out her hand to him. Hank set his beer down on an end table and stood with her. He turned to face her and took the offered hand. He was entranced. As soon as Hank's back was turned away from the stage, Matt saw Erica give Christy the finger. Some of the other girls rolled their eyes.

Christy was only paying attention to Hank. "Come on," she said. "Let's catch up."

She led Hank over to the bar where Matt was doing his best to blend into the background. He didn't know whether or not he should leave, but Christy seemed to know what she was doing and she's the one who'd brought Hank over.

"This is Matt," Christy said. "He's the new manager. He can run your card, unless you'd prefer to pay cash."

"Card's fine," Hank said. "But I wanted to check in with

you on something first. In case it may . . . alter the price."

Christy's smile didn't falter. "Sure. What did you have in mind?"

"Well . . ." Hank hesitated. "I've been reading the Internet."

"Uh-oh." Christy pretended to be concerned.

"I read about this thing. I think it's called the Pullman's Pushcart?" He said it like a question.

"I'm not sure I've heard of that one," said Christy.

Hank gave a nervous little smile as he held up his phone. The screen glowed brightly in the dim light. "I got it here on my phone."

Christy took the phone and squinted down at it. "Hang on," she said. She opened a little clutch purse and pulled out a small case. The case held a pair of reading glasses. She slid them on and glanced up at Hank, a little self-conscious. He was still staring at the screen.

"Hmm," said Christy. "That's creative. You might want to stretch."

"We don't have to do it," Hank said.

He started to reach for his phone, but Christy stopped him.

"No, it's fine." She put a hand on his arm. "It sounds interesting."

"How much do you think?" Hank sounded a little embarrassed to ask.

"Don't worry about it. Regular price." She smiled at him reassuringly. "It'll be fun."

Hank pulled out a thick leather wallet from his back pocket. "I figured if I was gonna try it, it should be with a professional." He handed her a credit card.

Christy passed the card to Matt and then pulled off her glasses. She locked elbows with Hank and started leading him out of the parlor. "Come on. Let's get you showered up." She pointed to something on the phone. "I'll see if we have one of *those*."

Matt watched them go and then looked down at the card. Christy had given him a rundown of how to use the card reader, but he knew he should wait until they were finished. It was like opening a tab at a bar. Hank might decide he wanted to buy another round.

Matt clipped the card next to the cash register.

A phone rang from the foyer. He started to head out to answer it, but Erica beat him to it. He looked in to see if he could help in some way. Maybe they took reservations.

"It's for you," she said and pointed the phone at him.

"What?" he said. "That doesn't make any sense."

Erica covered up the mouthpiece. "He asked for Matt."

"Who is it?"

Erica put the phone back up to her ear. She sighed before asking, "Who is this please?" She listened and then pointed the phone back at him. "He says his name is Boba Fett."

Matt's throat suddenly dried up. "I'll take it upstairs."

A minute later, his hand shook as he picked up the phone on Uncle Quent's desk. "How did you get this number?"

The last time he had heard the voice on the other end of the line, he had just been punched in the face. Matt rubbed his nose at the memory. It still ached.

"For registered mail, phone number is required. Like letter from uncle," said Thug Guy. "How is he, by the way?"

"Dead," said Matt. He eyed the cigar box sitting on the desk.

"Sorry to hear," said Thug Guy. "I guess that means you cannot ask him for money."

Matt opened the cigar box. The pistol was still there. There were also a couple of cigars he hadn't noticed before.

"Well, he left me something."

"Hopefully, piggy bank . . . with much cash," said Thug Guy.

"Close. A business."

"Is not restaurant I hope? So unpredictable. Always closing. I meet many who want to be . . . uh . . . Iron Chefs? Now need joint replacement because of me."

Matt pulled out one of the cigars and held it up to his nose. He took a sniff. He didn't know how cigars were supposed to smell, but this one smelled like a horse barn he had once crashed in over night. Not a bad smell, but he wasn't sure he wanted to light it on fire and force it into his lungs.

"It's a brothel," said Matt.

"A what?" asked Thug Guy.

"A whorehouse," he said. "It's called the Golden Delicious."

"So you are pimp now?"

Matt put the cigar back in its box. "I was told that I was not."

There was a pause on the other end of the line. Then Thug Guy came back on. He sounded cheerful. Too cheerful. "Good news! Am coming for visit."

"That's really not necessary," Matt said.

"It really is," said Thug Guy. "And when I get there you will have something for me."

14

Foster sat on the playground swing outside the orphanage. He didn't push off or pump his legs. The swing didn't move at all. He just had to be outside right now and the swing seemed like a good place to sit. He needed the fresh air. He had almost hyperventilated when he'd left the girl in the motel room, not out of fear but in a desperate attempt to flush the metallic scent of blood and death from his nostrils. He could still smell it if he sat too long in the TV room. That could have been his imagination, though. Either way he needed to be outside.

The rusty chains gave a slight squeak as he shifted his weight, and he stared down at the music box in his lap. He didn't dare open the lid. Instead, he turned it upside down to look at the engraving on the bottom. The symbol looked more familiar now. It wasn't one that he had drawn on *her*, but it might have been another word in the same language. There was also a single line of text carefully written in small letters underneath the symbol: I WISH I HAD MORE TO GIVE. The ink was blue and faded, probably from a ballpoint pen. Some of the letters were missing entirely. Foster used to touch the message when he was a kid, imagining it was the closest he would ever get to the woman who'd written it. When the letters had started to fade, he'd stopped touching it, fearing that it might rub off and be gone forever.

He absently traced a line in the dirt beneath him with the tip of one shoe. Then he stopped when he realized what he was doing. It was just a line. Not *the* line. No patterns or symbols. He did notice something on his shoe, though. The stain stood out clearly on his cheap sneakers. Blood. He bent down and frantically rubbed his thumb over it to wipe it off. As he did, his vision started to blur.

"I'm sorry," he whispered. "I'm sorry. I'm sorry. I'm sorry."

It wasn't until a teardrop hit his shoe that he realized he was crying. That made him cry harder. He buried his face in one elbow and let the tears flow. Each sob emptied his lungs a little more until he had to gasp it all back in at once. That gave him the strength for a wail. He wasn't just miserable. He was angry. With a primal grunt, he blindly flung his music box off into the weeds of the playground.

He took three deep breaths and blinked back the last of the tears. He stood and sighed, then looked around. His music box had landed near the merry-go-round. It was a small one, of course—no horses, just handles. It didn't even spin anymore. It listed on its side with one edge buried in the dirt. Foster reached down to pick up the box and heard something click underneath the rusting ride. He bent down on one knee to look.

A small fuzzy creature peered out at him like a tiny bridge troll. It was a toy of some sort. It kind of looked like a bird but at the same time it looked like a fat rodent. One eye was open wide while the other was frozen in an eternal wink. Its mouth looked like a stubby beak, and its fur might have been purple before years of exposure had drained the color from it. Somehow, it moved.

Ancient plastic gears clicked and grinded as it came to life. An ear twitched, and its good eye blinked. Then it spoke. "Ooh . . . Ha ha ha! *Zzzt*—"

Foster flinched, setting him off-balance. He dropped the music box and threw himself backward. He didn't get very far before plopping down on his butt. He started to scramble to his feet when it spoke again.

"What's wrong? Nobody wants to give you a push?" the thing said.

Foster eyed the toy as he snatched up the music box and held it to his chest. The toy seemed familiar suddenly. What was it called? A . . . a Furby, he thought. But he was pretty sure that had never been one of its standard phrases.

"Relax, Foster. It's me." It still sounded like the Furby, but he recognized the cadence of the Woman in the Garden.

Foster caught his breath and drew up his legs to sit a little more comfortably. The Furby waited patiently, cocking its head from side to side and making a little humming noise. Finally, Foster was ready to talk.

"I'm still here," he said. "You said I could come with you." He wasn't sure if he was angry, or pleading, or whining. "You let *her* in."

"I need my daughters with me before I can open the garden to others," said the Woman in the Garden. "We need to make it ready."

"Daughters?" Foster said. "You need more?"

"Yes."

Foster shook his head. "Why? How . . . how many?" He didn't let her answer the questions. "You didn't say anything about that before."

"You were eager to start," she said.

"I wasn't." Foster tried to convince himself. "I wasn't! I

just want to leave. Nobody wants me here."

"I do," she said. "I need you *there* . . . for now."

He sniffled. "It's hard."

"Come inside," said the Woman in the Garden. "It's snack time. You'll eat and calm down. And then we can talk some more. I want to show you something."

Foster made his way back to the TV room. He didn't bother taking the Furby with him. It had returned to being a lifeless, forgotten toy as soon as she'd stopped speaking. He did have a snack, though. All those tears had left him thirsty. He pealed the top off a plastic tray of cheese and crackers, then washed that down with some flat soda from a half-empty two-liter bottle.

"Better?" the Woman in the Garden asked.

Her voice seemed to come from the storybook like it had in the motel room. The book was open to a pop-up scene of a vegetable garden. A friendly scarecrow hung from a pole in the back, while the Woman in the Garden watered a strawberry patch in front. Foster knew that if he pulled the tab at the top of the page, it would make the strawberries grow. There was another woman he hadn't seen before bent over tending the plants.

He shrugged. "I guess."

"I want to show you the good you're doing," she said. "I left you a window into my world. It's here by my story."

The storybook wasn't by a window. He had tossed it next to his duffel bag over by the wall that he used to practice his drawings. He did see the red plastic View-Master, though. It was already loaded with a reel. He picked up the toy and looked skeptically at the plastic lenses. He used his breath to fog them up and then cleaned them with his sleeve. Then he held the View-Master up to his eyes.

In it he saw the garden in a rounded, square frame. It was

flat compared to the pop-up book, but the rows of vegetables appeared more realistic and the scarecrow looked like it didn't want to be friends anymore. The woman bent over tending the patch of strawberries wasn't just a vague illustration—he saw Vicki. She was wearing a simple white dress, something a Mennonite wouldn't be ashamed to own. Her face was expressionless, and she stared right at Foster with eyes that were a solid milky-blue.

Foster flinched when the Woman in the Garden whispered in his ear. "See? Nothing to be sorry about. She's right where she needs to be."

Foster took a closer look. Vicki didn't look happy. More like a doll posed for a photo.

"Are you sure she wants to be there?" Foster asked. "She looks sad."

"She is sad. And lost. And pathetic," said the Woman in the Garden.

Foster pulled the lever on the View-Master and changed the scene.

Now the Woman in the Garden was standing with Vicki under the oak tree. One of her arms was wrapped around Vicki's shoulders while the other reached out to the owl in one of the branches. Vicki held a white bunny in her arms, and her head was cocked to one side as though she was about to ask a question. Her face still didn't show any emotion.

"I thought you wanted her there," said Foster. "You said she was coming home."

"I do want her here," she said. "And I want her to be worthy of being here. She will be soon."

"When you talk like that, my head hurts," Foster said.

"Pull the lever," the Woman in the Garden told him.

Foster pulled, and a new picture clicked into place.

This time there was no garden. There was a forest trail. The forest was impossibly dense, with the background fading into mist. A young woman was walking the trail. She glared back over one shoulder. It was hard to tell if she was worried she was being followed or angry at what she was leaving behind. She may have just finished crying. In her arms she carried a small potted tree. Foster recognized its leaves—an oak tree. He also recognized the girl. She would grow up with that tree to become the Woman in the Garden.

"Look, I didn't start this," she said. "I was orphaned just like you. I didn't have a choice. I had to grow up fast and find my own way."

"Didn't you tell me this story already?" Foster let the View-Master drop from his eyes. He expected to see her standing right next to him, but she wasn't there.

She whispered to him anyway. "Not all of it. Pull."

Slide. Click.

The new frame showed a naked man standing in the garden. Her garden. He was backlit like some kind of rock star. Animals seemed to be paying homage as he looked down at his own hands in awe. It was a bit melodramatic . . . and, Foster hoped, disproportionate.

"You went to Sunday school right? Genesis. Chapter one, verse twenty-six. It's like the *first* page of the Bible," she explained. "'And God said, Let us make man in our image, after our likeness; and let them have dominion over the fish of the sea, and over the fowl of the air, and over the cattle and over all the earth, and over every creeping thing that creepeth upon the earth.'"

"Creepeth?" Foster asked.

"Don't interrupt," she snapped. "Pull."

Click.

The naked man looked surprised to see a naked woman

standing next to him. She had her own special effects and entourage of animals. It was her again—the younger version of the Woman in the Garden.

The Bible refresher continued. "'So God created man in his own image, in the image of God created he him: male and *female* created he them.'" The Woman in the Garden repeated herself for emphasis. "Male *and* female." Then she continued, "'And God blessed them, and God said unto them, Be fruitful, and multiply,' and blah, blah, blah."

"So, you *are* Eve, then? I thought you said there was another woman named Eve." Foster was just trying to get it right for himself now. "You don't seem like the Sunday school Eve."

"No," said the Woman in the Garden, "that bitch doesn't show up until the next chapter."

Click. Foster didn't remember pulling the lever that time.

A naked man was laying in the dirt, his eyes rolled back into his head. He was still in the garden, but it was night and all the plants were silhouettes or blending into shadows. Except where the plants were splattered with blood. The man's chest had exploded open, pale ribs jutting up toward the sky through blood and gore. One of them was jagged where it had been broken off. The Woman in the Garden was sitting on the ground cradling the man's head in her lap. She was covered in blood, too. Her eyes were squeezed tight, and tears were streaming down her cheeks.

"'And the LORD God caused a deep sleep to fall upon Adam,'" she said. "This is from Genesis, chapter two, verse twenty-one. 'And he slept: and he took one of his ribs, and closed up the flesh instead thereof.'"

Foster was too shocked to say anything. His finger worked on its own. *Click.*

A woman was standing under an apple tree. This had to

be *that* Eve. Her skin was translucent. The only thing that looked solid about her was one of her ribs. The rest of her was in various stages of being put together, layer by layer. A snake was curled up in the apple tree watching her being made. A man was also watching in the background. Adam's chest was whole again. His eyes were a solid, milky-blue.

"And the rib, which the LORD God had taken from man, made he a woman, and brought her unto the man." The Woman in the Garden paused. When she continued, she spoke slowly and clearly, letting each work sink in. "I am nobody's rib."

There was one final frame in the View-Master. Foster slowly clicked it into place.

The Woman in the Garden was kneeling down planting the sapling she had been carrying earlier in her pot. She was in a new garden with seedlings just starting to poke out of the soil. The dark forest from the first frame was in the background. Foster thought she was alone until he spotted the owl watching from one of the distant trees.

"So you left?" Foster asked. He was whispering now, too.

"I had to," the Woman in the Garden said. "I would have been mother to you all. And I wanted to be. So now I'll care for the sad, and the lost, and the forgotten. But they have to find me first. Like you have."

Foster set the View-Master down and rubbed his eyes. "That story kinda just sounds like a typo. Like it just got told out of order."

"Doesn't matter. If people want something enough, they'll believe in it."

15

The sticker on the back of Matt's laptop read, *I heart Turing*. Instead of the word *heart*, though, there was a picture of a heart, and the heart picture was made out of a series of 1's and 0's. Matt knew that the 1's and 0's spelled out the word *heart* in binary. He knew that because he had looked it up online after he'd stolen the laptop from a tourist at a bus station in Reno. He went on to learn all about the life and times of Alan Turing, father of computer science, and while Matt didn't normally use his computer for much more than porn or cat videos, he did think Turing was a pretty cool guy.

Right now Matt did not *heart* Turing, or computers, or cat videos, or even porn. Right now he was on hold with tech support for his new financial software.

He leaned forward in Uncle Quent's chair, squinting at the all the different menu options. Uncle Quent apparently kept ledgers, but when Matt had flipped through them, they made about as much since as Turing's 1's and 0's. He was hoping to bring the Golden Delicious into the twentieth century. Apparently, that required waiting on hold for ten minutes listening to the Muzak version of "The Final

Countdown."

Matt was rocking out to the chorus when the music suddenly cut out and was replaced by a male voice. "Hello, sir or madam. My name is Sean. How may I help you today?"

He couldn't quite place the accent, but this guy didn't sound like a *Sean*.

"Oh, hey," said Matt, "Yeah, I'm using your financial software. Well, trying to, anyway. I'm in the . . . service industry, and I want to add some new products to my sales list."

"Sean" had a reply almost before Matt finished talking. "Our software comes with an extensive taxonomy of generic and specific product types. Are you sure there's not one already on the list that you could use?"

Matt looked at a sticky note next to his laptop. "Some of our services have custom names. I'm pretty sure they're not on there."

"Can you give me an example please?" asked Sean.

"Uh . . . well, there's a service called the Pullman's Pushcart that—"

"One moment please. Let me just do a search." Sean was getting ahead of himself.

Matt tried to explain. "Like I said it's probably not in the—"

"Not in our primary list, let me just look online."

"You might not want to—"

Apparently Sean had found some results online. "Oh! Oh my God!"

"Yeah. That's probably the one," said Matt.

"Okay . . . uh . . . okay. Right." This part didn't seem to be on the script that Sean was reading from. "Yeah, just click on the pencil icon next to the Services tab."

Now they were getting somewhere. Matt clicked on the little pencil button. "All right. Done."

"Great. Next you should see a list of categories," said Sean. "Click the add data icon."

Matt saw a square icon and a cylinder icon. He tried clicking the cylinder. "Okay. I think I got it." The list went blank. He was pretty sure that wasn't supposed to happen. "No, wait. I clicked the cylinder. Was that right?"

Sean sounded disappointed in him. "That's not the next step." Of course, that's when Matt saw a plus icon a little to the left of his pointer.

"Yeah," said Matt, "I think I screwed up. How do you go back?"

"What does the list display now?" asked Sean.

"It's blank," said Matt.

"I see ... how blank?"

"All the way blank."

There was a pause. When Sean spoke again he sounded hopeful but doubtful. "Did you back up your work?"

"How do you do that?" asked Matt.

"Please hold." The Final Countdown returned.

Matt leaned back in his chair. "Shiiit." The word came out as a long sigh.

"You want me to take a look?"

The voice startled Matt. It came from the room instead of the phone. Matt jerked his head up and saw Adam staring at him.

"Hmm? You know how to use financial software?" Matt was dubious.

"No," said Adam, "but I play *Minecraft*." He said it like it was a valid qualification.

Matt hung up the phone. "Well, you probably can't break it any more than I have. But shouldn't you be doing your own homework?"

"I'm done. I was looking for Mom. Sometimes she sneaks me down to the break room so I can watch TV. I looked down from the top of the stairs, but I didn't see her."

"She's probably in the parlor," said Matt. Then awkwardly, "Or . . . you know."

"Yeah." It looked like Adam *did* know what his mother might be doing at that very moment. He didn't seem depressed about it; he just seemed resigned to a boring evening. "That's all right."

Matt pushed back from the desk and stood up. "I'll tell you what. You take a look at this, and I'll go see if she's around."

Adam perked up a little. "Okay. Thanks!" He took Matt's spot at the desk. He was already clicking and typing as Matt left the room.

As Adam had said, Christy wasn't in the foyer. It wasn't really her job to keep an eye on the phone or act as a hostess—all the girls took turns with those duties depending on who was busy—but Christy ended up spending a lot of her free time by the reception podium so she could check on Adam, at least until he went to bed.

The parlor sounded busy. The light, ambient background music had been replaced by something more driving and thumping. A group of enthusiastic guys sat in a circle made up of a couple of couches and a love seat. The men were all in their midtwenties, and each had a drink in one hand and dollar bills in the other. Somebody had brought one of the barstools into the center of the circle. A man sat on it, bare chested and sightless, his own necktie acting as a blindfold.

Two of the girls were keeping him busy. Matt was starting to get to know the women who worked here. He was pretty sure Kendra was teasing the guy's nipple with her tongue while Liz bit and pulled at his earlobe. His buddies took turn whispering tortures or delights into the girls' ears and then tucking bills into their garters. Matt suspected there would be more tortures than delights before it was over.

Christy wasn't there, so Matt went to the girl fixing drinks at the bar. Before his call with tech support, Matt had been looking at the money they had pulled in so far since he'd gotten here. A good chunk of the money came from drinks—either liquid courage to work up the nerve to request other services—or parties like this one.

Matt leaned across the bar to be heard over the music. "Amber, right?"

Amber smiled at him. "Yeah," she said. "Down here, anyway. When you're signing my checks upstairs it's Jessica Dobbs. What's up?"

There were a lot of names to remember. Matt was going to need to make flash cards. He smiled back at her. "Things seem lively."

Amber jiggled her cocktail shaker with a flourish and then poured a line of shots. "We booked a bachelor party."

"That seems dangerous," said Matt. "How many weddings have we ended?"

"The wife booked this one," said Amber. "She gave us some specific instructions. They have boundaries. But there's always wiggle room." She gave a teasing grin as she loaded the shots onto a serving tray.

"Is Christy with a client?" Matt asked.

"No, she has an appointment coming up, though." Amber stepped out from behind the bar and lifted her tray. "She's probably prepping the party room."

Matt walked down the hall, the thumping music receding a bit. Now it just sounded like a racing heartbeat. He decided he was going to figure this place out. It seemed to be working on autopilot, but he felt kind of useless, like a freeloader. Which he was, he supposed. So far he hadn't really done anything useful to contribute to the business. He thought he was going to start by getting the finances in order, but now that was in the hands of a nine-year-old. Maybe Christy would have some ideas. She seemed to know this place inside and out.

Matt opened the door to the party room. "Hey, Christy, Adam was—"

Erica cut him off. "You keep walking in on me. Makes me think you're hoping for another free peek."

She was sitting on the edge of the bed near one of the nightstands. The silver tray that normally held the room's champagne glasses had been cleared off . . . to make room for the line of cocaine. Next to the tray was a small brass cylinder that somehow looked familiar to Matt. Erica held a glass straw between her fingers like a cigarette. There was no powder on her nose but half the line was gone.

Matt wasn't quite sure how to react. "Is that . . . ?"

"Coke?" Erica suggested. "Yes. You want some?" She offered him the straw.

Today she was dressed like a stewardess. Not a modern unisex stewardess but more like a fantasy stewardess from the sixties who might refill your scotch before accepting your membership to the mile-high club. Somehow she made it look intimidating. Maybe it was the uniform.

"No," said Matt, and because he couldn't think of a real excuse, he added, "I had a big lunch."

She stood, smirked, then she slowly bent over to the tray and put the straw up to her nose. She gave him an exaggerated wink before holding one nostril closed and sniffing up the last of the powder. She threw the straw and the cylinder into a clutch purse, and then used one finger to wipe up the last traces of dust. She stepped over to Matt and offered her finger to his mouth.

"Seems like you don't know what you're doing here," she said.

Matt looked down at her finger, not daring to move his head. "Christy said Quent didn't really allow drugs."

She rubbed her fingers together until the powder was gone. "Well, you're not Quent."

She reached down and took one of Matt's hands. He started to pull back but stopped when she raised an eyebrow. She was either scolding him or challenging him. Either way, he gave in, and she guided his hand up the side of her body and then over her breast. There was a lot of polyester between his hand and her skin, but he could still feel her nipple, already stiff.

"In fact, you don't seem to be *anybody*. You're just kinda along for the ride, aren't you?"

He swallowed. "I'm somebody."

"You sure?" she asked. She pushed into him a little and ground her hips forward. "Anyway, who do you think I got this stuff from?"

Matt could feel himself getting hard. She pulled back her hips and then pressed forward again, starting a rhythm. It began to match the thumping music from the parlor. He would be crazy to leave right now. It was a bad idea to stay but crazy to leave. Her free hand slipped past his waistband and found his ass. She squeezed it as she bit her lip and gave a little moan. It looked like a move she practiced and used all the time. Matt didn't care. The last time he'd had sex it was after last call at a bar in California. Everybody who had still been at the bar had scrambled to make friends as quickly as possible. It had seemed more like an act of desperation then. Now somebody was literally trying to get into his pants.

Then she looked up at him. Her eyes were glazed over, and she seemed to be focusing on something well behind him. She wasn't really there, and she didn't really want to be with him. He was just another customer, which meant there was something she wanted from him.

Matt pulled back. He was painfully aware of the bulge in his pants. He had been on the run long enough to get a feel for how stupid he was being at any given moment. If he was being a typical dumb guy, he usually just went with it, figuring he could fix the fallout later. When he moved past that into how-are-you-not-dead-yet stupidity, his self-preservation kicked in. Fight or flight. It was usually flight.

"I better go," he said.

She didn't look surprised or disappointed. "Yeah, that sounds like you."

Matt retreated to the hallway.

At the end of the hallway there was a door that led to the backyard. It wasn't much of a yard, though. Weeds pushed up through the pea gravel, and paint flaked off an old storage shed. Matt closed the door behind him and sat on one of the three steps leading down to a patch of nothing. He stared at the empty space.

"What's got you all moody?"

He looked up to find Christy leaning against the house, her arms crossed. She flicked the ash off a cigarette and blew smoke out the corner of her mouth.

Matt really needed to start looking around more when he opened doors. These women seemed to be ambushing him everywhere he went. "Nothing," he said. It didn't sound convincing at all so he added, "Everything."

Christy pressed the cigarette to her mouth. "Yeah. Me

too."

Matt had never seen Christy smoke before, and she never smelled like she did. After his encounter with Erica, though, he certainly wasn't going to call her on it. Instead, they just hung out in silence for a couple of minutes, Christy smoking and Matt throwing little pieces of gravel toward the shed.

He pointed his chin toward the shed. "What's that?"

"Not sure what it used to be," she said. "Quent used it as storage."

"Do we have much to store?" Matt asked.

"When people set down roots they always end up dumping a bunch of crap they thought they needed," she said.

Matt flicked another stone. "I don't know if I can do this."

"Of course you don't know," said Christy. "You've been here less than a week."

"What if I can't? People shouldn't have to rely on me."

Christy bent down and stubbed out her cigarette in the dirt. "I asked myself that same question every day for a year after Adam was born. Sometimes I still ask myself. People get used to weird shit. This whole city proves that."

Matt stood as she came over to the steps. "Adam wants to watch TV. He's done with his homework. And he might be my accountant now."

Christy led the way back inside and gave a soft laugh. "He probably deserves some milk and cookies, then."

16

Laura Deans, aka Vicki, had been laid bare on the metal autopsy table. Her eyes still stared up in wonder. The medical examiner had made multiple attempts to close them but had only been successful for a minute or two before they slowly pried open on their own. Dani had worked with this ME—Garret—a number of times, but this was the first time she had seen him express any emotion about a case. He kept delaying his report to the sergeant, saying he needed to do more tests or wait for more results, but Dani guessed he was just in over his head with this one.

"You still with me there, Garret?" asked Dwayne.

"Yeah," he replied. "It's just really fucked up."

Dwayne looked up from his notepad. "I know."

"No, I mean, *really* fucked up," Garret reiterated. "Who would do something like this?"

"That's what we're trying to figure out," said Dani.

The autopsy had been completed, but it was hard to tell where Garret might have made his incisions. He must have spent hours getting the skin back in place, and with the blood washed off, the pattern of the cuts were made clear. Or the *cut*, according to the report that Dani had read.

Garret was sitting on a stool next to the table. He still wore his scrubs, but his paper mask was hanging around his neck. He just stared at the body. "The cut was so *intricate*. The blood was drained in seconds," Garret said. "And it was drained *evenly*."

"What does that mean?" asked Dwayne.

The ME reached up to touch his chin with a finger but then realized at the last second that he was still wearing his gloves. "The entire cut, following these patterns . . ." His finger traced a swirling line in the air. "It would need to be made in seconds."

"That's impossible," said Dani.

Garret nodded. "That's right."

Dwayne was actually being pretty patient with Garret. People had been hounding the sergeant all day asking for quotes or updates on the case—the mayor's office, the sheriff, the local news station, the Guardian Angels. They all wanted answers. He was good at fending them off, or if that failed, having Dani fend them off. Still, she could tell that Dwayne wanted answers just as much as the Guardian Angels. And so far, Garret had provided more questions than answers.

"What made the cut?" asked Dwayne.

"Some fucking psycho." Garret said. He said it under his breath, but it was loud enough for them to hear.

Dwayne raised an eyebrow. "Got that part. But what did he *use*?"

Garret held up a box cutter. It looked like it had just been pulled out of the package. It was the standard kind that took disposable blades—simple, gray, utilitarian.

"One of these," Garret said. "New. Or very well cleaned. There was no residue of anything in the wounds. Except . . ." Garret trailed off and looked a little queasy.

"Except what?" asked Dwayne.

"You can still smell the strawberries," said Garret. "Even through the blood and . . . stuff. Strawberries or something. In the ink."

"Fluffleberry," said Dani. "We think it's called Fluffleberry."

Dani held up the evidence bag containing the pen from the crime scene and offered it to Garret. The pen still had blood on it, but it had been dusted for fingerprints. Garret didn't take the pen all the way out of the bag, but he used two gloved fingers to pop the cap off. Then he held the purplish-pink marker up to his nose. He took a quick sniff and then a longer one. From the look on his face it was the same smell.

She thought he was going to vomit, but then he let out a shallow, wet burp. "Don't worry," he said. "I'm a professional."

Dani was skeptical, but then again, at least he wasn't wearing a toothpaste mustache.

"What about these patterns?" she asked.

"Well, they don't have any medical significance. The killer wasn't aiming for any particular vital organs or arteries. He still hit several, of course, though he didn't take anything with him that I could find. No souvenirs."

Dwayne jotted down some notes. "Then why do it? Anger?"

"Like I said, the cut was careful and precise," said Garret. "I don't think it could have been done in a rage."

"Maybe he got off on it," said Dwayne.

"He didn't leave any . . . fluids behind," said Garret. "I did find a hair that didn't belong to the victim, though. It's prepped for DNA profiling."

"Great. Let me know when you have the results," said

Dwayne. "Hopefully we'll have something to compare it with soon."

"Do you have a suspect?" asked Garret.

Dwayne didn't answer. He clicked his ballpoint pen closed with a thumb and flipped his notebook shut. "Rush order. I'll sign off on it."

They had more than a suspect. They had the killer dead to rights. And they were ready to move in on him.

An hour later, the sergeant introduced Dani to a conference room full of sheriff's deputies and police officers. There were no rivalries here. Everybody played ball for the Las Vegas Metropolitan Police Department. The LVMPD or "Metro" was a joint police force that serviced both the city of Las Vegas and Clark County. The group in this conference room had been assigned to a special-investigation task force specifically created to catch Laura Deans's murderer. Some were liaisons to other departments, to keep them informed and help chop through red tape; others were more directly involved. One of them was the sheriff of Clark County. All of them were staring at Dani.

Dwayne introduced her as the lead investigative specialist, so she guessed that made it official. She tapped a button on her laptop, and the projection screen behind her filled with a blurry image of a man looking furtively over his shoulder as he walked away from a motel parking lot. It was the best they could get from the ATM across the street.

"We're looking for a guy named Stephen Foster," she said. "Age thirty-five. Brown hair. Brown eyes. Five foot seven and about one hundred sixty pounds. In this picture, anyway." She tapped again, and the image was replaced with a mug shot from about ten years ago. The man looked a lot younger, though. Prison must not have agreed with him. "This was him when he first went in for burglary and possession of narcotics." She tapped again, and a second mug shot filled the screen. "Here he is again two years later for more of the same." Another tap and another mug shot. "And again three years after that."

Stephen Foster had aged with each shot. He didn't look hardened or more dangerous, just more desperate. His clothes and hairstyle were basically the same in each picture. In the final one, his eyes looked hollow and lost, like he'd just woken up from a dream and didn't know where he was.

"He's currently out on parole . . . for good behavior." She didn't mean it as a joke, but it still got a few chuckles.

Her next series of pictures showed a number of crime-scene markers next to dark smudges or smeared blood on cheap motel furniture. "Several fingerprints from the crime scene match Foster's record in the NCIC database." She showed a picture of the Fluffleberry marker. "We don't have a murder weapon, but we do have Foster's fingerprints on the pen used to draw on the victim's body. And we do know what kind of murder weapon to look for." Her final image was of a simple gray box cutter, blade extended.

Dani looked over at Dwayne to see if he wanted to add anything. He just nodded for her to keep going.

"Foster's landlord says he hasn't seen him around for several days now," said Dani. "His previous employer said he fired Foster the day before Laura Deans was murdered. He also said he caught Foster masturbating in the women's bathroom." Dani cringed as she said it, waiting for the inevitable lewd comment. It didn't come, and she relaxed a bit. "This guy is obviously broken, and he'll probably kill again if he can. So we won't let him. We know who he is. We have numbers on our side. He's alone, and he's no criminal mastermind."

■ ■ ■

The rest of the day was spent mobilizing Metro on a countywide manhunt, which to Dani, seemed more like being an air traffic controller than a cop. Scheduling was a nightmare, and it meant more work for everybody, especially her. Dwayne volunteered his squad to coordinate the effort, so as the lead investigative specialist, Dani was on the phone a lot. She went over her briefing half a dozen more times with different branches of Metro, and her inspirational speech at the end became more and more cranky as the day wore on.

Still, Foster was one man in a city of over two million people. Apparently, things weren't going to happen over night. To prove the point, Dwayne sent Dani home just after midnight. She was reluctant to go. Reports of the manhunt—and about three cups of coffee—had her wired as she got in her car. She knew she should go home and at least veg out for a bit, even if she couldn't sleep. Instead, she talked herself into another way to unwind.

Dani started her car but didn't drive off. She tapped her phone to wake it up. Then she tapped into her messaging app and flipped the phone sideways to use the keyboard. Erica's name autocorrected to *AbjectErica* as she typed out a text with her thumbs.

Dani5oh: *U up?*
AbjectErica: *Duh! It's not dawn o'clock yet.*
Dani5oh: *Working?*
AbjectErica: *Depends on you. Have you met Translantica?*
She could be your pre-flight entertainment.
Dani5oh: *It would be nice to just see Erica.*
AbjectErica: *Sure. lol*

AbjectErica: *You ok?*
Dani5oh: *Rough week.*
AbjectErica: *I have the cure for that. Coming over? It's pretty slow tonight.*
Dani5oh: *How about your place?*
AbjectErica: *We could do that. The place is a mess, though.*
Dani5oh: *Sounds perfect.*
AbjectErica: *Give me 30 mins.*
Dani5oh: *See u there.*
AbjectErica: *:-) xxx*

■ ■ ■

Erica lived in a condo close to the Strip. It was ridiculously expensive, but then Erica's paycheck was probably three times what Dani's was. Also, Erica wasn't putting anything into retirement just yet. She was focused on the here and now, as long as here and now looked like the cover of a fashion magazine. Dani worried about her sometimes. What they had together was barely more than a series of one-night stands, but she still felt like they had a connection. Like maybe they shared some kind of inside joke about how relationships really worked.

Erica opened the door in her bathrobe. It was a chocolate-colored satin, so soft that the little belt holding it closed had a hard time staying in a knot, or Erica had left it loose on purpose, more likely. The condo wasn't big, but it was very nice. The recessed lighting was dimmed, and the Strip glowed off in the distance through the living room window. Dani could hear the shower running in the background, and wisps of steam were escaping through the partially opened bathroom door into the hallway.

Erica's fingers teased at the hem of her robe where it

covered her breasts as Dani stepped inside. No dramatic poses, no one-liners, just a simple smile. This was the real Erica, not a persona she folded up and stored in her closet at night.

Dani smiled back. "Hi."

"Hey," said Erica.

Dani slid her arms underneath Erica's. Instead of lust, she felt relief. Relief that she was finally with somebody who wasn't relying on her. She could put herself entirely in Erica's hands tonight if she wanted to, and Erica wouldn't mind. She started by laying her head on Erica's shoulder rather than turning toward her for a kiss. It felt like slipping into a warm bath.

Dani took a deep breath and surprised herself when it caught in her chest. She wasn't crying. That would be silly. She didn't need to do that. And those weren't tears she was trying to blink away. She was just tired.

Erica's arms tightened around Dani's back and pressed her closer. Dani took another deep breath.

"Do you want to talk about it?" Erica asked.

"Yes," said Dani, her voice a little hoarse.

"*Can* you talk about it?"

"No."

Erica broke the embrace and started leading her toward the bathroom. "Maybe you can at least forget about it for a while."

The steam felt wonderful, and the tiny bathroom was filled with the scent of Erica's shampoo. Both the mirror and the glass shower door were fogged up, making everything look soft. She was kind of glad she couldn't see her own face. She was sure it was splotchy, and she was suddenly aware of how she must smell after twelve hours in the office bull pen.

Erica closed the door after them and stepped up behind Dani. She reached a hand around and popped open one of the buttons about midway down Dani's uniform. Her lips pressed against Dani's neck as her hand pushed inside her shirt to find her breast. Then her fingers grazed over the cup of Dani's bra and squeezed up from the bottom.

Dani shut her eyes as Erica's tongue flicked out against the base of her ear. It tickled, but instead of moving her head away, Dani tilted it to expose more of her neck and used one hand to lift her hair out of the way. The tickling was followed by nibbling. Then Erica's fingers slipped above the cup of Dani's bra to tease out her nipple. She pinched lightly before taking her hand away. She must have licked her fingers because when they returned to Dani's breast, they were slick and warm. Her finger rolled around Dani's nipple, pushing a little more firmly with each circle.

Dani was breathing faster now, the rhythm matching the rotations of Erica's finger. Actually, she wasn't sure if her breath was matching Erica's fingers or if Erica was timing her fingers to Dani's breath. Either way, both sped up, and Dani realized that other parts of her body were moving in time, as well. Her own hand started rubbing Erica's hip. The satin belt gave way, but she kept her hand on the robe, liking the way the material slid over Erica's body. Her hips also started to rock, pushing back, then up, forward, back, then up.

After one final pinch and nibble from Erica, Dani had to turn around. It didn't make sense to wear clothes anymore, and all of a sudden she wanted to be out of them as soon as possible. For Erica, that was easy. One quick flick and her robe fell into a puddle on the floor. That simple smile was still there, now with a hint of a dare. Dani peeled her own shirt off and released her bra with a quick twist of her fingers. She was still wearing her belt. Erica seemed to be enjoying Dani's frustration as she clawed the buckle open and gave it a yank. She unbuttoned her pants and the weight of the belt carried them to the floor. There was a loud *thunk* as gun, ammo, cuffs and Taser hit the tile.

They stood there for a second, eyeing each other and gasping in the steam. Dani wasn't sure who moved first, but suddenly their bodies collided and their lips pressed together. Somehow they ended up in the shower.

Erica pulled back to let the water from the showerhead fill up the space where their bodies met. Her hand reached down between Dani's legs and found no resistance. Erica pushed up with her middle finger, and Dani's head arched back at the pressure. Two more thrusts and Dani was up against the shower wall. Erica leaned in and kissed Dani's neck. Her tongue traced a line along her neck, across her breast, and down her belly. It lingered for a second at her navel, which made Dani squirm a bit. She looked down at Erica and found her staring, waiting. Then with their eyes locked, Erica continued her slide down Dani's pelvis and between her thighs. Erica's tongue was poised like a finger, pointing out where she intended to go next. Then she lunged in, and Dani lost all sense of time.

The water was cold before they were finished.

They recovered in bed. The satin sheets were cool against her skin as Erica kneaded her shoulders with a firm, steady grip. Dani must have even dozed off for a bit because she woke to the sound of typing coming from the kitchen. Dani rolled over and looked out the bedroom door. She could see Erica at a small breakfast table, lit up by the glow of her laptop screen. No doubt she was updating her status page with snarky comments about her day's work. Dani didn't follow it too much, afraid of what she might see.

She sat up and scooted to the edge of the bed. Her clothes were still in the bathroom. She was a bit chilly now, too, since Erica kept the air-conditioning on all year round. Dani hated the idea of putting on her uniform again right away. Maybe she had time for some tea and a bite of whatever was in the fridge before she had to leave. She would borrow a shirt until then.

The nightstand had two drawers. The top one didn't have any clothes in it at all. Instead, there were some scattered bits of jewelry, a dog-eared paperback of Stephen King's *Rose Madder*, and a framed picture. The picture was of a young girl dressed like a princess at Disneyland. The girl was pretending to kiss Goofy on the cheek with the iconic fairytale castle in the background. Goofy was covering his bucktoothed mouth as if he was embarrassed. The man standing next to them was smiling and giving the girl bunny ears with two raised fingers, his expression frozen in an eye roll.

Dani opened the second drawer. She had the strange sensation of seeing something familiar in a completely foreign context, like opening your closet door to find a winter wonderland inside. The box in the drawer was something that she saw regularly at work, typically at the firing range where a plain brown paper box like this one held fifty rounds of pistol ammunition and was usually accompanied by testosterone-fueled one-liners like *Come get some* or *Game over, man*. Here, the box was nestled between faded cotton panties and wadded-up nylons. There could be anything inside.

It turned out there *were* bullets inside this box. They just weren't for shooting.

The box currently only held about half the number of bullets that it should. Several of those were missing their slugs, which now rattled around on the bottom of the box. That didn't make any sense. Why would you take the gunpowder out of a bullet? Maybe to use the powder for something else?

Dani's mind raced through all the fetishes she knew of. Dripping candle wax was a thing. Maybe flash burns were, too?

One of the empty cartridges had tipped over, and she picked it up. Underneath was some powder. It didn't look right at all—too fine and too pale. She touched her forefinger to the powder, then rubbed it against her thumb. Definitely not gunpowder. Her training kicked in and told her something she didn't want to hear.

She decided to put on her uniform, after all. She rushed through it, not bothering to look for her panties or tuck in her shirt. Her gun belt felt heavy, and all the stress she had been feeling rushed back when she fastened the buckle. A tear crept along one cheek. She hated that and practically scraped it off with one hand.

Erica called out from the kitchen. "You up already, baby?"

Dani's reply was to slap down a fistful of bullets on the table in front of Erica's laptop. Erica looked startled, but Dani could tell that she instantly understood the situation. So Dani just started yelling.

"You told me you were done!"

Erica's reply was too calm. Slow, like she was talking to a child. "I told you I was *quitting*."

That *really* pissed Dani off. "Which was a lie!"

"No," Erica said. "I was quitting. Uncle Quent was helping me. He . . . left."

Dani crossed her arms. "So you dove right back in? You couldn't ask me for help?"

Erica closed her laptop. "No. I couldn't."

"What? Why not?"

"We're not close like that," Erica said matter-of-factly.

Dani had to just stand there for a moment. What was tonight all about, then? Erica had taken care of *her* tonight. It wasn't just a fling. She had to feel it, too, right?

"We could be," Dani finally managed to say.

"I need you here," said Erica. "Something to look forward to. Something to make the day worthwhile. I don't want to hate you."

Dani shook her head. "I can't deal with this right now. There's too much going on."

Erica's voice was quiet. "See, like that. Do you really think you could help me in your spare time? That's not the way it works."

Dani wanted to lash out again, but she found that she couldn't. Instead, she said, "I have to go."

She could feel Erica's eyes on her, and when she left the room, she heard Erica say, "Sure. I understand."

It was almost a whisper.

17

Matt held up the jar and gave it a shake. One lonely maraschino cherry spun around in a whirlpool of syrup. He was going to need more. It was partially his fault. When he was bored and his sweet tooth got the better of him, he would pop the neon-red balls into his mouth like candy, which they practically were. He was trying to find other ways to keep himself busy.

He figured he should try to learn how to mix their top-selling cocktails. He was about to attempt his first umbrella drink. It recommended three cherries. While most of the alcohol sales at the Golden Delicious were either bottled beer or shots—that made it easy for Matt to cover the bar most of the time—clients did occasionally order something more complex. Sometimes the guy ordering the drink was just trying to sound impressive, or sometimes he had a sweet tooth like Matt.

There was a convention in town, and the parlor was in full swing. Something to do with sales. Most of the guys here were wearing suits, so Matt guessed they were unwinding after a hard day spent trying to impress one another. He had run more than one corporate credit card for drinks. Charges from the Golden Delicious would show up later as *QBJ Hospitality Services* on a credit card bill. Just vague enough to be easily justified on an expense report. All the rooms were occupied, and the girls were doing their best to keep the rest of the customers entertained until something freed up.

Matt caught Christy's eye before he left the parlor to track down more cherries. She was dealing cards for a game of strip poker. The customers had the option of buying extra cards at five dollars a pop. Even so, Christy and the girls were holding their own. They were going to have to start cheating or these guys were going to be stripping for each other. Probably not good for business. From across the room, Matt held up the near-empty jar of cherries and motioned to the doorway. She nodded.

On his way toward the break room, he saw Amber/Jessica pinning one the suits up against the wall in the hallway. She had a wicked look in her eye as she flipped the guy's tie back over his shoulder. He was still wearing his convention badge, announcing him as Douglas Merrill from Spokane, Washington. Doug was clearly transfixed by Amber as she walked a pair of fingers up his chest and slid one knee between his legs. They were obviously up next for the party room. Matt hurried past.

When he opened the door to the break room, he caught Adam midbite as he crunched down on an Oreo. He was sitting on the couch in front of the TV. A small blue creature wearing a white hat poked its head out the window of mushroom-shaped house. Its eyes turned into animated hearts as another small blue creature walked by. This one wore a white dress. She taunted him by cocking her hips to one side and touching her long blond hair.

"Hey," Matt said as he walked through toward the kitchen.

Adam didn't look up from the TV, but he did return the, "Hey."

Adam's homework was sprawled out all over the breakfast table. He wondered how much homework a nine-year-old was supposed to have. What grade was that? Third? Fourth? Matt never had homework when he was growing up. He was never really in a grade. His aunt Rose had taken care of most of his education when he was that age, and he wouldn't be done with "school" until all his work was completed for the day. She had taught him Math and English. She was strict, but her lessons were a relief compared to his father's. Her lessons made sense, or at least they had eventually. They were based on logic, or rules, or at least things that people all tended to agree on. Things that didn't change much.

His father's lessons had been based on belief. The rules seemed to change with each lesson. He constantly had to learn new words to go with the new rules. Sometimes they would be in English but the language would sound different and words would be spelled differently. Sometimes they weren't English words at all, and he had to learn a new word or phrase in Latin or some other language that wasn't even spoken anymore. When Matt had asked why, his father had told him that the words didn't have direct translations, and that he would have to learn how to think with symbols instead of words. Whatever that meant.

Aunt Rose had tested him, but she had also praised him, even putting stickers on his work sometimes. Gold stars or scratch and sniff. His father never had stickers, and his tests hadn't been measured in points. Matt either failed or succeeded. When he did succeed, his father would immediately explain how it could have been done better.

Matt shook his head, bringing himself back to the

present. His eyes refocused on one of Adam's notebook pages. It was covered in one big doodle. It had loops, lines, and patterns. The whole thing looked organic, too, like it had come out of the boy's mind and flowed directly onto the page without thought. Parts of the doodle looked familiar, but Matt couldn't quite place them. He stared at it for a second and was impressed when he realized that the doodle was created with one long elaborate line.

Matt set his jar down on the counter next to the sink. The lone cherry drifted lazily in the sticky goo, and he opened a drawer to pull out a fork.

There was a thump against the wall just outside the door. Amber must have brought Doug farther down the hallway looking for a little privacy. Her voice was muffled, but Matt could still hear her chatting up her client. "Come on, baby. Show me what's stretching out those tighty-whities."

Adam obviously heard them, too, though he didn't seem too fazed by it. He reached for the TV remote and tapped on it a few times. The volume got a little louder, and a little blue creature with a beard declared, "We must help all the creatures of the forest!"

Matt unscrewed the lid off his jar. He eyed his cherry and speared at it with his fork. He missed. "What are you watching?" he asked Adam.

"*The Smurfs.*" He sounded slightly disappointed.

"Do they still make Smurfs?" asked Matt.

"Not these ones," said Adam. "My mom found them on eBay."

Matt tried again for his cherry, and Adam ate another cookie.

An old wizard shook his fist at the Smurfs as they hid in a hollowed-out log. "I'll get you yet! You hear me?"

This time Matt heard Doug's voice in the hallway. "Uh,

just to warn you . . . It's, uh, *fun-sized* . . . like Halloween candy."

"Short and sweet?" asked Amber. "Are you gonna dress it up?"

"Ha ha ha! Silly old man!" said a Smurf.

Matt finally gave up on his fork and plunged his hand into the jar. He was going to eat that damn cherry.

"Aren't you a bit old for the Smurfs?" Matt asked.

"Probably," said Adam. "But I still kinda like them."

As Matt finally bit down on his prize, he thought about asking Amber to find another corner of the house to conduct her business. He washed his hand and wondered if either of them would even notice if he stuck his head out the door.

Adam sidelined him before he could make up his mind. "Did you hear about that woman they found at the motel?"

Matt had seen the story on the news. It was hard to miss. There weren't a lot of details being given yet, but the reporter had mentioned the victim's name and her prior conviction of prostitution.

"I think I heard something about that," Matt said. "Pretty messed up."

Adam stared straight ahead, but it was pretty clear he was no longer watching his show. "Mom used to go out on jobs. She would go to casinos and hotels."

Matt opened a cupboard to look for another jar of cherries. He hoped he sounded confident. "I'm sure nothing like that would happen to your mom. She's pretty smart."

"Yeah," said Adam. "Still."

Matt stopped his search to look over at Adam. "I know. It's scary."

The boy gave a half shrug. "Uncle Quent had a gun. He showed it to me one time." Adam turned to meet Matt's eyes. "That's probably yours now, I guess."

"Yeah," said Matt. "I think I've seen it around." He opened another cupboard and found what he was looking for next to a bottle of chocolate syrup. He took the jar and went over to the couch. "Your dad will catch whoever did that."

Adam was watching his show again. Or at least pretending to. "I know."

Matt looked at the door. He thought he heard a soft moan coming from the hallway. He decided to have a seat on the couch. He twisted the lid of the jar and offered Adam a cherry. "What's that cat's name again?"

Adam considered the cherries but went with another Oreo instead. "Azrael. He's funny. He's the best part of the show. I wish we had a—"

Adam was interrupted by the guy in the hallway. "Oh yeah! Just like that! Blow that little pig!"

Apparently, Amber wasn't waiting for a room, after all. "Mmm. I'm like the big bad wolf, baby. I'll blow your house down."

"—a cat," Adam finished.

Adam tapped the "volume" button some more, and they both stared at the TV in awkward silence.

Adam closed up his Oreo bag and looked sideways at Matt. "Why do they always have to sound like that? It's always the same thing. They sound stupid."

Matt nodded. "Guys get stupid around girls."

"I mean the girls." Adam turned to look at Matt. "That's not how they sound at breakfast."

"Well," said Matt, "I don't know. I guess maybe they have to stoop down to our level. They're just making love."

Adam turned back to the TV. "It's not love."

"No," said Matt, "I guess not."

18

Foster wasn't very good at social media. He also didn't use the site that most people used. He had three friends who followed him, but he was pretty sure two of them weren't real people. One "friend" was called ShakespearDisciple. He posted quotes from the Bible rearranged into iambic pentameter. ShakespearDisciple had thousands of friends and had been a featured contributor promoted on the log-in page, which was how Foster had found him. Another was called Kothlar. He had found Foster somehow. He kept sending Foster messages in broken English about great websites that promised all kinds of things to ensure that his penis would be "3inch maxibig," would have "formidable uptime," and that there would be "no more boxing the Jesuits." The public library computers blocked all those websites, though, so Foster would have to make due with his current penis. He was pretty sure he could hold his own against a Jesuit in a fair fight, anyway.

CandyCaneCandice was a real person. She was the reason Foster created an account in the first place. He liked to check in to see what Candice was doing occasionally. He never posted or sent her messages. He wouldn't know what to say. Plus, all her other friends seemed to have just the right clever response or inside joke to post. He was pretty sure anything he posted would be glossed over and forgotten immediately. He hadn't checked in on Candice since she had gotten him fired from the Tail Spin. To his surprise, she hadn't unfriended him yet. Maybe she'd forgotten.

Candice didn't post a lot, just the occasional selfie along with her work schedule. There were no posts about the night she yelled at Foster in the women's restroom. She did make a post the night after, though. Foster clicked on the picture to get a better view. Candice and another dancer stood chest to chest. They were both topless, but their bodies were pressed together in a way that hid their nipples. Candice was holding the other dancer's hip with one hand while she made bunny ears with the other. They were both puckering their lips for the camera.

The post below the picture read, *Come make a sandwich with us tomorrow night at the Tail Spin! Two-for-one lap dances until midnight! We'll be the bread; you can be the meat!*

She certainly didn't seem disturbed at all by the previous night's freak-out. The event that had changed Foster's life wasn't even hinted at in her eyes. He stared at them for a long time to make sure.

Foster got some odd looks from one of the librarians as he sat there. She pushed along her cart and stopped every few paces to restack a book or two. Each time she started pushing her cart again, she would look at Foster and squint, obviously hoping to catch him in some kind of heinous act. He wasn't doing anything wrong, though. Not yet.

The Woman in the Garden had him walk to the library instead of taking the bus, which was fine; he needed to stretch his legs. He had been practicing more with the pen, and all the practice made his wrist stiff and his feet sore, so he was glad to get out of the TV room. He was getting good, though. New lines. New swirls. New patterns. It was like typing on a keyboard. When you typed, words became patterns that your fingers just knew how to make without thought or concentration. His lines were starting to get like that.

She had made him take a watch with him on his walk. She had given him a list of street names and told him to write down the exact times when he was supposed to walk from one street to the next. The path wasn't straight, and he often found himself doubling back for no good reason. Sometimes he walked down a street that he could have sworn hadn't been there before. It all seemed ridiculous to him, but she was pretty insistent on sticking to the directions. She and her owl stared at him with big, unblinking eyes and made him promise to follow the schedule. He did and hadn't asked any questions. At exactly 12:03 p.m. he had started walking his cryptic route toward the library. He had arrived at the library at precisely 1:47 p.m. She'd said he could take the bus home as long as he stayed in the library the whole time and then ran out to catch the bus at 3:17 p.m.

He looked at his watch. He still had another forty-six minutes.

He clicked on Candice's news feed. It listed posts from people she followed, things she'd "liked," and when somebody else mentioned her in his or her posts. According to her friend, AbjectErica, she and Candice were out on the Strip at that very moment. Apparently, AbjectErica was much better at social media than either he or Candice were. AbjectErica had 23,267 friends, but you didn't have to be her friend to view her posts. They were open to just anybody.

AbjectErica listed her "likes" as the Golden Delicious, the Tail Spin, and Lashtastic Dungeon Supplies. There was a link to each, but just like the helpful links from Kothlar, each of these links were blocked by the public library system. Foster scrolled through her posts for the day and stopped at the first one that mentioned Candice.

AbjectErica – 5 hours ago
This week is so fired! New boss started off as a douche and just keeps getting douchier. It's like he's been practicing! I may need to start looking for a new place to set up shop. Anybody have a dungeon for rent? ;-) Also, had a fight with my girl. :-(Couldn't sleep last night . . . in a bad way. I'm hoping breakfast on the Strip with CandyCaneCandice will help me take my mind off things. Will post pics! #WhereIsMyDramaflage
67 Likes
Comments

CandyCaneCandice:
Looking forward to it! LOL

OrganiGasm:
There are plenty of fish in the sea.
 AbjectErica:
 Oh yeah? Are there plenty of perfect, glowing, goddess fish in the sea?
  OrganiGasm:
  Who is this mystery girl? Can I meet her?
   AbjectErica:
   Sure. Just go rob a 7-Eleven. She'll find you.

JackOnJackOff:
I have a sorrow boner for you :-(

QuiteContraryMary:
You seem like such a normal girl.
   AbjectErica:
   Yes, I do seem that way. ;-)

Foster clicked LIKE because it seemed like the thing to do. His gaze shifted to AbjectErica's profile picture. She was looking up at the camera and giving more of a smirk than a smile. If you took away the lip ring and half the eye shadow, she looked just like a dancer who used to come in when he'd first started working at the Tail Spin. She'd gone by just Erica back then. Foster couldn't remember why she left.

He scrolled to the next post. This one had a picture at the top. Erica and Candice stood side by side with the Strip in the background. Erica was holding Candice close as she bit Candice's ear lobe. Candice was smiling and trying to pull away. A man and woman, obviously tourists, were walking past behind them. The man's head must have spun around to check them out right when Erica was taking the picture. His eyes were clearly focused on Erica's ass.

AbjectErica – 4 hours ago
Pre-brunch snack! CandyCaneCandice is salty-sweet! What buffet should we go to? Must include mimosas. We'll bring the eye candy! #HideYourHusbands
103 Likes

Comments
SnakeEyed69:
I HEART CandyCaneCandice!!!
   AbjectErica:
   Come see her tonight at #TheLandingStrip

This time Foster didn't click LIKE. He wasn't sure he liked this at all. Candice was carrying on like she *hadn't* just destroyed a man's life. In fact, she and her friend seemed like they wanted to find somebody else to toy with. Somebody they could pretend to be friends with before reducing him to tears in a bathroom stall as he knelt in jizz and soapy water. Foster looked for a "Hate" button but couldn't find one.

The next post was worse. Erica sat at a restaurant table in the picture. It looked like a nice place—vases of fresh flowers decorating tables with crisp white table clothes—but Erica looked sloppy drunk. Her eyelids seemed uneven, and her sundress was slipping off one shoulder. Candice must have taken this picture because Erica's hands were occupied. One was holding a champagne glass at an alarming angle; the other was grabbing the ass of a passing waiter. The waiter looked surprised, and it wasn't clear if he was going to be able to keep his serving tray balanced.

AbjectErica – 3 hours ago
On the one hand I'm completely drunk . . . End of story.
#CantUseMyWords
74 Likes

Comments
BatCountry:
I'll finish that story for you. I promise you a happy ending ;-)

MyPrettyZombie:
Hope you left him a good tip!!!

AbjectErica:
Words . . . words . . . words . . .

"Well, that waiter probably lost his job!"

Foster must have said it out loud because the librarian looked up from her cart to glare at him. She shelved another book without taking her eyes off him. There was almost nobody else in the library, so he wasn't sure whose sensitive ears she was trying to protect. That reminded him: he wanted to check out a couple of storybooks before he left. The Woman in the Garden had started another project in the TV room, and they had used up all the books they could find at the orphanage.

He still had some time, so he went back to Erica's posts. The next one in the list had another picture. This one looked like it was taken at the same restaurant, only this time the view was from underneath the table with the crisp white tablecloth. Erica's legs were spread apart, pulling the fabric of her sundress tight. The camera flash washed out the picture but lit up Erica's hot-pink panties nicely. Silk, based on the glare of the light reflecting off them. The dimple in the center of the panties made Foster forget that he was angry for a second. He almost missed Erica's hand under the table flipping him the bird.

AbjectErica – 3 hours ago
See! I DO wear panties ... sometimes. CandyCaneCandice
forgot them today #CamelToe
223 Likes

Comments
OMGinMyPants:
Mind = blown. But not like a bomb. Like a blowjob!

8InchesLimp:
I want to do bad things to you. Butt things.
    AbjectErica:
    We're having a sale on bad things at
    #TheGoldenDelicious. Butt things cost extra . . .

Candice must have taken that picture, too. At least she hadn't posted a picture of her own legs spread apart. Had she? Foster looked. No. He looked again. Still no. That was a relief . . . Right?

The next picture was of Candice, but she was no longer at the restaurant. It looked like she had hailed a cab on the Strip and was just about to get in. She had stopped to turn toward the camera and blow Foster a kiss. She was still thinking about him. He knew it.

AbjectErica – 30 minutes ago
Bye CandyCaneCandice! Thanks for holding my hair back for me in the ladies' room. LOL. I have to get back to work soon, too. Those asses aren't gonna whip themselves. #HiHoHiHo
112 Likes

Comments
AllTheBacon:
Your whole situation disgusts me.
    AbjectErica:
    At least I HAVE a situation :-
        SniffTheGlove:
        Hey AllTheBacon! Go drown yourself in a lake of fiery dicks!
            AllTheBacon:
            Umm, no.

Foster agreed with SniffTheGlove. Fiery dicks aside, these guys didn't know Erica, or Candice, or what kind of situation they were in. Foster did. These guys couldn't judge them. Foster could. And now he felt like he owed it to Candice to pay her a visit and hear her side of the story. Hear why she'd decided to toss their friendship away. Maybe it was a mistake. Maybe they could be friends again. Maybe he could get his old job back and things could go back to the way they were. If not, he still needed some closure, and he was sure she did, too.

19

Matt was thinking about masturbating. He wasn't really horny, but the thought just occurred to him that he hadn't taken the time to *indulge* himself since moving into Uncle Quent's place. It seemed odd to him once he'd realized it, but then he remembered the job he had as a pizza delivery guy in Arizona. It was a great job if you were lying low and might have to run at any moment. Most of the time you were in a car with food and a pocket full of cash. For some reason, he had hated it, though. Maybe it was the uniform, or maybe it was the fact that people were always hoping he would fail at his job so they could get a free pizza. He hadn't eaten pizza the whole time he'd worked there.

Matt could go without pizza for a month, but he was pretty sure he would break something if he didn't clear the pipes on a regular basis. He was ready to work through the problem. He just needed to do a little *research* online in the privacy of his office.

It was just after breakfast, which meant that most of the girls wouldn't show up for a few hours, unless there was some kind of special event booked. Matt checked the schedule before heading upstairs.

All clear.

He stepped into his office and pulled the door shut. He pushed the button to lock the door and then closed his eyes to start getting into the right frame of mind.

"Rough day already?" said a voice.

It was not a sexy, fantasy voice inside his head. It wasn't even a female voice. Matt felt a little sick when he recognized the accent. His eyes shot open.

Thug Guy was sitting behind Uncle Quent's desk. There was a black leather bag next to him. Matt didn't like the look of that bag. It looked like one of those antique doctor's bags that contained scalpels and bone saws. He also had Matt's laptop open in front of him.

"Need LOLcat maybe?" asked Thug Guy. "To take mind off things?" He spun the laptop around so that it was facing Matt. There was a video up on the screen, ready to play. A cat stared sullenly from a tub at a man who was giving it a bath.

Matt had seen that one actually. A few seconds into the video, the cat would claw its way up the man's leg and tag him in the junk for good measure. The man then gave a high-pitched howl only to be matched by the cat's own howl. It was pretty funny.

Thug Guy tapped a button but nothing happened. He looked perplexed, but his expression was exaggerated, as though he was playing to an audience. He slammed a finger down on the button a few more times.

"Hmm," said Thug Guy. "Does not want to play."

Keys exploded off the keyboard along with shards of glass as Thug Guy bashed the laptop into the desk over and over again. He was not calm as he did it, either. A rage built up in him from out of nowhere and left him breathing hard after the laptop was reduced to chunks of plastic.

Matt backed up into the locked door behind him. He thought about running. He knew he wouldn't get very far and it would probably be more painful for him if he ran.

Matt put a hand on his forehead and squeezed his eyes shut. "You could have just taken that and sold it or something."

"Is more dramatic this way," said Thug Guy. "And loud." He had caught his breath again. The rage seemed to have left as quickly as it had come. He took a step to the side and offered Matt the desk chair. "Please. Have seat."

Matt edged around the desk to the chair. He thought about the last time he'd sat down with Thug Guy. Matt knew it was a bad idea, but he couldn't think of any good ones. He kept his eyes on Thug Guy while he slowly sat down. He gave Matt a reassuring smile and then sucker punched him in the gut. Matt didn't really say anything, but the air forced out of his lungs made a noise that sounded like, *"Huuh!"*

Matt fell into his chair. His whole body tightened up as it bent over on itself. The pain in his stomach was overshadowed by the fear that he had forgotten how to breathe. He tried to make his lungs work, but his throat caught and he coughed instead. His eyes started to water, and a blurry version of Thug Guy casually walked around to the front of the desk.

"Being business owner not quite what you expect?" asked Thug Guy. "Me, I have no . . . uh . . . head? . . . for business."

Thug Guy sat down in his own chair. He leaned forward on the desk, resting on his elbows. Then he gestured toward the shell of the shattered laptop with a finger. Matt might have flinched, but he was concentrating too hard on not passing out.

"I have example," said Thug Guy. "I let you come here. I think maybe you could get money from uncle. Pay off debt. As you know, new birth certificates not cheap. This was bad investment. You cannot even check e-mail anymore."

Matt was finally able to suck down some air. He took in too much and immediately coughed again. His next breath was ragged, but the air was finally going in the right direction. The one after that started clearing away the dark spots that had been floating around in his eyes. Thug Guy waited patiently.

Matt lifted his head up and tried to focus on the man across the desk from him. His eyes locked on the bird skull perched on Thug Guy's hat. "People use phones for e-mail now." Matt gulped down more air. "The laptop was just for porn." Another gulp. "And LOLcats." Being a smart-ass was hard work.

Thug Guy leaned back. "Ha! Smart guy. Maybe is hope for you yet."

Matt's eyes slid from the bird skull over to Uncle Quent's cigar box. He rested one hand on top of the desk.

"Just thought of funny thing," said Thug Guy. "If uncle had not died and did not leave you this place, you would still be in same business, but I would be pimp. For you."

Matt didn't have a reply to that. His breaths were coming easier now, and his mind was racing through all kinds of stories that had bad endings. His hand inched a little closer to the cigar box.

Thug Guy opened his bag. Then, very carefully, he lifted out something black and fluffy, and set it on the desk between them. A crow stood on Uncle Quent's desk. Its black feathers had a slight sheen to them, as if they had been dipped in oil, and its head was cocked to one side so that it could focus on Matt with one eye. It stood absolutely motionless. Matt realized it wasn't alive when Thug Guy adjusted it so that he could look at the bird's face. "A gift for you. To remind you I'll be back soon."

He leaned forward, and Matt thought he was going to kiss the bird. Instead, he breathed on one of the eyes to steam it up. Then he polished it with his thumb. He turned the bird back to stare at Matt and stood up. "Time for going-out-of-business sale, I think."

Thug Guy turned his back to Matt and started heading to the door.

Matt's hand crept forward. "Well, I could—"

Thug Guy cut him off. "Was not question. Call me when it is done. I left number . . . in cigar box."

Matt started to feel sick. He wasn't sure if it was from the fist in the gut or the thought of reaching into the box. Thug Guy opened the door. Matt's hand stopped moving forward. Thug Guy paused in the doorway but didn't say anything before continuing on.

Matt laid his head down on the desk as the door shut again. He took a deep breath and sat back up. He used the desk phone to call Information. He gave the operator the city and state. When the operator asked for the listing, Matt paused for a second and then said, "A real estate agent, please."

"Which one, sir?" the operator asked.

Matt had no idea. "Whatever's at the top of the list is fine." There was a reason why people named companies things like AAA Cabs or A-Plus Locksmith. Matt was quickly connected with Apex Realty.

■ ■ ■

He met with Peggy Lynn later that afternoon. She and her assistant showed up in a white SUV with the Apex Realty logo painted on the side, which was, more or less, just a triangle with a dollar sign in the middle. Her appraisal seemed to have more to do with raw numbers and computer printouts than curb appeal. In fact, she barely looked at the place before coming up with a selling price. She asked Matt how many bedrooms and bathrooms there were and whether or not there were any standout features like a mezzanine or a butler's pantry. He wasn't quite sure how to describe the old embalming room in the basement so he didn't mention it. As it turned out, the upstairs landing overlooking the foyer counted as a mezzanine, so she seemed pretty happy about that.

When she finally did ask Matt for a walk-through, the fact that it was a working brothel didn't seem to faze her in the slightest. Some of the girls were there getting ready for work, but Peggy's smile never faltered. She focused on areas that might need damage control or creative touch-ups. She spitballed ideas and her assistant took notes. Peggy did raise an eyebrow when she saw the VIP room and suggested they might store some of the "furniture" during the open house.

Soon, they'd settled on a description of the brothel: *A unique heritage home with endless possibilities is waiting for YOU to unlock its hidden potential. Quiet neighborhood. Easy highway access.*

The asking price was a little lower than Matt had hoped, but she showed him several printouts that indicated she was right on the nose. Before he was even done reviewing the listing agreement, Peggy's assistant was pulling out a signpost from the back of the SUV. He signed the document, and they chatted a bit while her assistant hammered the post into the front lawn.

"We'll need to dress it up a bit," Peggy said, "but I think we can get you a decent price. Potted plants do wonders." She pointed down at the clumps of weeds pretending to be the front lawn. "And we can spray this with some green fertilizer. Do you have any funds to repaint?"

Matt looked back at the house. He had never really noticed the flaws until now. Some of the paint *was* starting to flake off. And yes the lawn did look like crap. There was no extra money to fix it up, though. And no time.

"No," Matt said. "I just need to sell it fast."

"So you can come down on the price if needed?" asked Peggy.

He nodded. "Whatever it takes."

Peggy's assistant stopped his hammering. He spoke but not to either of them. "Hey, kid. You sure you should be heading up there?"

Matt turned around and locked eyes with Adam. He must have just gotten home from school. His backpack hung loose off his shoulders, and his thumbs were hooked under the straps. He looked confused. He turned away to look back at the signpost.

Peggy and her assistant suddenly realized they had tasks to do somewhere away from the awkward silence.

When Adam turned back to face Matt, the confusion was gone. It was replaced with anger. Matt couldn't think of anything to say as the boy pushed past him. He kept his eyes on the ground as Adam slammed the door.

20

Foster pulled a dishtowel off a hook by the stove. It featured a black cat with big, bright-yellow eyes. Behind its head was either a halo or maybe the setting sun, and the animal seemed to be sitting on a fence. Next to it were the words, *Chat Noir*. Foster didn't speak French, but he figured he now knew how to say *black cat* if he ever needed to. He didn't know if Candice had been to France or just dreamed of going there one day, but the rest of the apartment was decorated with similar knickknacks. He sat down at the dining room table and started to clean his box cutter.

Candice was in the living room. If he turned around in his chair, he would only be able to see one arm stretched above her head and her eyes staring up at the ceiling in wonder. That was good because he wouldn't want to see the rest of her. Foster had tried to stare straight ahead at the wall when he went back into the room to get his box cutter. He had focused on a framed poster of the Eiffel Tower. The photo featured an attractive couple locked in a passionate kiss with the tower in the background on a bright, cheery day. The red spray covering it now, made it look like the couple had been caught in the middle of an apocalyptic hell storm.

Foster clicked the blade open. The tip was broken. He was going to have to fix that. He dug around in his pocket and found a dime. He used it to loosen the screw holding the handle together. When he pried the handle open, he found more blood to clean. Some new, some old.

As he scrubbed, Foster turned slightly toward the living room. "It was good seeing you again, Candice."

She didn't reply, of course, and he knew she wouldn't. He wasn't crazy. He knew she was in the garden now. He just hadn't gotten a chance to say everything he'd wanted to before Candice had started acting all panicky. She'd stopped listening and kept saying she was going to call the police. That's when he had to end their conversation.

"I just wanted to let you know that I don't blame you for losing my job," he said to the empty kitchen. "I mean, I *did* blame you. You *did* get me fired. But I can see now that working there wasn't very healthy for me, and you probably did me a favor."

He tipped the handle, and the razor blade fell out into his hand. There was more blood underneath. The *chat noir* was starting to look like it had gotten into a fight.

"I still consider you a friend. I know we all have our good days and our bad days. Lord knows I've just wanted to explode some days after hearing how some of those guys treated you. Oh man, the things I've imagined doing to them! I'm sure you were just having one of *those* days. You can't take it out on them. They pay the bills. So I understand why you took it out on me."

The box cutter was as clean as it was going to get. Foster flipped the razor blade around so that the unused end pointed outward. He slotted it into place and then reassembled the handle.

"That said, I know you're better than that. You're the only one who saw the potential in me. That's why I wanted to come see you again. I'm glad we were able to talk and work some of this stuff out."

He gave the blade a few test clicks, in and out.

"I'm sorry about the stun gun . . . and the chair." Foster had had to improvise when she wouldn't stop moving.

There was a little basket on the kitchen counter. It held some keys and a few stray coins. It also held Candice's cell phone. It was a nice one, and she had decorated it with a pink case that had a white cartoon poodle on it. The screen said SLIDE TO UNLOCK and when Foster slid his finger across, it didn't ask for a password or anything.

"I'm just gonna clean up your phone if you don't mind," said Foster. "Delete our little conversation from earlier."

Foster tapped an icon. No password needed for that one, either. Candice's status page came up. He started scrolling through her messages.

Foster turned toward the living room again. "Hey, MilkMan wants to know if you're gonna be working at the Landing Strip tomorrow," Foster tapped the "reply" button. "Don't want to leave him hanging." Foster mouthed the words as he typed.

CandyCaneCandice:
Sorry, MilkMan. Hanging out with an old friend, then off to visit Mother. #TheGarden

Foster continued to scroll and found the message he had sent earlier. It was short and simple. He'd just asked if they could get together to talk about the incident at work. He had apologized for whatever he had done to make her angry and just wanted to know how she was doing. She had replied almost right away. She used a lot of capital letters and exclamation points to explain that she was the one who should be apologizing, that she didn't know what had come over her that night. She said she felt awful about what she had said, and in fact, she didn't remember half of what had happened. They agreed to meet up after work at a coffee shop.

But Foster had never showed up at the coffee shop. Or at least, he hadn't gone inside. Instead, he watched her from across the street. She waited for a long time, too. When she had finally given up and left, he followed her home. She was really surprised when he knocked on her door. She seemed baffled at first and then concerned. He had been hoping for a nice quiet conversation with just the two of them. He wanted to show her the storybook and tell her all about the garden. But she had stopped listening.

Foster deleted their messages.

"I wish I could have come with you," said Foster. "I know you're probably scared. It's always hard going to a new place and trying to make new friends."

Foster went back to Candice's status page. There was a button to list all her friends. He tapped it.

"Maybe I can help you out with that. Send you a familiar face to help make you feel at home."

At the top of Candice's friends list was:

AbjectErica
The little devil on your shoulder whispering wicked things in your ear.

21

Sam was starting to sweat. He unbuttoned his cuffs and rolled up his sleeves to try to keep cool. It didn't work, and he started to suspect that he was sweating for an entirely different reason. It had been a long time since he'd ventured down the forest path, but everything seemed familiar, and he could tell that he was almost at the clearing. That meant he would see *her* soon, and he would have to finally figure out what to say to her. He had spent most of the journey running through different scenarios in his mind. He'd started each one differently—sometimes he was witty, sometimes he was sincere—but they all ended with her casting him out of the garden. Like last time.

He had put it off long enough, though. Bethel had invoked the pact, and the first sacrifice had been made. The Woman in the Garden would know that Sam was involved. He had to make sure *that* wasn't going to be a problem. She was dangerous, and summoning her went against the dictum that gave the Grigori its existence—*watch and be wakeful*—which was pretty vague, but probably didn't include letting a myth bleed into the world of sound and fury, even if it was just Las Vegas. Still, the last time the

Grigori had just *watched*, an inquisition had spread through Europe and made it all the way to the New World before it had finally died out. While that was an interesting time, it was hard to test one's soul when people were being tortured for something as meaningless as not singing the right hymns. Desperate times called for desperate lovers. In this case, that was literally true.

Sam didn't sleep—the Grigori didn't need to—so he didn't have the luxury of dreaming. His mind didn't get the chance to entertain itself at night while all the day's thoughts were unpacked, hosed off, and folded up nice and tidy for the next day. He did daydream, though. He had plenty of time for that as he dealt blackjack, ran his club, or handed out stripper cards on the street corner. He met the same people over and over again, and each of them seemed to have the same story to tell.

Your luck is going to turn around any minute? Double down.

You just want to dance for a couple weeks to make some quick cash? There's the dressing room.

Your girl only gives you blowjobs on your birthday? Call the number on this card.

His answers were automatic, and he didn't really have to focus on the job. Maybe he was just getting sloppy.

When he did daydream, he often found himself on this very path, with *her* waiting at the end. Sometimes they talked, sometimes they fought, and sometimes they fucked. It was a daydream, though, so it was always cranked up to eleven. When they talked, they unlocked the secrets of the universe. When they fought, oceans boiled and stars fell from the sky. And when they fucked, they created new religions. The reason he wanted her was the same reason they could never be together. They would unmake each other, and quite possibly, everything they touched.

The tree line ended abruptly, and Sam used his hat to shade his eyes from the sudden brightness of a clear blue sky. The garden opened up in front of him. Sam guessed that, from above, it might have looked like a perfect circle in vast sea of ancient wood. There were trees in the garden, too, but they were much younger and grew in groups that looked too perfect to be natural. Except the oak tree in the center of the garden. If anything, it looked older than all the trees in the surrounding forest. It was scarred and gnarled, and looked like it had fought to survive for hundreds of years rather than being cared for and nurtured. As Sam stepped into the garden, an owl screeched from the branches of that tree.

Sam hadn't been to the garden in a very long time, but it looked different every time he visited. It was constantly changing to reflect what people expected an ideal garden to look like. It needed a lot of work, and *she* never stopped tending to it. But she seemed to have some help now.

A young woman stood up from her work near a patch of strawberries. She faced Sam, but her eyes were blank and colored a milky-blue. She was wearing a white sundress and a linen bonnet. There was a faint swirled line on one of her cheeks, like a scar that had faded into her skin a long time ago. She didn't speak, and she didn't blink.

Sam started walking toward her. He followed a path of loose pebbles. To either side he saw bushes growing new leaves as they stretched toward the sky. He watched an apple hanging from a small tree turn from a light shade of green to a dark shade of red. A butterfly was disturbed as a rose bud spiraled open. It flew along side Sam for a while before a gust of wind caught it and took it up to the great oak. It fluttered and danced until he lost sight of it in the branches.

Then *she* was standing in front of him, the Woman in the Garden.

"Samael," she said. "Your name was not invoked."

He looked at her, drank her in, and let his mind flood with memories of a simpler time. She was wearing a white sundress, as well, but hers had embroidered flowers reaching up from the hem toward her waist. Her gardening hat had been decorated with a velveteen ribbon, and it had a lace veil that hung from the brim to protect her eyes from the sun. Or maybe to hide them from Sam. In one hand, she held a pair of gardening shears like a weapon.

"No," said Sam. "I guess it wasn't. Folks don't really do that anymore. Only a few still know how."

She patted the closed blades of the shears against her open palm. She was waiting for more.

"It's been a long time," said Sam. "With our recent arrangement, I thought a visit was in order."

The butterfly found its way out of the branches and drifted down to rest on a sunflower growing next to the strawberry patch. The girl in the bonnet turned her head to look at it.

"Really," said Sam, "I just wanted to see you. How are you doing?" The question seemed inadequate. None of his daydreams started with small talk.

His expression must have seemed genuine, though, because the Woman in the Garden lowered her shears and her lips parted in a tight smile. "It's good to be with my daughters again."

The girl with the bonnet held out a finger to the sunflower. The butterfly took flight but then settled on the flower again.

"Daughters? I only see the one," said Sam.

"Another is on the path," she said, "and still more will

follow. Our supplicant is playing his part well."

"It will have to end soon, you know," said Sam.

"I don't know why you care so much."

"It's my job."

"You've ignored your job before."

Samael used to carry a sword formed of molten glass. Its edge had constantly sharpened itself, even while it was cutting through iron and bone. Blood had never clung to it, because it was continuously being remade. He had used the sword in service of the Elohim, carrying out their decrees swiftly and efficiently. He didn't feel alive unless he was commanded to action. He *was* his job. Or he had been, until he'd entered the clearing and had seen the old oak for the first time.

Sam took off his hat and held it up to his chest. "I still think about you and our time here."

"I needed someone after I left *him*. I needed to forget *his* paradise," she said. "You came."

"I came to kill you," said Sam.

"But you didn't," she said.

"How could I?"

"Easily. With your sword. That was their command, wasn't it?"

Her daughter still had her finger extended to the butterfly on the sunflower. A slight gust of wind bent the flower, and the butterfly's wings fluttered. This time in came to rest on the girl's finger.

"They thought they knew my nature," said Sam.

"Clearly, they did not," said the Woman in the Garden.

"I didn't know myself until I met you. I would have stayed if you had asked," he said.

Sam looked at the girl again. The butterfly had crawled along her finger into her open palm. Her blank stare didn't change at all as her palm closed into a fist.

"I know," said the Woman in the Garden.

This wasn't going at all as he had imagined. The passion that they had felt together in the past was nowhere in her eyes. She didn't seem happy to see him, but she didn't seem mad. He remembered the last night that they had lain naked under the oak, out of breath and with the smell of sex still heavy in the air. The branches of the tree had lit up with swarm of fireflies, their glow streaking and blurring together. She had looked at him like he was the only man in the world. She cast him out the next morning.

The Elohim might have taken Sam back after he left the garden. He never asked. His sword had hardened into a hazy useless lump. He had tapped it against a stone, and it had shattered into a thousand shards. He had seen the best that life had to offer and had seen it taken away. Instead, he wandered. He drifted in and out of the cities of man, and he started to notice them suffering the same tragedy he had. The story was always the same, but the details were always different. That's when he had started *watching*. He had hoped to learn how they made peace with their suffering and healed their hearts. Instead, he learned how to lie to himself.

"So why didn't you?" asked Sam. "You said yourself you needed someone to share this with."

"No," she said. "I needed someone to *want* me. If you had stayed, we would have burned brightly for a time. Maybe a long time. But then passion would fade away. It might have left us broken and hollow, or we may have become so entangled that one could not exist without the other. Either way, the garden would have withered, and I would have been forgotten."

The owl screeched again. At first Sam thought it was just

emphasizing her point, but then her gaze shifted from him to the path behind him. She lifted the veil over the brim of her hat, and Sam saw true concern in her eyes.

"If I were forgotten, who would care for my daughters?" she asked.

Sam followed her gaze to a girl standing naked at the edge of the clearing. Apocrypha scrolled over her body from head to foot, the red line still weeping fresh blood. Her eyes were the same milky-blue as the other girl working the garden, but instead of a calm, vacant stare, this new girl's head whipped around franticly, as if she had never been outside before.

"Like I said, it will have to end soon," said Sam.

"Everything has its season. Again and again," said the Woman in the Garden. "You agreed to help me, and I agreed to help you. You'll get what you want."

"I doubt that," said Sam, but the Woman in the Garden was already walking toward the forest path and her new daughter.

22

The house was quiet. Yesterday there had been a lot of shouting, door slamming, and creative insults, but today it was spooky silent. Christy had hurried Adam out the door early in the morning. Apparently, they were splurging on breakfast out somewhere before Adam had to be at school. Christy hadn't come back yet.

The night before, Matt had tried to have a calm conversation with the girls. He wanted to explain what was going on. It was nothing personal; he *had* to sell. He was deep in debt, and he really had no choice. He might have even tried to explain how he'd gotten into debt in the first place, but nobody had wanted to listen.

Peggy had scheduled an open house for the next day, but she said there was a couple that was eager for a walk-through this afternoon. Matt figured there were a few things that couldn't easily be explained away that he should take care of before they arrived. One of them was the glowing neon sign that said "Golden Delicious" in the front window. The couple probably wouldn't believe that he was just a big fan of apples.

Matt unplugged the sign and then dragged a chair over

to the window where it was displayed. He winced as he stepped up. His stomach still felt like he had spent all last week doing crunches. The fist-sized bruise right above his belly button looked too small to be causing so much pain. He didn't know where Thug Guy had gone after his visit, but the crow he left on Uncle Quent's desk freaked Matt out so much that he hadn't been able to sleep until he'd locked it away in a drawer.

The sign came down easily enough. It usually hung from a chain that looped over two hooks above the window. It had obviously been set up so it could be taken down quickly if the need arose. The dust on the sign suggested that the precaution wasn't needed very often. Matt carefully lowered it to the floor by the chain and then, just as carefully, lowered himself down. He took a deep breath and started hauling it toward the back door.

It was heavier than it looked and kind of awkward to carry. It kept banging into his shins as he walked down the hallway. He tried to minimize the damage by keeping his eyes on it and shuffling sideways. He would have missed the fact that the door to the VIP room was open if he hadn't bumped against the wall and knocked the picture of the fan dancer off its hook. He reached out with one hand to try to catch it, which let the sign come down on his foot. The pain of his pinkie toe getting smashed made him suck in a quick breath, and the picture fell to the ground, shattering the glass in the frame.

"Fuck!" He said it with a hiss from the pain. Then he looked at the picture and said it again, drawn out with disappointment. "Fuuuck."

"What the hell?" It sounded like Erica's voice.

Matt looked through the door of the VIP room. Yep. It was Erica. She had a tape measure in one hand that gave a crack as the tape wound itself back into place.

"You scared the shit out of me," she said.

At least he wasn't the one being surprised to see somebody this time. Actually, he *was* kind of surprised.

"What are you doing here?" he asked. "I thought I was being shunned."

"I didn't come here to see you," she said. At her side was a mannequin wearing a black vinyl gimp suit. They both seemed to be glaring at him.

"Oh," said Matt. "Are you working? Because the real estate agent is coming by soon."

"No," she said. There was a lot of contempt in those two letters.

"So, what are you doing?" he asked.

"I'm trying to figure out where I'm going to store a St. Andrew's Cross when you sell this place." She pointed her tape measure behind her at the large X-shaped piece of bondage furniture that dominated the room. "I'm sure Uncle Quent would have wanted me to have it. It has sentimental value."

"That's fine," said Matt, "but they're gonna be here soon. I was hoping to throw a sheet over *that*. Over this whole room actually."

Erica rolled her eyes. "Good luck."

Matt bent down to start picking up glass from the frame. "Hey, have you seen Christy?"

"Yes, she asked me to give you this."

Matt looked up at Erica and found her free hand giving him the bird.

"That's—" Matt started.

"Oh and here's mine." Erica clipped the tape measure to her pocket and then flipped him off with her other hand.

"—great," he finished.

Matt went back to picking up glass, and Erica went back to measuring.

"Okay, okay. I get it," said Matt. "I'm a dick. I admit it."

Erica hooked the lip of the tape measure to the top of the cross. She had to stand on her tiptoes to do it. "That's the first step to recovery."

"It's not like I have a choice," grumbled Matt.

Erica carefully pulled down on the tape measure, holding the top in place as best she could. That thing had to be seven feet tall. "You were born that way?" she asked.

Matt piled his bits of glass on top of the picture, using it as a plate. "Well, I am from a long line of dicks and assholes, so yeah, I guess so."

Erica glanced over her shoulder at him. "Uncle Quent managed to turn it around."

"What was he like before that?" asked Matt.

She paused before replying. "He was a dick and an asshole."

Matt left the sign leaning up against the wall in the hallway. He kept his eyes on the pile of glass he was carrying and slowly made his way toward the workbench in the VIP room. He set the shards down and looked up at all the tools of the trade on the pegboard. They were hung neat and orderly. It wouldn't take him too long to throw them in a pillowcase and stash them in a closet or something. The gimp-suited mannequin might be more of a problem.

He turned back to Erica. " Okay, look. I'm just trying not to get punched anymore this week."

She crossed her arms. "You're in luck. People usually have to pay me to punch them."

Matt pointed at the mannequin. "So where can I stash this for now?"

"Your bedroom?" Erica suggested.

"There's gonna be an open house," he said. "All the rooms will be on display. There shouldn't be gimps in any of them."

Erica's shrug seemed like another middle finger. "Well there's that old shed out back. It's full of shit. You should feel right at home."

He didn't ask her for help hauling it out.

■ ■ ■

By the time Peggy arrived, Matt had taken care of about half the things he'd wanted to. All the porn was gone from the party room, the VIP room was as empty as he could make it, and the parlor looked like Hugh Hefner's eccentric dining room rather than Hugh Hefner's private strip club. It was still pretty ridiculous, and Matt hoped Peggy was really good at her job.

The couple she'd brought with her seemed perfectly ordinary. They were introduced as Ted and Paula Baker when Peggy led them into the house. The foyer was pretty impressive and looked completely normal, and thankfully, Peggy took the opportunity to start her sales pitch there.

"Architecture like this is pretty rare in Las Vegas," she said. "The city's just too new. Most of the neighborhoods aren't even fifty years old. I could find you a dozen houses that look like they were built for the Jetsons, but a Victorian is a real find."

Ted Baker put on his poker face. "The neighborhood's not the best, but the price got our attention."

"You'll get a lot for your money, too," said Peggy. "It has lots of hidden amenities that just need a little polish."

The Bakers seemed to agree, and they oohed and ahhed in all the right places as Peggy pointed out "vintage flourishes" and the "turn-of-the-century mezzanine." She made a grand sweeping gesture as she led them through the double doors into the parlor, as if she were showing them some kind of secret inner sanctum. The effect worked for a second, and then Matt could see the questions starting to form in their expressions as they took in all the details. He quickly moved to stand in front of the bar to try to obscure the Golden Delicious logo etched into the mirror behind it.

Peggy must have seen their enthusiasm waver as she quickly added, "This would make an elegant dining room. Perfect for entertaining. The wet bar in the corner comes with a draft beer tap system and wine storage."

Paula slowly turned and scanned the room. Then she paused and looked back at Matt. "You certainly do like red velvet, Mr. James."

"I find it to be calming," said Matt. It had been the first thing to pop into his mind.

She wasn't buying it. "And is . . . is that a stage?"

Peggy gave a sideways glance at Matt. "Mr. James, didn't you say you were in the entertainment industry?"

"I was," Matt said. "Turns out I wasn't very good at it." Matt tried to turn it into a joke. "Stage fright."

He got no laughs.

Matt took that as a sign that he should probably make himself scarce for the rest of the tour. Peggy seemed pretty good at conjuring up semiplausible explanations on the spot. That's why she got a commission. Matt didn't trust his own ability to maintain a web of half-truths for very long. Hell, he was on the run and he still used his real name most of the time.

"Please excuse me," Matt said, "I'm just gonna run to the restroom." That was actually true.

He left Peggy and the Bakers to discuss the dual-toned

walls and the wooden molding that divided the colors. It was apparently called a chair rail for some reason, and Mr. Baker seemed very interested to know why.

Matt used the upstairs bathroom. He figured he had a few minutes while Peggy talked up each of the rooms below. He splashed some water on his face and reminded himself that it would all be over soon. In fact, the way he saw it, aside from the bruised ribs, this was actually a good thing. Selling the house would pay off his debt, and then he would be free to find some other town to hide in. He was thinking he might try the Pacific Northwest. It was kind of trendy now.

Then he heard Mr. Baker say something like, "What the hell?" from downstairs. It was muffled but loud enough that he must have been raising his voice.

Matt sighed at himself in the mirror and headed down. By the time he got to the foyer, Mr. and Mrs. Baker were already on their way out the front door. Mrs. Baker's cheeks were flushed, and her lips were pinched together. She stared straight ahead and ignored Matt entirely. Mr. Baker looked like he'd just stepped in a pile of dog shit. He stopped when he saw Matt.

He started in a low voice but raised the volume with each word. "We are not buying a whorehouse!" He stormed off after his wife before Matt could reply.

Peggy followed on his heels. "The price is negotiable," she said. "Imagine what the place could become." And then she was out the front door, too.

Matt called out to her from the front door. "Did you tell them it was a mortuary first?"

Peggy tried to calm the couple down but it was clear that they weren't coming back in. She gave Mr. Baker the price sheet and made hand motions that seemed to suggest that he should call her when they'd had some more time to think about it. Mr. Baker responded by handing the paper back and getting in his car. Peggy put the paper in her folder and turned toward the house. Her smile faltered for a second and then returned. When she got back to the front door, Matt stood aside for her to enter, but she remained where she was.

"Mr. James," she said, "we have run into a bit of a snag."

Matt nodded. "Did they look under the sheet? It's hard to hide a big bondage cross like that. I'm surprised they knew what that thing was. They must watch some pretty obscure porn."

"It wasn't the St. Andrew's Cross," said Peggy.

"So you know what it is, too?" asked Matt.

Peggy answered that question with a glare. "We didn't even get to that room. The tour ended in the kitchen. Where they met one of your employees. You may want to have a chat with her."

"Oh," said Matt.

"I'll work on the Bakers," said Peggy, "but I think it's best if we concentrate on the open house at this point."

"Sure," said Matt.

"And it may be a good idea if you left that to me," she said. "Alone."

Matt apologized and thanked her, then apologized again. Peggy's smile seemed forced, but she kept it up during the whole conversation.

As she got into her car, Matt wondered if the smile would come crashing down all at once or if it was stuck in place and would need to gradually melt away.

"Erica," he muttered to himself as he headed for the kitchen.

She stood at the sink wearing rubber gloves. Not sexy

nurse gloves. Thick, yellow, cleaning gloves. The sink was full of bubbles. She was even wearing an apron.

"Hey, Erica," he said, trying to be cool. "I didn't realize you were still here."

"I had a few things to clean up," she said.

"It sounds like you met Mr. and Mrs. Baker."

"Sure. We had a little chat," she said. "They seemed nice."

"It was hard to tell," he said . "They left so quickly."

"Huh. Maybe they realized what an asshole you are."

"I didn't get a chance to be an asshole to them," said Matt.

She shrugged. "Must have been something else, then."

Erica stopped scrubbing and pulled a large glass dildo out of the sink. She used the dishtowel that was draped over one of her shoulders to start drying it off. Then she set it on the dish rack next to the others. She smiled and started scrubbing the next one.

23

Dani looked up just in time to see a coffee cup midflight. It shattered against the wall next to a whiteboard in the LVMPD war room. Ceramic shards bounced across the stained carpet. Luckily the cup was empty, so they wouldn't need to clean coffee off the pictures clipped to the board. Foster's most recent mug shot stared blankly out next to crime-scene photos and a scribbled timeline.

Most of the officers in the war room had been working double shifts. The conference room was the largest they had in the building, but all the workstations and bodies made it seem cramped. The exploding cup startled them, but maybe not as much as it should have. Their eyes all looked from the dent in the wall over to the sergeant, who was now yelling into his cell phone.

"Yes, I know there was a patrol on that street! I'm the one who scheduled it!"

Dani didn't know who Dwayne was yelling at, but whoever it was, they were taking the full force of his pent-up frustration. The sergeant hadn't slept since the second victim was found, and the only thing Dani had seen him eat or drink came out of the mug that just flew across the room.

The call must have been the most recent in a long line of patrol reports. Each car had a picture of Foster taped to the dash, and each officer had a copy on his or her phone. Chances were, whoever Dwayne was unloading on was just as frustrated as he was.

Dwayne wasn't done yelling. "Canvass the whole goddamn street if you have to! Somebody must have seen what direction he came from!"

The sergeant didn't wait for a reply. He jabbed a finger at his phone and then slammed it down on the table he was using as a desk. Dani gave the phone a fifty-fifty chance of survival. Dwayne pressed the palms of his hands against his eyes for a second before exploding again. This time he didn't have anybody in particular to yell at so he just started ranting at the whiteboard.

"Where is this motherfucker? We know his name! We have his picture! This city isn't *that* big!"

All the other officers in the room looked from the sergeant to Dani. She was the investigative lead, but she knew that Dwayne was blaming himself. She got up from where she was working and went to sit at his table. He looked up at her as she came over and lowered his voice just a bit.

"If he was smart, he would have moved on by now," he said. "But now we have two dead women. And one of them used to work at the same fucking place that just fired him."

"We talked to Foster's former employer," she said. "He told us he warned all the women who worked at the club." Dwayne already knew this, but she told him again anyway.

He lowered his voice a bit more. "I guess he wasn't very convincing."

She looked down at his desk. The victims stared back at her. Each of them had been recreated by laying out a series of autopsy photos. All the cuts lined up from photo to photo. There were Post-it notes next to some of the photos with questions or comments. No wonder he threw the mug. You couldn't think about anything else with those eyes constantly watching you.

The sergeant was looking down now, too. "There has to be some kind of meaning here." he said. "A message or a statement."

He was slipping into bad habits again. Stating the obvious. Not a good sign. He was losing focus, and the stress was obviously getting to him. Maybe he needed to throw more mugs to let off some of that steam. She wanted to help him. This is where she usually stepped in to start piecing things together. They had both studied the patterns on the victims numerous times, as had the medical examiner. So far, none of their theories were sticking.

"Well," said Dani, "the cuts don't seem to be random. They're almost identical on each body." She used a pen to point out identical symbols on each woman's belly. "We know he draws them ahead of time and the cuts are very precise. It's like art or some kind of writing."

"So what does it say?" asked the sergeant.

"I've worked with an artist to draw them out," she said, "and I've made a few calls but . . ." She ended the sentence with a shrug.

Dwayne looked up at the whiteboard again, staring down Foster. "Maybe he's just fucking with us? I certainly feel fucked with."

Dani leaned back from the table but kept her eyes on the photos. "Sir, maybe we *should* hold a press conference."

"And tip our hand?" He started to shake his head, but then stopped and looked at her.

The sergeant had the support of the department with

regard to how much information to communicate to the press. His original plan was to keep Foster in the dark long enough to quickly track him down. Somehow that hadn't worked. Now Dani didn't see the benefit. Foster had killed again even without seeing his handiwork splashed all over the nightly news. And she was sure he would do it again. It'd be better to have the press working for them at this point.

She looked up at him. "It doesn't seem to matter anymore."

Dwayne closed his eyes and stretched his neck from side to side. It made a couple of popping sounds. Then he sighed and looked back at Dani. "No," he said, "I guess it doesn't."

He looked defeated, but that could have just been the lack of sleep. She certainly hoped so. He got up, looked at the white ceramic fragments on the carpet, and then went in search of a new coffee mug.

She didn't see much of him for the rest of the day. He did come back into the war room once to announce that he would be holding a press conference the next afternoon. Then he went home.

Most of Dani's time was spent making sure patrol schedules were updated and reviewing the reports that came in from the officers canvassing the neighborhood near the most recent crime scene. She followed up on a couple of leads, but information seemed spotty. One man said he'd seen somebody who looked like Foster staring at his watch and talking to himself as he walked down the sidewalk heading away from the apartment complex. But that was *before* Foster had entered the apartment complex according to security footage from the parking lot. Then another man swore he'd seen Foster waiting at a bus stop not far from the second victim's apartment building. None of the bus drivers who picked up at that stop remembered seeing Foster, though one did recall seeing a homeless man playing with an Etch A Sketch.

Between reports, Dani reviewed all the evidence from the crime scenes again, looking for any similarities that might point to some kind of pattern. So far she hadn't found anything useful. The first victim was probably a stranger to Foster; the second one was an ex-coworker. The first victim hadn't put up any kind of fight; the second one had been subdued with a stun gun and then knocked unconscious with a dining room chair. The only thing consistent was the pattern of the actual cut. So that's what she was digging into now.

Looking at the whole design was too much. She didn't recognize it at all. She broke down the pattern into pieces, scanned them into her laptop, and cleaned up the images to focus just on the lines themselves, rather than the torn skin they were made from. She sent a number of these scans to a consulting professor at the University of Las Vegas. The professor said it looked stylized, like calligraphy, which would make the symbols in the pattern harder to identify, but that she would see what she could dig up. Her best guess was that they were religious in nature.

Dani was doing some digging of her own online based on what the professor had told her. She started by simply typing the phrase "crazy cult symbols" into a search engine. Within a few clicks she found a site dedicated to the translation of Enochian letters and phrases. The site looked pretty batshit crazy. It said that Enochian script was used to record the names of demons and angels, and that it was even spoken by some who claimed to be possessed or speaking in tongues. The site also had animated images of the devil from *South Park* at the top of each page, so it wasn't a source she was going to officially reference. Even so, she thought she saw something familiar in the way the script was written. Or maybe she just wanted to see something familiar. It was hard to tell anymore.

When she finally looked up from her laptop, she was alone in the war room. She vaguely remembered waving to somebody who'd said they were calling it a night. That seemed like a couple of hours ago now. She leaned back and stretched her arms upward. Something smelled. She suspected the thing that smelled was her.

She began to gather her things. A shower and change of clothes were long overdue. If she couldn't sleep after that, she could always fire up the laptop at home.

Her cell phone buzzed, and the screen lit up with caller ID. It was Erica. Her finger hovered over the IGNORE button. She had received a couple of texts from Erica since their last night together. They were one-liners like, *How's it going?* and *Thinking of ya.* Dani hadn't returned any of them. She hadn't felt like smoothing anything over. She still didn't, but she picked up the phone anyway.

"What? I'm busy," she said.

There was a slight pause. Then Erica said, "You work too much. You should come over and play."

Dani's mood should have been pretty obvious, but it sounded like Erica was choosing to ignore it. That tore open the wound from the other night, and Dani felt herself getting angry. She almost hung up, but she didn't want to keep it building up inside her anymore. She didn't want to lose it on the job like Dwayne. Her coffee cup was metal, and if she threw that, it might bounce back and hurt somebody.

"Some of us don't get to play all day," she snapped. "Some of us have to stop bad people from doing bad things."

Another slight pause. Maybe Erica was trying to calm herself before responding. This time it didn't work. "Hey! I'm just trying to make you feel better. You don't have to be all bitchy!"

"Sometimes I don't want to feel better," Dani said. "Sometimes I want to feel what I *should* be feeling."

"Why?"

"Because it's real and it needs to be felt."

Dani heard Erica sniffle and take a breath before replying. "I can't afford to be depressed."

Dani slammed her laptop closed and stood up. "Well, you do your job and I'll do mine."

No reply to that. Just more sniffling. Dani hadn't seen Erica cry before. She was glad she couldn't see her now.

"Look," Dani said, more calmly this time, "watch the news tomorrow at six. Tell the girls."

"Okay." Erica's voice sounded hoarse.

Dani gritted her teeth and a knot twisted in her stomach. "And Erica?"

"Yeah?"

"Don't call me anymore."

24

Matt stood on a stack of furniture in Uncle Quent's office. At first, he had just tried a chair, but that didn't get him enough height. There was an end table by the love seat, so he dragged that over and balanced the chair on top. It was a bit sketchy. From the top of the stack he was just inches away from the symbol carved into the ceiling beam. He supposed he could have gotten a ladder, but it was all the way out in the shed. He wobbled a bit as he reached out to the symbol, and he realized how little it took for him to risk personal injury these days.

He had been spending a lot of time staring up at that symbol. He assumed Quent must have put it there. It would be too much of a coincidence otherwise. He did ask himself why Quent had felt the need to put the symbol in his office at all when he had worked so hard to leave all that behind. He knew Quent had the same brand he did on his wrist. That was part of the process. You took the oath, and then you took the brand when you were initiated as a Scholar.

It was the coin nailed into the center of the symbol that had finally made Matt start stacking furniture. From the desk chair he couldn't recognize where it was from. Now at eye level, he still had no idea. There was writing around the edge, though. The letters were badly worn, but he could make out enough detail to know it was in Latin. His childhood education had taught him that much at least. In the center was some kind of coat of arms and above that was the year 1577.

It looked rare and expensive. Not something that you nailed into the ceiling. Unless it was a sacrifice. Matt knew all about sacrifice, personal and otherwise. It was his unwillingness to sacrifice that made him leave the Scholars—and his family—behind. He could have handled nailing coins to walls, but they had given him a knife instead of a hammer. Of course, nobody ever really left the Scholars. They just ran and hid for as long as they could.

Maybe Quent had taken up old habits again. Symbols and sacrifice went hand in hand with Scholar rituals. Maybe he had traced the diagrams and recited the formulae one more time. Or maybe he had never stopped. It could have been to keep him hidden, or to protect the house, or maybe to draw power for some other purpose. Each ritual was a sort of transaction. If you wanted power, you had to pay for it. If Uncle Quent had put this symbol on the ceiling, then he had paid with more than just the coin. Matt figured he better leave it alone.

Now he just had to figure out how to get down.

As he was starting his descent, he heard the front door to the house open and then close. Christy and Adam were already here. They hadn't spoken to him in a couple of days, but he'd heard them earlier down in the break room. And Thug Guy hadn't been by since the house went on the market. Matt's stomach tightened at the thought of another *pep talk*. His foot missed the edge of the end table, and he lost his balance. He grabbed the chair for support, but it just followed him down to the floor. No blood, but he landed hard on his tailbone.

He thought he heard laughing downstairs. A woman's voice. He couldn't imagine women laughing around Thug Guy. Matt grabbed the edge of the desk and pulled himself to his feet. His back complained a little but less than he thought it would. It would probably hurt a lot more later on. The front door opened and closed again. More voices. They were muffled, but they sounded familiar. He supposed he should go check it out.

From the top of the stairs he could hear a little more clearly. The voices were all coming from the parlor now, and someone had turned on the TV by the bar. As he was about to start down the steps, he saw Adam coming through the foyer from the break room. He looked up and saw Matt, as well. Matt wanted to say something to break the ice—a joke, a smart-ass remark, or even just a hello—but his mind wasn't working fast enough, and Adam turned away to head into the parlor.

He listened for a bit. He heard Christy's voice and then Erica's. He heard some of the other girls, too. Maybe the former employees of the Golden Delicious were planning a mutiny. They sounded happy to see one another but also a little nervous. They were too eager to laugh at each others' jokes. He heard the intro to the nightly news start up on the TV, and then Christy hushed the girls. Matt made his way down to the entrance to the foyer. He didn't think he could pull off walking in to face them all again, but he did stick his head in to see what was going on.

The girls were crowded around the bar. Some already had drinks in front of them. Adam was there, too, sitting on one of the barstools in front of his mom, who was behind the bar. She had the remote in one hand and was aiming it at the

TV to turn up the volume. Everyone was quiet by the time the news anchor started talking. Over her shoulder was a splashy graphic of a chalk outline next to the silhouette of a palm tree.

"We're broadcasting live from the Shady Palms apartment complex in Los Prados, the scene of the latest in what appears to be a series of gruesome murders." Her tone was even, with just the right amount of concern. "Mike?"

The camera cut over to a reporter standing in front of the entrance to an apartment complex. True to its name, there were a number of palm trees growing next to the two-story buildings. They weren't luxury apartments, but they didn't look run-down, either. As the reporter started talking, the camera zoomed in on one apartment door that was blocked off by yellow crime-scene tape.

"That's right, Deborah," the reporter—Mike—said. "Police responded yesterday morning when a concerned neighbor reported a strange smell coming from the apartment of Candice Brookes."

The camera zoomed out again, and now there was a woman standing next to the reporter. She wore a uniform. Matt guessed she was a maid at a hotel or something.

Mike motioned a hand toward the woman. "With us now is—"

The woman leaned over to the microphone and cut him off. "Call me Bethel."

Adam looked up at his mother. "Do we know her? She looks familiar."

Christy didn't take her eyes off the screen. "No, honey. Now be quiet."

The reporter leaned back a little from the woman, who was right in his face. "I know this is hard for you, but can you please describe what you saw?"

It didn't seem too hard for her at all. As the camera focused in on Bethel, a graphic appeared at the bottom of the screen labeling her BETHEL, CONCERNED NEIGHBOR. She seemed excited to be on TV. A bit too excited, really. Maybe nobody ever paid much attention to her.

"It was bad," she said. "Real bad. You don't even know. That's the last time I walk into somebody's house when I smell something *nasty*. There was blood on the walls, blood on the floor, blood on the ceiling." She started talking with her hands, pointing them in the air like pistols. "Like somebody filled a squirt gun with blood and went crazy. And that was just the hallway. I didn't even go into the living room where they found her."

The camera angled back to the reporter, but Bethel leaned into the frame as though she didn't want to give up the camera just yet.

Mike faced the camera, but his eyes kept flicking over to the woman as he talked. "Other residents of Shady Palms said that last night was calm and quiet. No screaming or other disturbances were reported."

The scene changed, and the screen now showed a police officer standing at a podium set up in front of an official-looking building, probably the police department or city hall or something. Attached to the podium was a tangle of microphones. It took a second, but Matt recognized the guy. It was Christy's ex, Dwayne. And the officer standing next to him was his partner, the woman who had "questioned" Erica the day they'd come by the house. Dwayne was grim-faced as he prepared to give his statement.

The reporter's voice continued even though he wasn't on the screen. "Earlier today, Sergeant Dwayne Murdock of the Las Vegas Metropolitan Police Department had this to say..."

Adam looked up at his mom again. "Hey, it's Dad!"

"Shh!"

The sergeant stared straight into the camera as he spoke. If he had any notes, he wasn't using them. "We want the people of Clark County to know that tracking down this criminal is our top priority. We believe he is targeting young women working as adult entertainers and that he has a history of working with those women."

Some of the girls exchanged glances, but none of them said anything. The frame changed to a mug shot, and it got everybody's attention again. In general, the man in the mug shot looked normal, but that's what they said about most serial killers. His *eyes* didn't look normal, though. They looked pleading and vacant, like he might be on death row. Unfortunately, that wasn't where he was.

The sergeant's voice continued. "We are currently seeking a man named Stephen Foster for questioning in relation to these crimes. If you see him, please do not approach him. Contact the local authorities immediately."

The scene returned to the news anchor. The graphic over her shoulder was replaced with a smaller version of the mug shot. Under the mug shot it read, STEPHEN FOSTER, MURDER SUSPECT and then listed the phone number for the police department.

"Please stay with us for continuous coverage of this high-stakes manhunt—"

Christy turned off the TV. Nobody said anything. Some girls were looking at each other, some looked at their drinks. Christy came out from behind the bar and put an arm around Adam.

It was Erica who broke the silence. "I knew her," she said. "Candice. She worked at the Tail Spin. I used to work there, too. I *just* saw her. We had drinks. It must have been the same day as . . . I just *saw* her . . ." She couldn't finish.

Erica's eyes were glassy as she turned away.

Christy left Adam to go wrap her arms around Erica. At first Erica looked stiff and uncomfortable. Then her whole body sagged. She started heaving silent sobs. Other girls joined in, wrapping their arms around both of them. Adam stayed on his stool. He looked like he didn't know what to do with himself. Matt backed out of the room before anyone noticed him.

He hid upstairs for the rest of the night. He couldn't get any sleep, not in his bed and not on Uncle Quent's love seat. He even tried the bed in the party room, since it seemed like it would be the most comfortable. That hadn't lasted long at all. The sheets were new, of course—he had replaced the satin sheets with cotton ones for the open house—one of the many things on Peggy's to-do list. It didn't matter, though. It was like he could feel the sex radiating out of the mattress itself. He finally gave up and went out to the break room.

He sat on the couch and flicked through the channels until he found an old movie to stare at—*Big Trouble in Little China*. Jack Burton let fly with fists and one-liners as ancient Chinese gods fought with lightning. It was strangely comforting. So much so that he must have dozed off for a good hour of it.

Too bad. He liked that one.

Just before dawn, he brewed a pot of coffee, drank it, and then brewed another for Christy. He figured he'd better fill up his belly with something, so he pilfered a couple of Adam's cereal bars. A hot shower woke Matt up the rest of the way, though it didn't make a whole lot of sense to bother based on his plans for the morning.

As he got dressed, he heard Christy getting Adam ready for school. He waited in his office until they were both gone. It would be better if they weren't here after he made his phone call. When he heard the front door close, he flipped up the lid of the cigar box. The pistol was still there. Lying on top of it was a scrap of paper with a handwritten phone number. His fingers only shook a little as he dialed.

■ ■ ■

Matt met Thug Guy on the front lawn. Thug Guy looked at the toolbox Matt was carrying with a raised eyebrow.

Matt set down the toolbox as he spoke. "Look . . . what's your name, anyway?"

Thug Guy crossed his arms. "You do not want to know me long enough to know my name."

"Yes, that's very mysterious, but here's the deal. Nobody's buying," said Matt.

"Not yet," said Thug Guy.

"There not gonna buy, not at a price that's going to make you happy."

"You owe us money. A lot," said Thug Guy. "Plus interest, of course."

"Yes, I do," said Matt. "And I'll get you that and more."

"Is that right?" asked Thug Guy. "How? You don't have business anymore."

"We'll reopen," said Matt.

Thug Guy snorted.

Matt pointed at Thug Guy and then himself. "*We* will reopen. As partners."

Thug Guy shrugged like he was making an obvious statement. "This is not our town. Is not possible."

"So expand," said Matt. "That's the offer."

Thug Guy narrowed his eyes and touched a finger to the bird skull on his hat. He was thinking things through. Matt just wasn't sure if he was thinking about the offer or which part of Matt's body to break first.

Matt opened up the toolbox. He reached in and took out a hammer. "You want to hit something? Fine. I can live with that, but I can't shut this place down. Not right now."

Thug Guy looked down at the hammer. Then he reached inside his pocket for something else. Matt let out the breath he was holding when it turned out to be just a phone.

Thug Guy dialed a number. "You go take care of your nose while I have a talk with boss."

"What's wrong with my—"

Suddenly, Matt was on his back. Thug Guy was looking down at him while he talked on his phone. Matt panicked a little when he couldn't understand what Thug Guy was saying. Then he realized Thug Guy was speaking in a foreign language. He nodded and smiled at Matt as he said something into the phone with a little laugh. That's when Matt noticed that his nose felt like it was full of crushed glass.

He probably *should* go take care of that.

Once the bleeding had stopped, Matt spent the rest of the morning in the backyard. He brought his toolbox and started working on the shed. He had to clean it out first and return some of the items to the house. He rehung the neon sign, set up the reception podium, and put the gimp-suited mannequin back in its natural habitat.

He was putting a few new nails into some loose boards when someone called his name. He stopped hammering and went around to the other side of the shed, the side that faced the house. Christy was standing there with her hands on her hips. She looked pissed but also a bit sad. Thug Guy was watching them from the back door. He leaned against the doorframe, arms crossed.

"It sold, then?" she asked. "I saw they took down the for-sale sign out front."

"What? No," said Matt. "I took that down."

"Why?"

"He is probably making big mistake," said Thug Guy from behind her.

She looked over her shoulder and then back at Matt. "Who is that guy?"

"Long story," said Matt. "He might be sticking around for a while, though."

"Good news," said Thug Guy. "I already move in. I take your room. You don't mind." It wasn't a question.

Christy stepped forward and spoke so that only Matt could hear her. "Why would he be staying here?"

"Because," said Matt, "we're reopening. And he's our new partner. Well, his boss is our new partner, technically."

"I'm not comfortable with that," she said. He knew she was thinking of Adam.

"Neither am I," said Matt. He glanced up at Thug Guy, who was still leaning against the doorframe. "But we'll be open again."

Christy reached a hand toward Matt's face. "Did he do that to your nose?"

Matt flinched back. "If he's going to hurt anybody, it will be me." He gave her a weak smile. "He's actually kind of reasonable. If you aren't a big smart-ass."

Christly looked conflicted. She glanced at Thug Guy and then at the house. Next she looked at the shed behind Matt. "What are you doing out here?"

"I'll show you," said Matt. "But I'll need a ride to the hardware store first to pick up a few things."

■ ■ ■

It was getting dark by the time he was done working on the shed. There was probably more to do, but he supposed it would never be perfect. He closed his toolbox and went inside. He could hear that the TV was on inside the break room. When he opened the door he was relieved to see that he wasn't welcomed by cold stares. Adam was in his usual spot on the couch in front of the TV, and Christy was at the table looking at something on her phone.

She stopped to give him a smile. "Hey."

"It's ready," said Matt.

"What's ready?" asked Adam. He hadn't turned to look at Matt yet, but when he did he added, "You look gross."

"I'm sure," said Matt, "but I smell worse." He looked from Adam to Christy and back again. "Are you coming or what?"

"Where?" Adam asked, standing up.

Matt jerked his thumb toward the backyard. "Outside."

Christy and Adam followed Matt as he led the way out the back door. Adam stood on the steps trying to figure out what he was supposed to be looking at. Then Matt plugged in the extension cord. The shed lit up like a carnival ride.

"I may have overdone it with the lights," he said.

Adam's feet made quick crunching sounds as he ran out onto the pea gravel. He stopped short at the entrance to the shed. A pirate flag hung down from a pole over the door. Instead of a skull there was a big yellow smiley face with an eye patch.

"What is this?" asked Adam.

"It's a playhouse," said Matt.

The boy turned to him. Adam looked like he was about to explain something that everybody should already know. "You know, playhouses are for girls. They like to play *house."*

"I bet they like to play pirates, too," said Matt. "Your mom would make a great Captain Hook."

"I heard that!" shouted Christy as she made her way over to the shed.

"That was a compliment," said Matt. "Everybody knows that Captain Hook is the coolest pirate."

She looked over to Adam who said, kind of reluctantly, "He's right."

"*Playhouse* is pretty weak for a nine-year-old," said Christy.

"Fine." Matt rolled his eyes. "Then it's a clubhouse."

He stepped forward and opened the door. All the junk had been cleared out. He'd thrown some away but most of it was down in the basement. A bulb in a plastic cage hung from the center of the room, and Christmas lights were strung up across all four walls. They were multicolored so everything had a strange rainbow hue to it. A few mismatched chairs surrounded a flimsy-looking card table in the center, and there was a short bookcase up against one wall. So far, the bookcase was empty except for an ancient CD player. Matt had unearthed it when cleaning out the shed. He wasn't even sure it still worked. He had also found a dusty old dartboard that he'd hung on the far wall. A few darts jutted out from it at odd angles.

"Decorate it any way you want," said Matt.

"Cool," said Adam. It came out understated, but the smile on his face stretched from ear to ear.

Something squeaked and Adam looked around. His eyes widened when they landed on something furry that was staring back up at him from a pile of blankets in the corner.

"Oh, and it comes with this." Matt pointed at the orange cat as it stretched and yawned. "His name's Azrael."

25

Lois sat on her couch looking out the window and thinking about how things changed. There are some who might say people never change. Lois didn't believe that. She didn't think that *she* had changed much over the years, but her husband, Neal, certainly had. And she wasn't sure if that was a good thing or a bad thing. Neal seemed pretty happy most of the time. He had his friends on the computer. They chatted all the time and got together to do . . . whatever it was that they did. Lois spent most of her day reminiscing about better times. She had built up quite the collection of happy memories over her seventy-three years, and she had very few regrets. She just didn't have a lot to look forward to anymore.

They had moved to Las Vegas in their thirties. They'd been on the same page back then. Neal had taken a great job building all those casinos. As soon as one had been finished, a new one would be waiting to be built or an old one would want to expand. The money had been good, and houses had been cheap. Everybody wanted to visit Las Vegas, but most of them didn't want to stay. So he worked, and she stayed home to raise their family. Their neighborhood wasn't the best, but all the houses had been new then, and it was far enough from the Strip to make it feel like the typical suburb of any quiet town.

Their kids—two boys and a girl—had enjoyed a good childhood. Lois had taken the time to raise them the way she'd wanted, and she'd loved it. Those years had seemed to stretch out forever, until suddenly they were over and the last of their children had gone off to college. None of them ended up staying in Las Vegas, and only their daughter still lived in Nevada.

They could have moved, she supposed. But life had its rhythms, and starting over seemed like a massive chore. The house was paid for and Neal's pension let them live comfortably, if not a bit frugally. Their days were filled with the routines they'd made for themselves. They spent half the morning just waking up and puttering around. By the time they were ready to do something, they were starting to think about lunch. After lunch, they might want to take a little rest. After that, there weren't a whole lot of hours left in the day. And they went to bed pretty early. They had some friends around, and they did try to get together every other week or so. They kept saying they were going to play bridge, but usually when they had folks over they all just ended up chatting and snacking.

If they were able to somehow find the energy to move, she wouldn't know where to go anyway. Her kids had their own lives with their own rhythms. One even had his own grandson. They were all busy raising their own families and making their own memories. She figured they wouldn't have much time for her. She would have to change to fit into their lives, and so far she wasn't very good at change.

"Suck it, newbie!"

Lois knew Neal wasn't talking to her. His was wearing

his headset, and he had his laptop open on his TV tray. He was playing his computer game. It wasn't exercise, but it did get his heart rate up for a couple of hours a day. Sometimes, the whole tray would wobble when he slammed the keyboard and shoved the mouse back and forth.

"You just got ganked, son!"

He also wasn't talking to either of their sons. They didn't play computer games. They had better things to do with their time. No, Neal had his new computer friends, and they were all part of a *clan* or some such nonsense.

She needed a drink. She usually waited until lunch before she had a little something to dull the joint pain, but today she didn't feel like waiting. She decided to make lunch a little early. She would make the drink first, though. Nothing fancy. Just a gin and tonic.

She finished the first one while she was still making her sandwich. It hadn't been a full glass, of course. She was pretty sure it was just a splash. She made the next one by the book.

As she laid a pickle slice next to her sandwich, she saw something move out the kitchen window. That window faced the street, and she could see somebody walking down the sidewalk. It wasn't an uncommon occurrence, but this person stood out. His clothes were dirty and stained. His face was grimy, and his hair was wild, like he hadn't combed it in weeks. But mainly he stood out because of the way he walked. He would walk at a normal pace and then stop all of a sudden to talk to himself. Then he might take a few steps back and cross the street, or he might continue on as if nothing had happened. She had seen him around for several days now.

She called out to Neal in the living room. "That homeless guy is back."

"Huh?" asked Neal.

"I think he's heading back to that old condemned school," she said.

"Uh-huh."

"I've seen him there a couple times. He just sits on that swing. Swinging like he does."

She heard Neal tap his keyboard and click his mouse.

She kept on talking as if Neal were actually paying attention. "Talking to that toy. It's sad, really."

"Yep," said Neal.

Lois took a sip of her drink and got out two more slices of bread.

"I'm gonna make him a sandwich. What do you think he'd like?"

"Food."

She poked her head into the living room. Neal's face was lit up from below by his laptop screen. It made him look uglier than normal. A wizard shot flames out of his hands at a woman with six arms. She wasn't sure which one was Neal.

"You ought to come with me," she said. "It'll do you some good. Get out of the house for a bit."

He didn't look up. "I'm playin' my *Warcraft*. 'Bout ready to ding." Apparently that meant no.

"Fine. I'm gonna take him an egg salad and maybe a root beer."

Tap, tap. Click, click.

She sighed and finished her drink. Then she made the sandwich. She put it in a bag along with a can of root beer and an apple for good measure. She put on her sweater and exchanged her slippers for some walking shoes. She headed out the front door, leaving Neal to his fantasy world. She already felt better about her day.

The old school was just a couple of blocks away. It hadn't been a school, though, had it? No, it had been an orphanage. It used to be run by Catholics, if she remembered correctly. It had closed down years ago when the new cathedral opened up downtown. She wasn't sure what had happened to all the kids. It seemed like something the state would take care of. Maybe they had a foster program. She wondered if she was too old to be a foster parent. She would ask.

Surrounding the orphanage was an old chain-link fence. It looked pretty run-down. It had those crappy green plastic slats that made a cheap fence look even cheaper. Big patches of the slats were covered in green paint where somebody had attempted to hide some graffiti. It hadn't made it look any better. The green paint didn't match the color of the slats, and new graffiti had been added over it anyway.

Lois went around the fence into a weedy playground. She heard something creak, but it was just the old swing set. She was surprised it was still standing. It was such a shame. She could remember walking past, years ago, to the sounds of squealing laughter and jump rope rhymes. Back then, a good jump rope rhyme could predict the future. She tried to remember the words as she looked around.

Ice cream soda, lemonade, punch. Tell me the name of my honey bunch.

Then you would recite the alphabet until the rope tangled you up. The last letter you said would tell you the name of your crush. Lois hadn't been very good. She'd never made it to *N*.

There was no sign of the homeless man in the playground, and the door to the building looked chained up tight. She was disappointed. She thought about leaving the bag of food by the swing where she had seen him once before, but she really wanted to give it to him in person. She wanted to hear a bit about his story. Maybe she could help him.

He could be around back she supposed. It would be a nice quiet place to rest, assuming the neighborhood kids left him alone. The cans and candy wrappers on the ground looked pretty old, and even the graffiti was fading, so she figured they didn't visit very often.

As she followed the fence along the side of the building, another rhyme came to mind.

Johnny gave me apples. Johnny gave me pears. Johnny gave me fifty cents to kiss him on the stairs. I gave him back his apples. I gave him back his pears. I gave him back his fifty cents and kicked him down the stairs.

Then she heard something quack. It was a tinny sounding quack, like a duck using an old microphone. But it sounded familiar.

She stopped and looked around. She didn't see anybody along the fence, and she was still pretty far from the back of the building. There was some plywood lying on the ground about midway along the building. It was littered with a few fragments of broken glass. She looked up at the building and saw the window that it used to cover. There was a voice coming from the window.

She hesitated for a second, but she wasn't sure why. She already knew that this poor man probably had some mental health issues. He seemed harmless enough, though. She was more worried that he was so far gone that nobody could help him. She stepped over to the window and looked in.

And there he was. He actually looked cleaner than she'd expected, and his skin was pale, not leathery and tanned from overexposure. He was sitting on an old beanbag chair in a room full of broken toys. The toys looked like they had been put on display rather than scattered around and forgotten. His back was to her, and he held one of the toys in his lap. It was round like a clock but it had pictures of animals on it instead of numbers. There was a big, red arrow in the center that pointed to a duck.

"I know, but how many more?" The man wasn't speaking to her. He was staring down at the toy. A See 'n Say—that's what it was called.

He pulled the cord on the See 'n Say, and the arrow started to spin around. It landed on a cartoon image of a sheep. A letter or symbol had been drawn over the sheep, but she couldn't make out what it was.

The toy spoke with a cheerful but staticky voice. "The sheep says, *Baaa.*"

The man was quiet for a second, and Lois was just about to say something when the man nodded and said, "I just don't know if I can keep doing it. I can't sleep. I keep seeing their faces."

Lois didn't know what to make of that.

The man pulled the cord again, and this time the arrow landed on a cow. It had a different symbol on it, but she couldn't make that one out, either. "The cow says, *Mooo.*"

This time he shook his head. "You're right. They shouldn't have to sell themselves like that. I know I'll see them again soon. Maybe we'll all have a laugh about it. And the blood doesn't bother me so much anymore. It's not that."

"The pig says, *Oink, oink, oink.*"

The man fished something out of his pocket. It was long and rectangular, and a dull gray. He ran his thumb along the side, and a blade clicked out from one end. "It's just . . . I can't sleep because their faces are so beautiful. I want to set more of them free. I don't think I should like it so much."

Lois's stomach twisted. She didn't normally watch the news. It was always so dramatic. Every rainstorm was a hurricane, and every criminal was a terrorist. Still, there were some stories you just couldn't avoid. Everyone was talking about those girls. Even Neal. His computer had told him about a murderer right here in Las Vegas. A man who killed women. Prostitutes.

"The cat says, *Meow*." Did he pull the cord that time?

All of a sudden, he sounded very defensive. "No, I don't touch myself! It's not like that."

This time he moved the arrow by hand, pointing it directly at the sheep once more. He pulled the cord. "The lamb says, *Mmbeh*." That wasn't what it'd said before.

The man seemed to calm down a bit. "Okay, I can do that. I have somebody else in mind. She tells everybody she's having a good time, but I think she's burning out. She seems ready to walk the path."

Lois's heart was thumping in her ears. She was afraid the man with the knife could hear it, too. She gripped the bag of food in a clenched fist. She had just wanted a little change of pace. To do a good deed. Feel like she could still be needed. She should have stayed home and taken her nap.

She should be running, maybe screaming. She knew she had to move, but her body was frozen in place. She had to turn as quietly as she could and put one foot in front of the other until she got to the road. Then she had to run. She couldn't stop. Not until she was in her house, on her couch next to Neal, with the phone in her hand and the police on the line. If she could do all that, she might start playing *Warcraft*.

26

Matt thought the man lying on the bed looked like a stage magician who had just made his own clothes disappear. He was naked and pigeon chested, but he still wore a top hat and sported a nice goatee. Sitting on his lap was a ventriloquist's dummy. It wore a top hat, too. And unlike his owner, the dummy still had most of his clothes on. He was dressed in a tux with tails, but his tuxedo pants were pulled down. Jutting out between the dummy's legs was an erection. Whether it belonged to the man or the dummy was hard to tell because it was completely covered by a pink French tickler.

"Hi," said Matt. "Mr. . . . Johnson? Really? That's the name you're going with?"

Mr. Johnson gestured dramatically to the dummy sitting on his junk. "And this is Wally."

They were in the party room. Matt stood next to the bed with Christy behind him by the door. She was hugging a short silk robe around her body and glaring at Mr. Johnson. There was a panic button hidden behind one of the nightstands, and Christy had pressed it a few minutes ago. It lit up a small red light behind the bar in the parlor, as well as one on the desk in the office. This was the first time the panic button had been used since Matt had taken over. He wasn't sure exactly how to react.

"It sounds like there's been a little confusion here," said Matt.

"I'm not confused," said Mr. Johnson. "She didn't give me what I wanted. She's a whore. That's her job."

"Well, now, her job is to entertain you on an hourly basis," said Matt. "So maybe you were confused on the services offered per hour?"

Wally turned his wooden head toward Matt. "She's a fucking whore!"

Not bad. Matt didn't see Mr. Johnson's lips move at all.

Christy was less impressed. She lunged forward at him. Luckily, Matt was between them. He held out his hands toward Christy to block her path.

"Whoa, whoa, whoa!" he said.

She stopped, but the look in her eyes was demanding blood. Matt kept one hand up in front of her, but then he pointed the other toward Mr. Johnson. The guy didn't seem fazed at all by Christy's reaction.

"Hey," said Matt, "no need to be rude. We're just having a customer service conversation here."

Wally's eyebrows waggled. "Maybe you should off-shore that shit."

Matt was reminded of his call to the financial software helpline. He wondered what Sean might say in this situation.

"You know what I'm gonna do?" asked Matt. "I'm just gonna look right past that so we can get to the point. You and Christy had an understanding."

Both Wally and Mr. Johnson turned to give Matt blank stares. Christy snorted and walked over to the nightstand where she had left her clutch purse.

Matt continued. "You agreed to the . . . *entrée* she was offering. But then you tried to add a *side dish*? One that we don't even serve here. Now she's pretty upset."

Mr. Johnson waved a hand dismissively. "Is this about money? Do you want more money?"

As he said that, Wally took the opportunity to bend over and start sucking on the French tickler. He made glugging sounds as he bobbed his head. It was kind of like when a ventriloquist drinks a glass of water while his puppet performs a monologue. Matt was beginning to realize that this was not really a customer service type of conversation.

"Well," Matt said, "no. I think what you owe us is an apology. This has been very traumatic." He couldn't take is eyes off the bobbing puppet. "You know . . . for all concerned."

Wally looked up from his work. "I'll tell you what. Why don't you and Nip Slip here go fuck yourselves off?"

Matt turned toward Christy and started walking her out the doorway. "This guy's a jerk. Let's just get him out of here."

Christy had something in her hand. A small cylinder of some sort. "Sure. One sec."

She stepped back inside the party room and closed the door. Matt stood alone in the hallway for a second. Maybe she forgot something. Then he heard Wally through the door.

"Oh, you want some more? I thought you might. Once you've had wood, nothing else is quite as good."

Christy didn't reply, but there was a faint hissing sound. It was followed by screaming.

"Ahh! Fuuuck! My eyes! Fuuuck!"

"I can see your lips moving this time," said Christy.

There was a sharp crack, like something got slapped hard. Matt was a little afraid to open the door now. Whatever it had been, it sounded like Mr. Johnson was still more concerned about his eyes.

"They're fucking melting!"

"You both need to work on your manners," said Christy.

Christy opened the door. She was carrying Wally's head. "They apologized."

Matt noticed a single drop of blood on her forehead. "Oh, you're bleeding!"

"No, I'm not," said Christy.

There was a whimper from the bed and something thumped to the floor. Christy closed the door and looked at Matt. She wasn't quite smiling.

"I suppose I should have taken care of that," said Matt.

"That's what managers are for."

Christy pointed Wally's head at the bandage on Matt's nose. "You've already taken one for the team."

"Yeah, well, I snore now," said Matt.

Something got knocked over as Mr. Johnson fumbled around in the party room. "Is anybody there? I'm fucking dying here!"

Matt raised an eyebrow at Christy.

"He's not dying," said Christy. "Unless he's severely allergic to pepper spray." She sounded hopeful.

"Okay," said Matt, "I'll see if I can get our new *partner* to help me take out the trash. My guess is, he'll just watch and laugh instead."

Thug Guy *did* laugh when Matt told him. He was in the kitchen standing by the sink with his sleeves were rolled up and his newsboy hat pushed back. He had a knife in his hand. It was the stubby one with the hook at the tip. From the break room, Matt couldn't see what Thug Guy was cooking up.

Thug Guy gestured to his ear with his knife. "I thought I hear moaning. Not the good kind. Is he dead?"

"What? No! Why would you think that?" asked Matt.

Thug Guy rolled his eyes and then looked down at whatever it was that he was cutting. "He could be bad for business. Maybe he tell people what happen. Maybe he tell cops."

Matt crossed his arms but lowered his voice. "I wouldn't kill him. That's crazy!"

Thug Guy didn't lower his voice. He held something with one hand and jabbed his knife into it with his other. "Is natural. The strong prey on the weak. You must kill to survive. Don't you watch . . . uh . . . Discovery Channel?"

Matt moved toward the kitchen, hoping Thug Guy would lower his voice if he got a little closer. "Nobody's going to *prey* on anyone. I just want to get him out of here. Beside, the cops aren't a problem. We have that covered."

He could see the kitchen counter now, and Thug Guy wasn't preparing a meal. Newspaper had been laid out over the counter. Lying in the center of it was a dead crow. Blood was pooling around it but not a lot. There was a cut between the bird's legs, and Thug Guy was using the hook part of the knife to tease something out of it.

Thug Guy didn't look up from his work. "Oh? Maybe I misjudge you? Maybe you are big-time criminal? A real gangster?" The sarcasm was clear, even with his thick accent.

The smell hit Matt as the hook pulled out some of the bird's organs. It reminded him of the animal cages at the zoo. Not rotten, but an exotic kind of stink. Something caught inside the crow, and Thug Guy gave a little tug. There was a popping sound, and another glob of bird parts spilled out.

Matt's throat felt thick as he swallowed. "I think gangsters plan their crimes. I just kind of blunder into them. So are you gonna help me?"

"Sure. I will help. Maybe I break something small as reminder."

"You mean on him, right?"

Thug Guy used his knife to scrape something into the garbage disposal. He looked up at Matt. "Sure."

Matt figured he'd better get back to Mr. Johnson in the party room. He also didn't want to learn any more about crow anatomy.

He left Thug Guy to clean up and went back out into the hallway. The party room door was wide open. Matt's stomach tightened, and he stepped quietly down the hallway like he was expecting somebody to jump out at him.

He slowly leaned his head into the room. "Hello?"

Nobody.

It was still early, so there weren't a lot of people in the parlor. That was good. At least there wouldn't be a big audience if Mr. Johnson decided to go *perform* onstage. Matt didn't hear any yelling so he guessed that wasn't the case. He slowly turned in a circle, trying to figure out where a deranged ventriloquist might hide.

"What are you doing?"

Matt looked toward the foyer and saw Christy just coming down the stairs. She had jeans on now and a loose-fitting blouse. Not her normal work clothes.

"Where's the puppet master?" asked Matt.

"Oh," said Christy, "he left. As soon as he could see again, he grabbed his clothes and ran. He couldn't see very well, though. I think I heard him hit a garbage can with his car. At least, I hope it was only a garbage can."

"Did he take Wally?" he asked.

"Most of him," said Christy. "I put his head on my nightstand."

"That's creepy."

"Maybe a little. I'll sleep fine, though," she said. "I think we still have Mr. Johnson's credit card at the bar."

"Drinks are on him, then."

"I'll have to have mine later. I'm heading over to Erica's. She wanted to talk."

Matt was surprised. "You guys talk?"

"Sometimes," Christy said. "She doesn't have a lot of friends. I think that's the way she wants it."

"What about the cop?" asked Matt.

"Dani? They broke up," she said. "That's why she wants me to come over. We'll probably also bitch about you. Because that's what you do when the boss isn't around."

Matt nodded. "That makes sense. What about Adam? We're not closing for a while."

Christy smiled. "He's in his clubhouse. I can't get him out of there. He'd sleep in there if I let him. Do you think you could check in on him in a bit?"

"Yeah, sure. I like it in there myself."

"Thanks. I shouldn't be too late."

Matt watched Christy go. Thug Guy must have been watching her, too.

"Very beautiful," he said.

Matt turned to look at him. Thug Guy had a knowing smile on his face, like they were sharing some kind of secret. Matt didn't like it. He decided to change the subject as quickly as possible.

"False alarm," he said. "Mr. Johnson found his own way out. You can go back to your . . . work."

Thug Guy tilted his head from side to side and shrugged.

He gave Matt another smile and lumbered back into the break room. Matt wondered who he was making his new crow for. Or maybe he just collected them as souvenirs from his travels.

Matt thought about heading out to the clubhouse now. The day had turned out to be stranger than most, and hiding away from the rest of it sounded like a good idea.

27

The SWAT van smelled like sweat. It was fresh sweat, but that didn't make it smell any better. Dani was crammed in the back with seven other officers. Each of them wore a helmet and layers of body armor. She was trying to think about her training. She had completed Dynamic Entry training a couple of years ago, but she wasn't part of the regular SWAT team. As the investigative specialist on the case, it was her job to help direct the team after the location had been secured. In a few minutes the side door would slide open and there would be no more time to think.

One of the other officers was bouncing his leg in a steady rhythm by the ball of his foot. Another leaned his head back with his eyes closed. Dani was nervous, but she clearly wasn't the only one sweating.

Dwayne sat up front with the driver. He turned back to face them as the van slowed, and it started making its way through residential streets. "No sirens. No lights," he said. "We'll park half a block up and approach on foot. We announce ourselves as we breach."

They had gone over all this earlier in the war room. Three separate times. With maps. He was stating the obvious again, but this time she thought it was more for the team than for himself. He was getting everybody focused before the doors opened and he yelled, *Go, go, go, go!*

"We want him alive," he said. Then he added, "I'm required to say that."

The tip had come in just a couple of hours ago. There were lots of tips coming in, though, and so far none of them had provided any significant leads. At first this one had sounded like it could be a dead end, too. Maybe just a nosy neighbor complaining about a vagrant. But the woman had been very insistent, so the call had gotten through the initial screening process and Dani had picked up the phone. The woman's name was Lois. Once she had calmed down and finished her rant about not being taken seriously, Dani started to run through her standard questions. Lois stopped her right there. What she had to say made Dani stand up and wave Dwayne over as she put Lois on speakerphone.

Lois spoke deliberately, like she was reliving the experience. Her description of the box cutter was what got Dani's attention. That and what the man had said when he was talking to himself. It was Foster. It had to be.

Everybody sat up straight as the van slowed to a stop. Dani adjusted her grip on her assault rifle and jammed the stock under her armpit. They parked next to a small house that had a car up on blocks in the driveway. Based on the layer of dust on the car, it had probably been years since anybody had worked on it.

There was a moment of absolute stillness as the sergeant checked in with another officer who had eyes on the abandoned building. It was like waiting for a roller coaster to crest the rise before the first big drop. Everybody stared at the sergeant's radio.

A hiss of static broke the silence. "Confirmed. No

pedestrians on the street. Green light."

"Go, go, go, go!"

Daylight lit up the interior of the van as the doors cracked open. The team was out in seconds and lined up on the sidewalk. They moved forward, crouched with their weapons angling out in front of them. The sergeant joined Dani at the rear of the column, radio in one hand, pistol in the other.

A man stepped through the front door of the house next to them. He stopped short, and a cigarette tumbled out of his lips as he gawked at the squad. He looked like he was trying to figure out what he'd done wrong. The second officer in the column jabbed a finger at the man and then at the front door. He had to do it again before the man got the hint and stepped back into his house. His face appeared in the front window a few seconds later.

The officer taking point got to the fence line of the abandoned building and dropped to one knee. He leaned around the edge of the fence and raised his rifle to cover the rest of the column as the team hurried past. The next officer stopped at a faded sign that read, TULE SPRINGS GROUP HOME and then did the same. Dani had a strange sense of déjà vu as boots trampled through the old playground. Cops and robbers. Cowboys and Indians. Duck, duck, goose. Kids were always hunting each other.

Officers stacked up against the wall next to the entrance of the building. Gun mounted flashlights clicked on. It was still early afternoon, but the building was boarded up, and it was going to be dark inside. It would take them time to adjust to the light. Just a few seconds, but Dani knew she could empty her rifle in just a few seconds. The lead officer unclipped a flashbang grenade to even the playing field. He looked back at the sergeant.

Dwayne tapped the rear officer and motioned him forward with a flick of his fingers. The officer ducked low and rushed up. He was carrying a small metal battering ram. The double door had a chain threaded through its tarnished brass handles, and one of the handles flew off in an explosion of splinters as the ram made contact. Both doors flew open, and dust billowed up like smoke. The entryway was inky black.

The lead officer stood with his back against the wall but directed his voice into the building. "Police! On the ground! Now!"

He didn't wait for a reply. His finger yanked a pin, and everybody ducked low as he threw the grenade into the darkness. There was a dull thunking sound as the grenade rattled across a linoleum floor. The shadows disappeared in a white strobe. It was followed by a thunderclap and then everybody was up and running.

At first, their flashlights just served to create cones of white smoke in the darkness. As bodies rushed in, the smoke swirled and started to disperse. Dani's flashlight lit up an old poster telling her to JUST SAY NO. She turned to the right and stayed low until she reached a corner. Then she spun around and aimed her rifle out into the middle of the room. It looked like a reception area. There was a low wall with a desk behind it across from her.

Somebody yelled, "Clear!" He must have been able to see more than Dani could.

Everybody was up and moving again. There were two doors leading out of the room and a hallway that stretched back deeper into the building. Dani stuck with the team on the right. Two officers covered the hallway but didn't move down. The other two got into position by one of the doors. Dani put her back to a wall and noticed that she was crunching through something on the ground. She looked down. They were papers of some sort. More fluttered down around her as she moved down the hall. She pointed her light at the wall and saw a row of children's drawing just barely clinging to the surface, held in place by ancient, yellowed tape.

One officer by the door nodded, and the other kicked it in with a booted foot. He stepped back after the kick, and the first officer rushed inside, weapon raised. Bathroom stalls were illuminated in a dancing beam of light. There was another kick, and then a woman's voice shouted, "Clear! Coming out!" She rejoined her partner, and they headed back toward Dani. Apparently, that was a dead end.

Another voice shouted, "Clear!" from the other side of the reception area. Dani turned and saw Dwayne motioning toward the hallway. Officers lined up along the walls to either side. The sergeant tapped one on the shoulder. The officer spun around the corner, low and already looking down the sights of his weapon. Officers leapfrogged down the hallway, a new one crouching down to cover the rest every twenty feet or so.

"Watch those windows!" The sergeant was pointing to some interior windows facing out into the hallway.

A team cleared the room. Some kind of administration office, Dani guessed. Another cleared a cafeteria and then went deeper in to clear the attached kitchen. Dani stayed in the hall with Dwayne. They had been in the building less than a minute.

"Light!" The officer on point in the hallway was motioning at a door farther down.

Dani saw a faint line of light spilling out from the crack beneath the door. She thought she saw movement in that light. It was hard to tell because her eyes had to keep adjusting from bright LED lights to dusty shadows. She also thought she heard something. Laughter.

Dani and the sergeant backed up two other officers that formed up on the door. Dani remembered what Dwayne had said about being a crap shot. She let him go first. He tapped the officer in front of him, and the officer's boot kicked out, the door exploding inward upon impact. Adrenaline shot through Dani's body like a jolt. She gritted her teeth and rushed in with the rest. She forced herself to exhale the way she did when she squeezed the trigger on her pistol. It came out as a low growl.

Nobody.

She still heard that laughter, though.

This room had more light than the others. The plywood covering one of the windows was gone, and the glass had been shattered. Toys sat on old shelves. They were evenly spaced out, and each one seemed deliberately placed, like tiny shrines to nostalgic gods. One of the toys was moving. It was a chubby-looking thing with a drooping eye and big pointy ears—a Furby? The fur it still had left was matted with mud or else falling off in patches. Its plastic mouth opened and closed in spasms as the gears that worked it slipped and stuttered. It made the laughter seem out of sync, like in an old kung fu movie.

One of the officers had his weapon pointed at the toy, but he kept his cool. "Clear!"

The sergeant pointed to the open window. "Check that! Circle around back."

The officer covering the creepy toy moved to the window. "Coming out!" Then he poked his head out, rifle leading the way. The other officer planted one hand on the window frame and vaulted out after him.

Dwayne was moving to follow the officers, but Dani put

a hand on his shoulder. When he turned to look at her, she pointed at the wall. Her flashlight lit up a mosaic made up of fairy tales. Pages had been torn out of dozens of storybooks and pasted to the wall from floor to ceiling. Knights and dragons, mermaids and pirates, castles in the clouds, and cats with fiddles—all ripped into fragments and remade into a new image. Or rather, the shreds of paper created the outline around the empty space that formed the image.

It was shaped like the silhouettes of three women holding hands under a tree with long snaking branches. Lines drawn on the wall decorated the silhouettes. Lines that told a story in a language they couldn't read. Lines that smelled like imaginary berries.

Dwayne lowered his pistol. "Well fuck."

His radio hissed. "Building clear. No contact."

Another voice came over the speaker. "No movement out front."

Dwayne mashed a button on the side of his radio as he held it up to his mouth. "Clear it again. All points. Check everything. Lockers. Kitchen cabinets. Crawl spaces. He had no way out."

"Understood."

He lowered the radio and looked at Dani. "Where is he?"

She slowly shook her head. "I don't think he's here."

She stepped closer to the mosaic and raised her flashlight again. The beam swept from one silhouette to the next. They weren't all the same. Two of the women had blue paper eyes. One didn't have any eyes at all.

Dani reached up to touch the silhouette. "I think he's looking for her."

28

"Azrael!"

"Azrael? Here, kitty, kitty, kitty!"

The sun was going down, and Adam wanted to make sure his cat found his way back home before it got dark. He wasn't a kitten, but he wasn't an old lap cat, either. Adam locked him in the clubhouse at night, and every morning he was yowling to be let out. Or maybe he was just yowling for his breakfast. He usually hung out in the backyard, but Adam had lost sight of him for a bit. He had been decorating the wall inside the clubhouse and bringing down some things from his room to make it a bit cooler.

Matt seemed all right, but sometimes he was pretty clueless when it came to kids. The CD player he had put in the clubhouse worked, but Adam didn't have any CDs. He did have his mom's old iPod, though. Its battery was starting to fade, so it needed to stay plugged in most of the time. Luckily, it had its own tiny speaker. He found that he could just plug it into the end of the string of Christmas lights. He also brought down some of his comic books and a few models he was trying to paint. The models were for a war game, but he had never found anyone to play with.

He had tried out the dartboard that Matt hung up. After Adam fiddled with the fins on the back of the darts, they had flown pretty straight. So far there were just as many holes in the wall as there were on the dartboard, and after one had bounced backward and almost hit Azrael, he decided to leave it alone for a while.

Still, he was glad to have his own space. The bedroom that he shared with his mom was pretty small. Her half always seemed to be much neater. That was probably just because she didn't spend much time in there. Adam's half was more comfortable. He liked to have his favorite things within reach of his bed, so it didn't make a whole lot of sense for him to put them away on the shelf across the room. Now most of that stuff was in the clubhouse. She seemed happy about that.

The cat wasn't allowed inside the house. Mom said it would be bad for business. People might be allergic. Or he might scratch the furniture. Matt seemed to like him, though, and was always giving him little bits of lunch meat. He even bought him some cans of fancy wet cat food, but Azrael liked the dry stuff better.

Adam rattled the bag of cat food. "Azrael!" That would get him running for sure.

He looked down the side of the house toward the front yard. He saw something moving, but it was just a little kid across the street. The kid had his arms outstretched and was pretending to be an airplane or something. Adam took a few steps to get a better look. The kid made engine sounds as he zoomed around on the sidewalk. There was a man walking behind him who was probably his dad. The kid made a U-turn and came right at the man. They were both smiling, and the kid's sound effects were interrupted by giggles.

The dad squatted down right before the kid was about to

crash into him. He scooped up his son and set him on his shoulders. "The clouds are up here, buddy." The kid laughed and stretched out his arms again as his dad continued down the street.

Adam could feel his face getting red. He hadn't felt that kind of sting in a long time. He didn't cry about not having a dad around. Not anymore. That's why he started to feel angry with himself when he realized a tear was running down one cheek. He rubbed it away with the back of his hand. He had a dad. They didn't play stupid airplane games, but he did come around. And he was a real-life hero. He was busy, though. He hunted down bad guys.

"Hey, Adam?" It sounded like Matt.

Adam walked back to the corner of the house. Matt was standing by the clubhouse. When he saw Adam, Matt held up an orange cat. "You lose something?"

Adam ran over to them. Azrael was biting Matt's hand and giving him a couple of halfhearted kicks with his back paws. His ears perked up when he heard the crinkling sound of the cat food bag in Adam's hand.

"I found him inside," said Matt. "He must have snuck in when your mom came out to say good-bye. He's kinda mad that I didn't give him any lunch meat."

Adam opened the door to the clubhouse. Azrael didn't wait for Matt to set him down. He kicked Matt one last time for good measure, and then leaped toward the door. The cat ran right between Adam's legs as he tried to get inside. Adam had to keep sidestepping so that he didn't trip over him. He poured some kibble into a bowl, and Azrael head-butted the bag out of the way to start getting at the food.

Matt ducked as he stepped inside. "Has he been keeping this place clear of Smurfs? 'Cause we can put down some Smurf traps, too, if he's being lazy."

"I haven't seen any," said Adam.

Matt looked at one of the chairs around the little table. Maybe he was afraid it would fall apart when he sat on it. He lowered himself down on it anyway. "I like what you've done with the place."

Adam folded up the cat food bag and put it up on the bookcase. "Thanks. I was gonna hang up a couple posters. Have you heard of the Imperial Academy Dropouts?"

"Is that a band?"

"Yeah."

"Sorry, you stop listening to new music when you get old like me. The last album I bought was by the Beastie Boys. And it wasn't even their latest."

Matt picked up one of the models on the table. Adam had just started painting it, so it still looked pretty plain. When it was done, it would be a badass armored warrior with a glowing sword in one hand and a machine gun in the other. Right now it just had its base coats of paint so it looked kind of cartoony.

"I know these guys, though," said Matt. "Warhammer 40K right? They've been around forever. I wanted to play but . . ." He just ended with a shrug.

Adam pointed out the symbol on the model's armor. "This guy's an Inquisitor. They hunt down chaos demons and stuff."

"Cool."

Adam picked up another model. This one had tentacles instead of arms. It still had a machine gun, of course.

"Do you have a dad?" It sounded strange as soon as he said it.

Matt paused for a second, but he didn't look at Adam like he was weird. "Kind of. I have a guy who showed me how to tie a tie."

"I've only seen you wear a tie once. At the funeral."

"Exactly."

Azrael hopped up on the table. His dinner had already vanished, and now he was looking for someone to pet him. He slobbered a little after he ate, and the first thing he did was wipe off his mouth by rubbing it on Adam's arm.

Adam had to put down his model to give his cat the attention he was demanding. "Was he nice?"

Matt scrunched up his lips. "Hmm. Sometimes, I suppose. They're not all great. Sometimes you're better off without one."

"I guess," said Adam.

"Seems like the police sergeant is pretty cool."

"He's cool. Mom won't let him be my dad, though. She says he didn't want a family."

Azrael flopped over and purred. A squad of space marines got pushed aside as he stretched out.

"He seems to come out here a lot," said Matt.

"He mainly wants to see her," said Adam. "He says stuff about wanting to go to the movies. But we never do."

"That sucks."

"Yeah."

Matt reached out a hand to give Azrael some more love, but the cat lifted its head and twitched an ear back. Matt wisely pulled his hand away.

"Your mom does a lot for you," he said.

"Yeah," said Adam. "She tries."

Matt reached into one of his pockets. He held out a pill between his thumb and finger. Adam cringed a little inside.

"She sent me out here to check on you," said Matt. "And to give you this."

Adam took the pill, but he didn't put it in his mouth.

"Thanks," said Adam. He said it the same way that

someone might say it after being dropped off at prison.

"She also said she would bring home burgers after her visit with Erica," Matt told him.

"She never eats burgers," said Adam. "She just likes to eat the fries. Sometimes she dips them in her milkshake."

Matt stood up and started heading for the door. "I do that. But I eat my burger, too."

"Maybe you can join us."

"Sure . . . well, you can ask your mom." Matt nodded toward Adam's hand. "Don't forget to take your medicine."

Adam rolled his eyes and popped the pill into his mouth. Matt smiled and left. As soon as the door closed, Adam spit the pill back out into his hand.

He used a fishing tackle box to store his paints and brushes, but he used it for something else, too. It was the kind that unfolded when it opened so that you could see all the different compartments. It was handy because it seemed like you needed a couple dozen shades of paint to get a space marine to look like it was ready to kick serious ass. The box also had a tray that you could pull out of the bottom. Underneath the tray was an old aspirin bottle. Adam opened the bottle and dropped the pill in with the others that he had spit out over the past few weeks. The bottle was half-full now.

He didn't like taking the pills. They made his stomach hurt, and his head got all fuzzy. When he took them, he just felt like sleeping or watching TV all the time. The tremors still came when he took the pills; his body just didn't react as much. He tried explaining that to the doctors, but they didn't listen. They had him try all kinds of different pills, some worse than others. When Adam tried to tell them the tremors still came back, they would always make him take more pills for a while and then switch him to something else.

Now Adam found it easier to just tell them the pills were working.

He had to be careful, though. When the tremors did come he had to find a way to stay calm. That was hard when his parents were yelling at each other. It was easier when he was by himself. Drawing also helped. He wouldn't draw anything in particular. Just lines. Lines that swirled, and curved, and sometimes exploded into little patterns, almost like writing. At first he had drawn on paper, but lately he had started drawing on the walls of his clubhouse. Just looking at the lines would calm him down. Then the tremors would turn into daydreams. And that wasn't so bad. He knew he said things during the tremors. He could never remember what he had said, but he wondered if it might be related to the things he saw in the tremor dreams.

He felt them coming now. It was like hearing two people talking as they walked down a long hallway toward him. Muffled rumbling at first. Slowly getting louder and clearer. Then he started to pick out patterns and phrases. When the sound seemed like it was right next to him, he started to shake. He reached into his tackle box and pulled out a Sharpie. He heard a click as he took the cap off the pen, and then the world shook apart.

The Christmas lights started to vibrate and shift out of focus. One second Azrael was sniffing his nose, the next he was running away. Space marines jumped across the table, and the gaps between the boards that made up the floor seemed to be getting bigger.

Adam felt his pen touch the wall. The rough scratching as the tip dragged across the wood. A line spiraled, crossed over itself, and then split off in a different direction. It was like drawing lines between the stars that formed a constellation. Only, instead of stars he was connecting ideas.

Then his hand pushed *through* the wall.

He was standing in a forest. It was still, and at first it was completely silent. Then he heard a bird screech off in the distance. The forest was dark and dense. It would take forever to walk through it, but he wouldn't know where to go anyway, so he didn't move. He looked down at his feet and saw that he was standing on a path. It disappeared into the darkness in both directions. He knew this was a tremor dream so he wasn't afraid. Soon the tremors would stop and he would see a new drawing on the wall in front of him.

He heard footsteps coming down the path. And then music. The tune seemed familiar, but if it was from a song he knew, he couldn't remember the words. Somebody was humming along with it. As he looked down the path, a man stepped around a tree and out of the shadows. His eyes were watching the trail as though he was concentrating hard on where he was going. He held a music box in one hand and almost dropped it when he finally noticed Adam.

"Jesus!" said the man. "You scared the hell out of me."

Adam didn't quite know what to say. Usually people couldn't see him in his tremor dreams, and nobody had ever tried to talk to him.

"What are you doing here?" asked the man. "Are you looking for the garden?"

Adam opened his mouth to ask, *What garden?* but what came out was, "Take-unto-you-the-whole-armor-of-God-that-ye-may-be-able-to-withstand-in-the-evil-day-and-having-done-all-to-stand."

The man closed the lid of his box, and the music stopped. "I don't know what that means. Who are you? Did she send you? Are you supposed to take me to her?" He sounded very hopeful.

Adam couldn't answer any of those questions. "The-

Lord-is-my-light-and-my-stronghold-Of-whom-shall-I-be-afraid?"

The man slowly shook his head, the hope draining out of his eyes. "No. She didn't send you. She wouldn't. She chose *me*. I send people to *her*. You're just another whisper left over in my head. You want me to step off the path."

Adam was afraid to open his mouth. This guy sounded seriously disturbed, and Adam didn't want to make him mad.

His mouth opened anyway. "Who-hath-cut-a-channel-for-the-torrents-of-rain-and-a-path-for-the-thunderstorm."

And it *did* make the man mad. "I know what you're trying to do!" He pulled something from a pocket, and suddenly there was a knife hovering a few inches from Adam's nose. "It's not gonna work. I'm almost there."

The man must have cut himself when he pulled out the knife because Adam saw blood starting to seep through his shirt down by his ribs. Adam clenched his jaw tight and then slowly lifted a finger to point to the man's chest.

As the man looked down, more blood spread across his shirt. At first it just looked like a shapeless splotch, but then a red line crept up his body in a curving pattern. The line spiraled, crossed over itself, and split off in a different direction. The man's eyes widened, and he dropped his music box to grab at his chest. He started to scream, but it was cut off.

And then Adam was staring at the wall of his clubhouse. The tremors were leaving his hand, and the world snapped back into place. The line he had started drawing now filled the wall, but the ink from the pen must have run dry because the last pattern was barely visible. The scream still echoed in his ears, and Adam wondered if maybe it had come from his own mouth.

29

The first bottle of wine had been almost empty when Christy arrived. Now Erica was finishing off the second. Christy had only refilled her glass once, and it was still half-full. It was late in the afternoon, which meant Erica was up pretty early. It also meant that she was having wine for breakfast. Christy wasn't sure why. It didn't seem to be cheering her up at all. And she certainly wasn't drinking to forget.

"I miss her," said Erica.

It wasn't the first time she had said that since Christy had sat down with her. They were in Erica's living room. Christy had only been there once before, but that was for a party, and it had been so crowded that she'd barely noticed the furniture. Now, with just the two of them, it looked like Erica had flipped through a furniture catalog until she found a living room she liked and just ordered everything on the page. It was nice and elegant, but it didn't really feel like a home.

"It's only been a couple days," said Christy. At first she had tried to distract Erica with gossip, hoping to get her mind off the breakup. It had worked for a while, but now it seemed like they were back at square one. Erica obviously had something she needed to work through.

"It feels longer," said Erica. "Especially with all that's been going on."

Christy took a sip from her glass. *Time to dig into it,* she supposed. "Did she say why?"

"I'm sure it's partially the stress of trying to track down that psycho," said Erica. "But mainly it's me. I'm not what she wants anymore. Not what she needs."

"I'm sure that's not true."

"She pretty much said it to my face. And I was too high to do anything about it."

Aha. So, this was depression mixed with *guilt.* Christy knew about the drugs—all the girls knew. It had been pretty obvious. But it hadn't been a problem for months.

She remembered when Erica had first started at the Golden Delicious. It hadn't seemed like she was going to be there long, which was what most of the girls told themselves when they started. That wasn't a bad thing. But Erica hadn't been looking for some quick money. She had been looking for the next step up, whatever that was. She had tried out porn for a while and even released a couple of videos, but she didn't get along with the people she was working with. From what Christy had heard, Erica tended to go "off script" a lot and made people bleed when they weren't supposed to. So that didn't last too long.

Erica went out with people who had a lot of money, but she never stayed with anyone for long. Either she got bored or they got hurt. She had never considered any of those relationships serious, and it didn't seem like she wanted to find somebody to take care of her. Not even Dani apparently.

Erica wasn't actually that great at seduction. She *was*

excellent at branding, and she had quickly made a name for herself. If you wanted to be tied up and whipped in Las Vegas, you went to Erica. Which was great for business at the Golden Delicious. Some guys saw her as a celebrity, and she seemed to enjoy the attention. She put a lot of effort into her costumes and routines. You always got a different flavor of Erica each time you visited.

The drugs were a problem, of course. They got her into a lot of parties, and she met some powerful people, but they also dragged her down. She never seemed to focus on any one project for very long. She wasn't able to build anything, and she didn't have anybody to keep her on track. Except for Uncle Quent.

"Oh," said Christy. "I thought you quit."

Erica couldn't meet her eyes. "Quent was helping me."

"Maybe I could help? Or Matt?"

"Matt? Didn't we just spend the last hour making fun of him?"

"He's not so bad," said Christy. "You heard about the clubhouse out back?"

"Yeah," said Erica. "I'm sure it's strictly 'no girls allowed.'"

"Well, we *do* have cooties," said Christy.

Erica smiled a little at that. "True." The smile didn't last long and vanished altogether after her next sip of wine.

Christy leaned over and put her hand on Erica's. "You should call her."

"She told me not to."

Christy gave her a knowing look. "Which means?"

"Okay. Maybe I'll try tomorrow."

"You should try tonight."

Erica stared into her wine for a few seconds.

"Fine," she said. "Tell Matt I may not be in. Either I'll be having make-up sex or I'll be too depressed to work."

"Okay," said Christy. "But if things don't work out, it might be good to be around other people. Plus, you could take out some frustration in the VIP room. And get paid for it."

"Sure," said Erica. She drained what was left in her glass.

Christy wasn't convinced that Erica would follow through, but there wasn't much else she could say without calling her an addict. Maybe a better friend would have done just that. The truth was, they weren't that close.

Christy set down her glass and stood up. "I should head out. My shift is starting soon, and I promised Adam I'd pick up dinner."

Erica stood up with her. "Well, thanks for stopping by."

Christy started to say something but stopped when Erica reached out and hugged her. It felt strange, coming from her, but it also felt sincere.

"I should be a better friend," said Erica. "I can be."

"I know," said Christy.

It was almost dark as she started driving back home. She could see the lights of the Strip in her rearview mirror. People had high expectations when they saw those lights. This was supposed to be the place where you could cut loose and be the person who you usually hid away from the rest of the world. It made it hard to live here, though. You got used to seeing those hidden people everywhere. Fantasy made flesh. It was like living in an amusement park. If you weren't having a good time, people didn't want to be around you.

Christy had lost herself in that fantasy for a while. She'd become an adult too soon. Instead of finishing high school, she'd learned about diapers and breast pumps. Her mom had helped out, but she also needed to work to support all three of them. Her anger and frustration with Christy had vanished the moment she held Adam in her arms. It had returned, however, when Christy started acting like a teenager again.

Christy hadn't gone to her high school prom. Nobody had asked her, of course. She didn't regret it. At the time, she hadn't wanted to run the risk of seeing Dwayne. Dwayne, whose life hadn't changed at all because he'd chosen not to let it change. She had tried to stay in touch with her high school friends, though. They invited her out after graduation even though she hadn't been part of the ceremony. A girls' night out. One of them knew the DJ at a club, and they got in without ID. It was awkward. Her friends didn't know how to talk to her anymore. Christy wanted it to be like it was before she had gotten pregnant, but it wasn't. They kept asking her about being a mother.

What's it like to have a kid?

How much did it hurt to give birth?

Should you really be drinking that cosmo?

Luckily, it had been hard to talk much at the club anyway. Christy lost herself in the music and the bodies dancing up against each other. It felt good not to think. So, she didn't think when the guy she was dancing with took her hand and led her out the door. There was a limo waiting outside, and it sounded like a good idea to go for a ride in it. Even sex had sounded like a good idea, until it was over.

It *felt* fine. It had been her first time since she had given birth, but that had been six months before. Instead of feeling utterly relaxed afterward, she felt anxious. She got dressed immediately, and the guy lying in the bed didn't seem surprised at all. He leaned over the edge of the mattress to pick up his pants. Instead of putting them on, he fished his wallet out of a pocket. He thanked her, and handed her something. She thought it was money for a cab ride home.

When she walked into the hotel lobby she saw it was a lot more. Five one-hundred-dollar bills.

He must've made a mistake. She started to head back to the elevator. He had been a nice enough guy. Quite a bit older than she was. Maybe he had just wanted sex, but that's all she'd wanted, too. She stopped walking as the doors slid open. It wasn't a mistake somebody would make. She let the doors slide close again. He had *paid* her. Her first reaction was to laugh. She ended up crying all the way home in the back of the cab.

Two years later, her mother had passed away. Acute heart failure. She was taken to the hospital on Wednesday. By Friday, Christy was living alone with Adam. Her mother left her everything she had, but they were renting, and the money had only lasted through the end of the year. And she still hadn't called Dwayne. They had to move into a smaller place, and Christy found a job as a cocktail waitress at a casino. With tips, it was enough to live on.

When Adam had his first seizure, Christy had to take off so much time that she lost her job. She had put the hospital bill on a credit card. When he had his second seizure, her credit card had been declined. That's when she had finally called Dwayne. Who was a complete ass. She tried to explain what was going on, but he had refused to listen. He went on about how he was with somebody else now and how he had debt of his own to worry about. She hung up on him when he accused *her* of taking Adam away from him.

Adam had been three and a half at the time, but he could tell that something was wrong. He brought her a Band-Aid after she'd hung up the phone because she was crying. It made her cry harder, which made him start crying. They held each other until the tears stopped. Adam was laughing again in half an hour.

Christy had hired a babysitter that same night. She'd gone out and come home with five one-hundred-dollar bills. That was six years ago.

Now, she wondered if she should be looking at other options. Dwayne was back in their lives. She didn't know what had changed for him, but he seemed genuinely interested in how they were doing. He had offered to help out with the hospital bills several times, and last time she had let him. With Quent gone, now might be the right time to make a change. Matt seemed to be doing the best he could, but he was mixed up in something way over his head. He couldn't control things the way Quent had been able to, and she didn't want to put Adam in the middle of any fallout. Too bad. Matt seemed to get along naturally with Adam, where Dwayne had to work at it.

Her stomach growled. She might actually get a burger for herself tonight. Normally that wasn't a good idea on a work night, but then again, neither was a growling stomach. She needed something to start soaking up the wine. She figured she should get an extra burger for Matt while she was at it. He was pretty bad about feeding himself. And she wanted him to be in a good mood if Erica did decide to come in.

30

Erica rolled the brass cylinder between her fingers. It felt heavier than it looked. The oil from her thumb left a faint fingerprint on the casing. She tipped it over and let the powder pour out. It was so fine that wisps of it lingered in the air as the rest tumbled down into the water. That was the last one. The box was empty. She pushed the lever and flushed away a thousand dollars' worth of bliss and suffering.

She knew she had to do it before calling Dani. If not, she would probably end up getting high all night. Odds were that Dani wouldn't even pick up the phone, but she might answer just long enough to tell Erica to go fuck herself. If that happened, she would end up emptying the box anyway. On the off chance that Dani stayed on the line long enough to have a conversation, Erica didn't really know what she was going to say. She would start with *I'm sorry*, and then see where things went.

Talking with Christy had helped. Erica had always admired her. She never hid who she was, even when she was with a customer. Erica could never put that much of herself out there. She was still trying to figure out who she wanted to be. It was hard to settle on just one life. Erica was happy trying on a different face every day. The problem with not knowing who you were was that nobody else did, either.

She tossed the bullet casings in the trash and sat down in front of her laptop. Maybe she would just check in on her news feed before giving Dani a call. She was procrastinating, but that didn't stop her from logging in. When she heard the knock at the door she felt a rush of guilt and embarrassment, like she had just been caught masturbating. It was probably Christy. Erica looked around for something she might have forgotten. After a quick glance, she didn't see anything so she pulled out her phone. She could pretend that she was just about to give Dani a call.

She held the phone up in front of her as she opened the door. "Did you forget something? I was just about to—"

It wasn't Christy.

The man in the hallway looked familiar, but Erica couldn't quite put a name to the face. The wine might have something to do with that. She didn't think he was a client. That was good. She never worked out of her apartment so if he was a client, that would make him a stalker, too. And she was in no condition to deal with a stalker. Maybe he was a lost delivery guy.

"Oh," said Erica. "I didn't order anything."

"Good," said the man.

He held something out to her. Was he selling something? She looked down in time to see a spark crackle between two bright metal studs.

She felt her body jerk on its own. Then darkness.

■ ■ ■

When she opened her eyes again, everything was blurry. As things started to come into focus, she realized she was on the floor. She must have passed out or something. Someone was standing over her. He looked concerned. He held something in his hand. When she recognized what it was, everything came rushing back to her. She wanted to move but all her muscles seized up. She managed to lift her hand off the ground, and she got her foot to move a few inches.

The man looked down at her and smiled. "Hi. I'm really sorry. It's just that, with the news story, it's hard to meet girls."

That was where she had seen him—on TV at the Golden Delicious. The police were looking for him. She didn't remember his first name, but his last name stuck out. Foster.

"N-guhhh," said Erica. Things were starting to get blurry again.

"You and Candice were friends. I was friends with her, too." He turned and closed the door with this free hand. "She mentioned you. Well, her phone did anyway."

"B-bastard!"

Her eyes weren't refocusing. Foster seemed to be drifting farther away, but she could feel him grab one of her arms.

"Don't worry, you'll be with her soon."

She slipped back into darkness.

■ ■ ■

The floor felt impossibly soft. Her foot slid across satin. She wasn't moving it, though. Four glowing white lights merged into two as her eyes strained to make sense of what she was looking at. They were recessed lights. She was in her bedroom, and she was lying in her own bed looking up at the ceiling. Then her other foot moved. She looked down at it and saw him there. He was tightening a black strap around her ankle. Her other ankle was already restrained.

"There you are," he said. "Hope you don't mind. I borrowed some of your things."

Her body was sore, but it wasn't clenched up anymore. Panic and adrenaline flooded her, and she tried to sit up. A tugging at her wrists held her firmly in place. They were restrained, too. Instead of black straps, her wrists were held by chrome handcuffs. Two pairs, lined with hot pink faux fur. They were hers. The opposite ends were locked to the headboard.

Foster looked strange. Then she realized why. He seemed a little embarrassed. "I found that *box* under your bed," he said. "You know the one I mean. I just want you to know, I was real respectful of your private . . . things."

He held something up in front of him. She knew what it was before the blade clicked into place. A box cutter.

"I am going to need to undress you, though," he said.

Fuck that. Erica drew in a breath to scream and realized he had used something else from her collection. A ball gag. She screamed anyway. And thrashed and kicked.

"No," he said. "Don't struggle. I don't want to accidentally cut you."

She thrashed harder. The handcuffs bit into her wrists, and she tried to yank a knee up as he leaned over her.

He pulled back and sighed. "Fine."

He put the knife down on her nightstand and pulled something out of his back pocket. It sparked and crackled.

Darkness.

■ ■ ■

This time she woke up to voices. She didn't know what

they were saying. One voice sounded like it could be a woman's, but her ears must have been struggling to work as much as her eyes were. She slowly forced her eyes to open. Foster was the only one there, and it looked like he was talking to himself.

"I saw him on the trail. I don't know who he was," he said.

He was sitting in her makeup chair, staring down at a flat red box of some sort. It had white knobs on top and some sort of screen. He turned the knobs and seemed to be listening to something. It looked too big to be a radio, and it wasn't making any sounds, anyway. He wasn't paying attention to her, so she decided to lie still and give herself time to think.

Her next thought was, *I'm naked.*

"I don't know. What's a Grigori?"

An Etch A Sketch. That's what he was staring at. She couldn't see what he was drawing, but he was concentrating very hard on it.

"No, he didn't look like that. He was a boy. Not even a teenager yet. He said something about God armor, and strongholds, and rainstorms. It didn't sound good."

Erica tried to look around with just her eyes. She was naked, but he hadn't done anything else to her. Yet. Her clothes were in a pile on the floor. She was still cuffed and strapped to the bed. He had used *her* cuffs. He hadn't brought any with him. Why not? Wasn't this his plan? He couldn't have known she had handcuffs or leg straps. Or did he? Panic started to flood in. She didn't want to freak out again. It wouldn't do any good. There was something about the cuffs she knew she was forgetting. What was it?

"It doesn't matter, right? This is the last one. Three daughters. Then I can be with you. Right?"

Three daughters? This guy was bug nuts insane. But she already knew that.

"Oh, she is?"

Foster sounded surprised. He turned to look at her and stood up. She saw what he had been drawing with the Etch A Sketch: a stick figure woman stood under a blocky tree. It was crude, but there might have been a bird perched up in the tree. The needle in the toy was still moving, but he wasn't turning the knobs anymore. A line carved its way through the silvery-gray dust on its own. As she watched, the line grew blocky leaves and then a blocky flower. When she glanced back at Foster, he was reaching into his back pocket.

This time Foster placed the stun gun deliberately on her thigh, right over her skull tattoo.

"Sorry, we're not ready yet."

Darkness.

■ ■ ■

Something tickled. It felt like a bug crawling slowly across her stomach. She went to scratch it away, but her hand was stopped by a tiny rattle of chain links. This time she jerked her eyes open, already breathing hard around the ball filling up her mouth.

Foster was straddling her. He was fully clothed, but his sleeves were rolled up. He was bent over, staring at her belly. One hand was pressing down on her rib cage while the other dragged something across her skin. She almost screamed but then realized she wasn't in pain. Instead of a knife, he held an orange felt-tip marker.

He looked up at her when she moved, but his hands never left her body. There was a strange smell in the room.

Citrus of some sort.

"It's called Orangealicious," he said. "It smells more like tangelo to me."

He was drawing on her. She couldn't see what it was, but it looked like it started on her left foot. His body was covering the rest.

Her hands were starting to get numb. The faux fur helped prevent cuts, but the cuffs were still tight against her wrists. She lifted a finger and felt it bump along the length of chain back to the base of the cuff.

Foster went back to his drawing. "These pens always make me hungry. I brought a pudding cup. Vanilla. But I'm usually less hungry after."

She wanted to say, *I get it. You're creepy,* but that would definitely get her shocked again.

He moved his hand from her rib cage to her breast. He didn't grope it, but simply lifted it up to make room for his pen. The line swirled around her breast, and then he moved his hand again so he could draw up toward her nipple.

"My hands are getting all glittery. Is that from your lotion?" His hand shook a little as the pen made a tiny circle. "Sorry. I talk a lot when I'm nervous."

She moved her finger along the edge of the cuff and then down to the keyhole. The keys were in the box that Foster must have dug through to find the leg straps. She actually kept the handcuffs attached to her headboard all the time. She thought they looked cute. She had other restraints she could use if she was in the mood for something more authentic. The cuffs on her wrists were more for show. So were the keys, if you knew about the tiny lever just to the right of the keyhole.

Erica spoke slowly and deliberately, but the ball gag reduced it to a mumble.

Foster scooted up along her body, and his pen reached her collarbone. He was now straddling her stomach and leaning close to her face to keep an eye on what he was doing.

He paused and said, "I'm sorry. What?"

Erica mumbled again. She tried to make up for her lack of words by using her eyes. She looked from Foster to her right hand and then back at Foster.

"What was that?" He leaned in closer.

A popping sound snapped the air when her forehead connected with his nose. It reminded her of the sound a drumstick makes when it's pulled off a raw chicken. He must have sucked in a breath as he flew backward because when he hit the ground he coughed and blood came bubbling out of his nose. She moved quickly and had one hand free before he even lifted his head. The next thing she did was pull that damn ball out of her mouth.

"I said this isn't the first time I've been tied up, asshole!"

By the time she had her other hand free, Foster had rolled over and was up on his hands and knees. Instead of lunging at her, he coughed again, gagged, and then threw up a puddle of blood. That gave her time to get one leg free. Then he was up on his feet. He didn't look too stable, though.

"Stop!" It came out nasally, like he had a bad cold. "You're ruining it!"

He took a couple of shuffling steps toward the bed. He must have lost his pen when he went sprawling. Instead, he yanked the stun gun out of his pocket. As he came toward her, Erica threw herself back onto the bed to brace herself, then she whipped out with her free leg. It connected beautifully with his groin.

"I guess we're both having a bad day," she said.

The stun gun rattled when it hit the ground. It dropped

much faster than Foster, who slowly sank to one knee. Erica rolled forward and clawed at the last strap. The pressure of the strap had caused her foot to fall asleep. Pins and needles fired up and down her skin as she finally loosened the strap and pulled her leg free. She lunged off the bed and immediately had to stagger back as her foot tried to wake itself up.

Foster was still kneeling. He was breathing hard, but instead of trying to stand, his other knee faltered and dropped to the floor. He looked broken and defeated. Erica reached down and grabbed the stun gun.

"My turn," she said.

She waited a second for the feeling in her foot to return, then gripped the trigger and stepped toward him.

There was a clicking sound, and Foster's arm shot out in a wide arc.

Erica's thigh burned as she stepped forward. Her foot twisted, and she slipped on something wet. She looked down and saw a pulse of crimson blood gush down her leg, then another. The slice in her thigh didn't seem like it should be bleeding that much. She immediately felt like somebody had plunged her into a bath of ice water.

She stood there for a second trying to regain her balance. It didn't come. Instead, everything started to feel numb. She heard the stun gun hit the ground but didn't remember letting go of it. The floor almost felt comfortable as she crumbled down to meet it.

Foster looked over at her. He looked sad. "I'm . . . I'm sorry. It's ruined. It won't work now."

When he stood, she saw the box cutter in his hand. It didn't even look like it had any blood on it.

From somewhere up above he said, "You won't be able to go home."

Erica didn't know what he was talking about, but she could see her clothes beside her on the floor—and the smooth white and sliver curves of her phone poking out of one pants pocket. It felt like she was using somebody else's hand to reach for it. She just wanted to hear her voice one last time.

"Dani . . ."

Her hand almost made it before Foster picked up the phone.

"Oh. I'm gonna need that," he said.

31

Matt was thinking hard about spoons. His coffee steamed in its mug as he sat at his desk, and he gave the spoon a swirl, watching the coffee mix with creamer as they spun together in a tiny whirlpool. He was supposed to be doing paperwork. Using *real* paper. He still didn't have a laptop so he'd borrowed some graph paper from Adam. It was actually a lot easier than the financial software he had been using. He didn't have to scan receipts or print out reports. Instead, he just shoved the receipts into a folder and added up the numbers with the calculator on his phone. It's not like they were ever going to get audited. He'd never really liked paperwork, though, and his mind was constantly wandering off. Right now it was wandering around in his past, remembering the theory he had learned about spoons.

A spoon was basically a handle with a scoopy-thing at the end. Of course, that description fit lots of objects— spoons, ice cream scoops, shovels, oars. The idea of a "scoopy-thing" with a handle was pretty useful. And that idea was just two other ideas stuck together. His father had called that concept a *monad*, a pattern of ideas. That was the crazy shit he'd started learning when he was Adam's age.

That and Latin.

Actually, he had learned snippets of Latin when he was even younger. He just hadn't known what they meant. One day, Aunt Rose took all the kids out to the garden. Matt had probably been about three, one of the youngest kids on the estate. She showed them a snail and told them how snails were bad for a garden. They ate the plants before they had a chance to grow into fruits and vegetables. If a snail ate just a couple of leaves off a new plant, that plant might die. Then it would never be able to produce ripe, yummy strawberries. She used strawberries to really drive the point home. Then she said a little rhyme in Latin after that and crunched the snail under her foot: *Contra vim mortis. Non crescit in hortis.*

Matt had thought it was funny. So had all the other kids. That was before he knew what killing was. Tiny feet pounded legions of snails into paste. And from that point on, there had always been strawberries growing in the garden.

That was the beginning of another pattern of ideas: sacrifice a thing to gain a thing. As more lessons were taught, that pattern became known as the Primary Monad. It was taught over and over again. Each time, there was a little more blood involved.

It started off slow. Lessons any kid would learn growing up on a farm.

Chicks were cute. You might even name one. But eventually you were going to have to kill it if you wanted to eat. Even if its name was Big Bird.

Goats would eat right out of your hand. That made it easier to slit their throats. They sounded like scared children as they sank down onto their knees to die.

Even a faithful companion would have to be put down if it cost too much to keep it alive.

Matt had always been presented with a choice, and his father had always been very careful to explain the consequences for each decision. Death was a necessary part of life. It was necessary to achieve your goals.

Hic locus est ubi mors gaudet succurrere vitae.

He had learned what that one meant: *This is the place where death delights in helping life.* It was actually a pretty common motto . . . in morgues.

Matt had learned these lessons with seven other children. Technically, they were his brothers and sisters; however, each of them had been adopted, including Matt. It was the same for his father, Uncle Quent, and Aunt Rose. They were related on paper and bound together by purpose. That was how the Scholars recruited. It didn't always work out, though. Matt's father used to have three other brothers and sisters. Two of them were dead, and the other was quietly locked away.

They weren't the only family like this. The Scholars had estates scattered across the globe. Each was structured the same way and was run according to "the Traditions." Matt didn't know where the other estates were. You had to graduate before you learned that. Graduation was the one Tradition that Matt hadn't been able to go through with. The sacrifice that cost too much. He was the only one, though; everyone else paid the price. Some more than others.

While he was a kid, Matt hadn't gotten off the estate much. All the children there were homeschooled, and the property was isolated enough so that visiting town required a car, unless you wanted to walk all day. They didn't live like the Amish, though. Matt hadn't known it at the time, but the estate always had cutting-edge technology when it came to research and communication. Matt had an e-mail account before spam existed.

They also had satellite TV. Matt watched a lot of movies, though that wasn't encouraged on the estate. As part of their studies, the children were given freedom to pursue almost any topic they liked in their spare time. The estate was better equipped than most colleges so a motivated student could dig into any subject as deeply as they wanted. If they were limited by the facilities on hand, new equipment would show up within days. And it wasn't just limited to the sciences. Art and music were fully supported, as well.

Sarah was one of Matt's sisters. She had spent most of her time analyzing the patterns of petal growth on different species of flowers. She started them from seeds and played music to them as they grew. She measured them, took pictures as their petals bloomed, and documented their rate of decay. For each pattern she found, she scratched mathematical formulas on chalkboards and fed them into a computer. Her printer would then spit out pages of musical notation. Matt had attended a recital once where her cello seemed to recreate the life and death of each of her flowers.

Aunt Rose had tried to help Matt find a similar passion.

"You seem to like your science fiction films," she said. "Have you thought about building your own rocket? Or a laser? Boys seem to like lasers."

Matt shrugged. "Well . . . I really like the *stories*."

She had found him in the rec room. He was sprawled out on the couch like only a tween could be, remote in one hand, corn chips in the other. He didn't pause the movie.

She moved to stand in front of the TV. "Perhaps you could create your own film? That's all done on computers now isn't it?"

"I suppose," he said. "But I don't really have a story to tell."

"Take somebody else's story, then. Make it your own."

"That seems like cheating."

Aunt Rose crossed her arms. "Cheating is better than failing. There's no reason for failure *here*. The opportunities you have are unique. They shouldn't be wasted."

Matt scooted himself up on the couch. "Maybe somebody else could take my spot. I'm not sure I belong here."

"Nonsense," she said. "Every one of you has a place here."

"What about Uncle Quent?" asked Matt. "I've heard you talk to Father about him."

"His place is here, too."

"He's never around. And I've seen the way you and Father look at each other whenever somebody says his name."

Aunt Rose had looked that way right then, actually. "Yes, well, he's on sabbatical. He'll come back. He just needs time to refocus."

"I guess I haven't found my focus yet."

"This is a time to explore," she told him. "Learn all that you can. Find out what's important to you. You'll naturally focus on that."

So Matt had explored. The regular curriculum included most of the subjects that any private school taught, with a couple of additions. Theoretical History was kind of like a critical-thinking class. The students learned about key points during history that caused humanity to swerve one way or the other. They investigated all the paths the world hadn't taken and argued about how it might be better off or worse for it. It sounded more fun than it actually was.

Inductive Symbology taught the students how to identify patterns and symbols in everything around them. They learned how to measure the effectiveness of those symbols and postulate how they might be optimized for greater impact. Matt based his final paper for the class on the symbols in *The Da Vinci Code*. He didn't even read the book; he just watched the movie. He got a D. His instructor informed him that he would have received an F, except that the movie itself was an excellent example of a symbolic idea optimized for the greatest impact. Matt didn't really know what that meant.

The course called Applied Monas Hieroglyphica was straight-up spell casting. Sure, it was all taught as if it were science, but it didn't feel like science when you were chanting in Latin while standing around a circle inscribed with ancient glyphs. The first theorem they learned to prove was that belief equaled reality. By the end of the first semester they were able to call upon the Divine Servants to place certain elements into their own dreams, like an ice-cream cone or a naked woman. That was crazy. Matt barely believed that it worked. There was no real physical evidence. They never heard voices, and nothing ever levitated or anything like that. But by the time they graduated, they were able to swap entire dreams with each other like trading cards. At least, some of the students claimed to.

Certain parts of the Scholars' training seemed very religious, but there was no priest on the estate and they never went to church. They learned about all kinds of religions. To Matt, most of them seemed to worship different flavors of the same god. They weren't taught that any one way to worship was the right way, but they weren't taught to be atheists, either. Instead, they were taught to believe in all of them, because they were all real and they all held power.

Angels and demons were just Divine Servants. If you asked the right way and paid the right price, they did pretty much the same thing. Both were vain, both were righteous, and both were willing to get their hands dirty. You just needed to negotiate. And that's were Matt had finally found some focus. Apparently, he exceled at getting others to do his work for him. As it turned out, that talent was highly valued by the Scholars.

Divine Servants could also become *familiars*. From what Matt understood, it was like entering into a contract. The angel or demon—or gremlin, or whatever—would give you a backstage pass to its specific sphere of influence. In exchange, it could ride you around like a pony if it wanted to. You had to be strong or you would be its plaything. All the Scholars had familiars. It was their last test before graduating.

Matt had thought he was ready. Sarah had thought she was, too.

She wasn't, though.

The last time Matt spoke with her, she had been lying restrained in her bed. He remembered it being cold even though there had been a log burning in the fireplace. The smell of burning oak mixed with the scent of dying hibiscus. One side of her face was swollen from when she had to be tackled to the ground. If they hadn't, she would have used her gardening shears to snip off more than just the tips of her fingers.

At first, she couldn't speak. Her familiar wouldn't let her. She shook and strained as spit bubbled out of her mouth. Matt didn't know what had gone wrong. The ceremony was always closed to the other students, and his father wouldn't give him any details. Matt wasn't even supposed to visit her until things had "settled."

He had visited anyway. He remembered taking out his iPod as he sat with her and pulling up a track. A cello drew a long, sad chord, and Sarah stopped shaking. He let the music just play for a bit as her whole body finally relaxed. He used his sleeve to clean up her face and waited.

One eyelid lifted halfway open on the undamaged side of her face. "'Oncidium Orchid,'" she said.

Matt looked at the iPod. It was the name of the track. "I didn't know which one to play."

"That's a good one. Not quite as flashy as some of the other orchids, but simple and beautiful."

Matt leaned in close to her. "What happened?"

At first, she didn't speak. She closed her eye and just hummed along with the music. Then she looked at him again. "I was nervous. And eager. I agreed to too much."

"Couldn't Father help?"

"Yes. I think he could have," she said. "He didn't."

"Why not?"

"He said the choice had to be mine. The familiar needed my oath, not his. I guess I didn't know what I was asking for. She seemed so nice before I made the offering."

"Maybe I can bargain with it . . . or her," Matt said. "I'm not too bad at that."

She tried to turn toward him but didn't get very far. "You have your own pact to make. You'll need your strength."

"I'm not gonna leave you like this," he said.

"I don't think there's much you can do . . . The sacrifice has been made. That's what we are to them—the Scholars. Just another sacrifice. We don't know what we're buying with our own blood."

The music faded out, and Sarah started to shake again.

Matt left that same night. He packed one bag—the same one that he had now—and left quickly and quietly. But Aunt Rose still met him at the door. She didn't say anything; she just gave him an envelope. Inside was some money and a Post-it note with a phone number written on it. Above the phone number was the word *home*. Maybe she figured he'd be back. Maybe he just needed some time to accept his fate.

He never called the number. By the time they started hunting for him, he was already three states away.

32

The paths were becoming more and more familiar. Foster almost didn't need her help anymore. Somehow, the Woman in the Garden knew all about the city he lived in or at least how to get from one place to another. That seemed odd since she never left the garden. In fact, Foster didn't think she *could* leave the garden. That's why she needed Foster. Maybe she had a map. One that used something other than GPS to tell you where you were. The paths she had him walk were never the same, but they did seem to follow a certain logic.

He was also starting to recognize landmarks. It's just that the landmarks were relative. When he saw a dog peeing on a tree or a bush, he knew to turn right. If the dog was peeing on a fire hydrant or a streetlight, he took a left. If a red car drove past, Foster knew to stop and wait until it turned, then go in the opposite direction. If a homeless person asked him for spare change, he gave it and would wait one minute for each coin he'd given. If the homeless person got freaked out and left, Foster knew that danger was near, and he should step out of sight. If somebody offered Foster some spare change, he knew he could take a shortcut.

He still followed her instructions, though. He had to

finish this tonight, and he didn't want to waste any more time. That woman Erica had ruined everything. Foster should have just used a chair to keep her quiet like he did with Candice, but that seemed a bit cold. He had been hoping to have some time to explain what he was doing. She would have thanked him. Now he had to improvise. Thanks to Erica, he was heading someplace new. The Woman in the Garden had given him clear instructions:

6:36 p.m. – *Turn toward the North Star and walk along the path of Paradise.*

6:43 p.m. – *A bus shall pass bearing the image of a great and meaty sandwich with fried potato sticks. Follow its direction along the Saharan road.*

6:46 p.m. – *Pass by Saint Clara, giving her no heed.*

6:47 p.m. – *Pass Saint Paula also giving her no heed.*

6:48 p.m. – *But pay heed to Saint Rita, who will, in turn, lead you to the Saint of Roses.*

6:54 p.m. – *Humble thyself and extend thy hands. Take the gift offered. Three coins of silver, each a different size.*

6:56 p.m. – *Step sideways between shadows and onto the forest path.*

6:57 p.m. – *Inspect the nearest tree for moss. Follow the path in the direction the moss grows.*

7:07 p.m. – *You will see strings of fairy lights settled onto a small cottage. This is not a house of good humor and merriment, but instead a house where men of common purpose form alliances.*

7:08 p.m. – *Knock thrice and enter, blade drawn, for it is guarded. There you shall find a prize most desired by a worthy daughter.*

All of which made complete sense to Foster.

When he saw the bus, the hamburger ad made him realize how hungry he was. Luckily, he still had that pudding cup. No time to stop, so he ate it as he walked. He found it funny that there were so many streets named after saints so close to the Strip. At exactly 6:54 p.m. he kneeled down on the sidewalk and held his hands cupped above his head, as though he was hoping it would rain and they would fill up with water. A man about to pass by was so startled that he took a quick step back and looked at Foster. Then the man reached into his pocket and practically threw change into Foster's hand as he hurried by. One quarter, one nickel, and one dime.

Foster saw the shadows flicker. The sun had set, and this street was far enough from the lights of the casinos that there were dark patches between streetlights. The patch to his right shifted. One second the shadow of a struggling tree was hiding a garbage can, the next it was hiding the mailbox on the opposite side. Foster didn't turn, but he sidestepped toward the tree. The tree changed. It was no longer surrounded by concrete, struggling to find water. Now it was an ancient sycamore, thick and strong. Everything got darker. There were no more streetlights, and the moon was hidden by the canopy of a forest. The street was gone, too, replaced by a narrow dirt path choked with weeds.

The moss on the tree pointed behind Foster, so he turned around and started walking. It looked similar to the path he had taken earlier that evening, but then these trails always looked similar. The forest seemed endless, and none of his walks ever took him to the edge or even to a clearing. It seemed like the kind of forest where fairy tales grew up to become nightmares. It made Foster nervous, and he started walking faster. He wasn't sure if that would mess up the timing of his schedule, or if the schedule knew that he would be walking faster at this point. He was relieved when he saw the lights right on time.

They weren't actually fairies, which was a little bit disappointing. Instead, they looked like Christmas tree lights drizzled over a forgotten shack. And calling it a *shack* was being generous. It stood just off the path. The lights didn't do much more than highlight its shape, and the trees growing closest to it seemed to bend slightly away from it, as if they were afraid to touch it. There was a flag out front, a smiley-face pirate flag. Foster wasn't sure what to make of that, but he did pause before stepping toward the door. His hand shook a little as he extended the blade on his box cutter.

He knocked one minute late. The first was just a tap that he barely heard himself. Then he clenched his teeth and put a little more force behind his knuckles for the remaining two. He almost took a step back when he heard a voice from behind the door.

"The-Lord-is-my-light-and-my-stronghold-Of-whom-shall-I-be-afraid?"

Foster remembered that voice. It was the boy from the path. The Woman in the Garden hadn't known who he was when Foster had mentioned seeing him before. Did she know he would be here? Was he the guardian, or was he the prize? Foster opened the door and stepped in.

The boy stood by the far wall with his back to Foster. The wall was covered with lines. The designs were similar to the patterns he had been taught to draw, but the style was different. So were some of the symbols.

As Foster was trying to take it all in, the boy spun around. He looked surprised to see Foster, which didn't make sense. He did knock, after all, didn't he?

"You're not Matt," said the boy.

"No," said Foster. "I'm not."

Foster looked around the room. There wasn't much to it. There was a table with some strange toy army men, paints, and brushes. The boy must have been working on them. One of the brushes still looked wet.

The boy's eyes darted around a couple of times and then focused on Foster again. "You were on that trail in the forest . . . But that wasn't real."

Foster stepped over to the table. One of the little pots of paint was open. Foster picked it up. Apparently, it was called Apocalypse Sunrise Orange. He spoke without looking at the boy. "That trail led me here."

The boy took a step back, pressing himself up against the wall. "I thought that was a dream. Why did I say those things to you?"

That was weird. Foster set down the paint. "I don't know. *You're* the one who said them."

"I don't think I did," said the boy.

Patterns and lines swirled all around on the wall behind the boy. Foster traced one in the air with his finger. "Did you draw those lines?"

The boy tilted his head back to look over one shoulder. "Yeah. I think so."

"What kind of pen do you use?"

There was a sharp hissing sound followed by a low growl. At first Foster couldn't tell where it was coming from. Then he looked down. A scruffy cat was trying to make itself look twice as big as it actually was. Maybe that was the guardian.

Foster raised his blade and looked at the cat. *Really, cat?*

The cat lunged. It was all claws, and teeth, and guttural sounds. It crashed into Foster like a gladiator. Before Foster could react, the cat raked his leg with a series of lightning-fast blows. It followed that up with a savage bite, its ears pinned back and its fur standing up.

Foster was wearing jeans, so he barely felt any of it. He reached down and grabbed the cat by the scruff of the neck. He had to give a couple of tugs before the cat's grip finally gave way. Foster pointed his blade at the boy and backed up a couple of steps. The boy was frozen in place. Foster opened the door. The forest and path were gone, replaced by the heat and stink of the city. He lobbed the cat outside. It landed on most of its feet and immediately ran off into the shadows of a nearby house. There were lights on in the house, and Foster heard music. He stepped back into the shack and closed the door.

"I know who you are," said the boy. "You're that killer on TV."

"No," said Foster. "I'm the killer in your playhouse." He looked down at his leg. No real damage. "I'm not sure if I'm supposed to kill you, though."

"It's . . . it's a clubhouse."

"Right. Not a house of good humor or merriment."

The boy's eyes were glassy. "Why are you doing this?"

Foster didn't like the look he was giving him. "I just want to go home."

"So go." The boy sounded like he was pleading.

"I need somebody to go with me," said Foster. "Somebody I think you might know."

33

Christy had forgotten to ask for one of those cardboard drink trays, so she had to juggle three milkshakes and a bag of hamburgers as she made her way into the house. Her purse hung from one shoulder, and it kept getting in the way as she tried to open the door. If she ended up dropping one of the shakes, that could be Matt's. Amber must have been keeping an eye on the foyer and rushed over to help, but by then Christy had already made it inside.

Amber closed the door as she eyed the armload of fast-food. "Your eyes might be bigger than your stomach."

"I sure hope so," said Christy. "If I eat one of these things, I'll just want to sit on the couch all night and binge-watch teen dramedies." She offered the bag to Amber. "Can you help me out and eat a handful of fries?"

Amber took the bag and looked inside. "Of course."

Christy rearranged the drinks in her arms to improve the odds that they might all survive the trip to the break room. "I'm sure Adam's starving. Things went a bit late with Erica."

Between fries, Amber asked, "How is she? Is she coming in?"

"I don't think so. Not tonight. Is it busy?"

"Not too bad. No requests for latex yet. Are you working?"

"Yeah," said Christy, "in just a bit. I need to make sure Adam eats at least one of these burgers. Shouldn't be too hard."

Amber handed the bag back and licked the salt off her fingers. "Okay, I'll let the girls know. Thanks for the lard."

Christy continued her balancing act down the hallway. She felt a little self-conscious as she passed by the open doorway to the parlor. Smuggling in that many calories might ruin the illusion of a sophisticated house of ill repute. As promised, it wasn't too crowded and nobody saw her sneak by. When she got to the break room, she pushed down on the handle with her elbow and then bumped the door open with her hip.

Instead of finding Adam pretending to do homework in front of the TV, she found Matt's new partner. Actually, they had never been properly introduced. Matt just referred to him as Thug Guy. Right now, Thug Guy had a magnifying glass held up to one eye that made it look freakishly huge. He was using it to look at the tip of a hot-glue gun.

Christy started to back out the door again, hoping he hadn't noticed her.

He did notice her. "You are not looking for me, I guess?"

Christy stopped backing out and put on a fake smile. "No. Have you seen Matt? I'm running a bit late."

Thug Guy looked over the rim of his magnifying glass at her. "Late for dinner?"

"I'm covering for Erica," Christy said. "She's out . . . sick."

A bead of glue was starting to form at the tip of the glue gun. "I'm sure she is out sick a lot," said Thug Guy. "Have not seen him. Maybe is hiding in playhouse again."

"He was looking in on Adam for me."

"Like good pimp."

Thug Guy brought the tip of the glue gun down to something on the table. Something covered in black feathers.

"He's trying to take care of us, so we can do our jobs," said Christy. That's when she realized what the thing on the table was. The body of a large black bird lay on its side. Thug Guy was placing a drop of glue in its empty eye socket. Christy's fake smile melted into disgust. "What are you doing?"

Thug Guy answered without looking up. "Arts and crafts." He carefully pressed a black glass ball into the glue. He lifted the bird a little so she could see its new eye. "The eyes give it life."

"You didn't have to kill it in the first place," she said.

"No," said Thug Guy. "But now it is . . . uh . . . immortal?"

"We eat in here, you know. And Adam does his homework at that table. Your hobby isn't exactly kid-friendly."

Thug Guy turned the body over and angled his glue gun down at the other eye socket.

"My father taught me when I was boy," he said. "We spent summers in cabin. We would hunt and collect mushrooms. It remind me of him."

"Oh," said Christy. "Where is he now?"

"He is buried behind cabin," said Thug Guy. He tapped in the other glass eye and stood the bird up to look at it. He gave a slight nod and turned the bird toward her. "Is not creepy. His heart gave up. He would want to rest there."

She wasn't sure if it was the smell of the glue or the smell of the bird, but she was quickly losing her appetite.

"Okay," she said. "Well, if you see Matt, tell him I'm looking for him."

Thug Guy put down his glue gun as Christy backed out into the hallway. Adam was probably still out in his clubhouse, so she figured she would check there first. If Matt wasn't there, she would head up to his office.

She made it as far as the VIP room before she felt a hand on her shoulder. She could tell by the meaty grip that it was Thug Guy's.

"You leave so quick," he said. "Let me help carry things."

His accent made it hard to tell whether he was actually concerned or just looking for an excuse to touch her. She turned to look at him, and it became pretty clear it was the latter.

"That's all right. I got it," said Christy.

He didn't move his hand. "So you only need Matt's help?"

She shrugged out of his grip and took a step back. "I can manage on my own."

That made him mad, and he stopped pretending to be helpful. He shot out an arm and grabbed her wrist. One of the drinks fell to the ground, and the lid popped off. There was a slosh of thick white liquid as vanilla shake pooled on the floor.

"To me, it seems you should take all help you can get," said Thug Guy.

Her bag dropped as she tried to pull away. It didn't work. "Let go!"

He leaned in close until he was almost nose to nose with her. Now he looked more amused than angry. "You know, me and Matt, we like partners. This make me your boss, too."

Christy met his gaze. She was sure *she* looked angry. "He

never said that."

"I am saying that." He cocked his head slightly.

Christy stopped trying to pull his wrist away. Instead, she let her hand drop down by her purse. She kept staring at him while she reached inside and felt around for her can of pepper spray.

"That's not the way it works," she said.

The last two drinks hit the floor as he pushed her up against the VIP room door. He pressed his body against her, pinning her in place. When she felt a bulge grind up against her hip, she pulled out the spray.

Thug Guy glanced down toward his crotch and then back up at her. "I can feel it working—"

Suddenly she was falling backward. Thug Guy fell with her and seemed just as surprised as she was. They landed on the VIP room floor. She probably would have been fine if there hadn't been a big pile of thug on top of her. As it was, she landed hard, and her breath was knocked out of her. Thug Guy recovered more quickly and was up on one knee before Christy could see straight again.

The door closed them in the room. Thug Guy stood up, and Christy took the opportunity to scoot away from him. Somehow, she managed to keep hold of the pepper spray. The lights were on but they were dim, casting the corners of the room in shadows, which is how most clients liked it. She didn't see any clients or any of the other girls in here, though. Instead, she saw Adam. He was standing by the closed door, and he had a blade to his throat. Panic rushed through her in a sickening pulse.

"Hi," said a voice. "Is this yours?"

Behind Adam was a man that Christy thought she must know. He seemed so familiar.

Adam swallowed hard. "Mom. It's him. That guy they're

looking for."

Christy's stomach roiled. This was the nightmare that crept into parents' minds when they watched their children sleeping: *What if my child was in an accident? What if he was abducted? What if his life was threatened? What would I do?*

The fear flooding through her body wouldn't let her think of any answers.

The man looked at Christy. "We heard you two bickering out in the hallway. Adam, here, said you were his mother."

Thug Guy straightened himself up and stared at the man. "Who is this?"

"His name's Foster," said Adam. "He's—"

Foster tightened his grip on Adam and held the box cutter up to his nose. "Shh."

"Okay," said Thug Guy. "Foster, is it? You are making mistake. My name is—"

Foster cut him off, too. "You aren't needed here."

Thug Guy's hands turned into fists. "Oh? Is this true?" He tipped his head from one side to the other, his neck making popping sounds. He looked like a boxer about to step into the ring. Before Christy could tell him not to, Thug Guy moved forward.

"Yes," said Foster. The simple word was punctuated by his hand slashing out with the box cutter.

At first Christy thought he'd missed. Thug Guy stopped moving and looked confused. She didn't see the cut until he tried to turn his head. Then a gush of blood sprayed up at an angle into the air. Thug Guy watched it with fascination. A second gush shot out before Thug Guy thought to cover his neck with his hands. Christy watched as blood flooded out between his fingers. He took a step back. Then a step forward. He tried to say something, but that just made bubbles come out of his neck. His hat fell off as he collapsed to the floor. The pale bird skull attached to it stared up at Christy.

"That was . . . easy," said Foster.

"What did you do?" asked Christy.

Foster looked at her. He gestured with his knife as he talked. "He didn't matter. You. You matter."

Adam was staring wide-eyed at the body on the ground. There was a line of blood splatter across his cheek.

Christy held out her hands in front of her. "Please. I'll do anything."

Foster pointed his box cutter at one of her hands. "Well, you can start by dropping *that*. It looks dangerous."

She didn't know what he was talking about at first, but then she realized he was pointing to the pepper spray she was holding in a trembling hand. It seemed like a toy now. She dropped it, and it rolled away into the shadows.

Foster nodded toward the black leather bench in front of the St. Andrew's Cross. "Is that a bed?"

"Kind of," said Christy.

"Please have a seat," said Foster.

The pool of blood around Thug Guy was starting to spread out across the floor. Foster shuffled Adam a couple of steps to the side to avoid getting it on their shoes.

Christy stood up on shaking legs. It took her a second to get her balance before she made her way to the bench. "Look, you can have anything you want. Just let him go."

Foster returned the blade to the soft spot under Adam's chin. "I think the only way I'm going to get what I want is by keeping him here. Now take off your clothes."

"Please," said Christy. "Not with him here."

"It will be worse if I have to cut them off you."

Christy forced herself to look at Adam and tried to sound reassuring. "Don't look, honey."

Adam's eyes drifted across the room like he was taking it in for the first time. "He's not alone."

"Shh. Honey, don't make him mad."

Foster looked down at Adam. He didn't seem mad. He seemed curious. "No. It's all right. Who do you see?"

"That woman," said Adam. "Your mother. Only . . ."

Adam didn't finish. His eyes started to flutter like they did before one of his episodes. Christy felt a tear sting her cheek. *Not now!* But then she thought, *Maybe it's for the best.*

Foster took away the knife and turned Adam's chin to look at him. "Only what?"

Adam's eyes stopped fluttering. They snapped wide open. "She doesn't look at you the way my mom looks at me."

"How does she look at me?"

"The same way men do when they see the women here. She looks hungry."

34

Matt watched Amber as she stripped off her bra for one of the customers. He wasn't trying to be a perv; he was just looking for a chance to ask her a question. Her customer was an older man who had those cool white streaks in his hair along his temples. That and the goatee made him look like he could be a Bond villain, especially if he had a cool accent. Matt hadn't heard him speak yet, though.

The man was sitting in an armchair in the parlor. He had Amber all to himself. The only other customers were being served shots by a naughty cheerleader at the bar. The man held up a twenty-dollar bill and raised an eyebrow. Amber raised an eyebrow of her own and leaned toward him. She used her hands to squeeze her breasts together around the bill. Then she straddled his lap and pressed herself against him while she made a little moan into his ear. Matt took that opportunity to come up behind the chair and ask his question.

He tried to just mouth the words, exaggerating each one and using vague hand gestures. *Have you seen Christy?*

That seemed to work because she straightened up and said, "Yeah, she was looking for you, actually. She's probably in the break room with Adam." She used her regular speaking voice, which made Matt feel like he was being a dork.

"Okay, thanks," said Matt. The gentleman underneath Amber turned his head to look at him. Matt took a step back. "Oh, sorry."

"This is Sam," said Amber. "He's been around awhile."

"Don't mind me," said Sam. "I'm just here for the show."

Matt was a little disappointed that he didn't have a British accent, or at least a German one.

Amber swung a leg around so that she was sitting in Sam's lap instead of straddling it. "She brought you a burger. And a *shake*."

Apparently, this was turning into a conversation.

"That was nice of her," said Matt.

Amber traced one finger along Sam's shirt collar. "You know what that means don't you?"

"She's trying to give me diabetes?" asked Matt.

"It means she was thinking about you," said Amber.

Matt waved it off. "It's just a shake."

Sam tilted his head and looked at him like he was a child. "It's never just a shake."

"Sorry?" asked Matt.

"A burger? Maybe that's just a kind gesture," said Sam. "Picking up dinner for the boss to put him in a good mood. But she bought you a shake. A *shake*. She had to think about what kind of man you are. Vanilla? Chocolate? Strawberry? That choice says a lot about your character. And a lot about what she thinks of you."

Matt gave Amber a sideways glace. "Does it?"

Amber nodded like it was obvious.

Sam continued his lecture. "Hell yeah, it does. What's your favorite?"

"I don't know," said Matt. "Vanilla?"

"Is that a question?" asked Sam.

"I mean, I guess it's vanilla," said Matt. "I've never really thought much about it. I don't think I ever get strawberry."

"That's sad," said Sam. "That tells me you've lost touch with your childhood."

Amber nodded again. "I like strawberry," she said.

Matt shrugged. "I don't know. I do goof off a lot. People say I'm childish."

"Being a child's not about goofing off," said Sam. "It's about exploring new things. Being a teenager is about goofing off."

"Oh," said Matt. "What's your favorite?"

"Are you kidding? I can't drink that shit," said Sam. "They don't even use real ice cream anymore."

"They don't?" asked Matt.

"You just pay attention to what kind of shake she got you," said Sam. "Is it the same as hers? Does she think you're alike? Maybe she got you chocolate. She might think there's a little mystery to you. Just watch out if she got you Neapolitan."

Amber was trying to be helpful. "That's when they put all three together."

Sam continued. "Then she doesn't know what to think of you. She's hedging her bets."

This guy knew a little too much about fast-food and the human psyche. Maybe he *was* a supervillain.

Matt suddenly felt a rush of paranoia. "You're not a ventriloquist, are you?"

"Uh, no."

"Good."

Matt left them to their armchair romance. Amber went back to work, this time spinning around and teasing the waistband of her panties. Matt thought it was a little bit creepy that Sam kept watching him instead of Amber as he left the parlor.

Christy wasn't in the break room. There was a new crow staring at him from the table, though. Maybe she saw that and decided to eat out in the clubhouse. Matt wouldn't want to eat in here, either. He wondered where Thug Guy was.

Matt turned down the hallway toward the back door. The lights in the hallway were dim and the red light above the VIP room door seemed to drain the color out of everything. Even so, he could see a bunch of trash scattered around on the floor below the red bulb. When he was a few steps away, he realized what it was.

He tapped on the door to the VIP room with one knuckle. "Hello?"

Christy answered. Her voice was faint like she was busy doing something. "I'm . . . I'm with somebody."

"Are you okay?" asked Matt. "It looks like the Burger King just threw up all over the floor out here."

"Sorry," she said. "Wasn't me. I'm just covering for Erica. One of her regulars stopped by. Let *Dwayne* know I'll have to reschedule his session."

Wait. What? None of that made any sense. *She* was the one picking up burgers today. She never covered for Erica. Nobody covered for Erica, because Erica wouldn't let them. And Christy would never have a *session* with Dwayne. This was crazy talk.

Then he noticed another pool of liquid starting to seep out under the door. This pool didn't look like milkshake. It was dark and syrupy. It also didn't come from any of the paper cups lying on the ground. Matt bent down and touched his finger to it. He held it up to his nose. It didn't smell sweet. It smelled metallic. He knew that smell.

He cleared his throat to try to keep the shaking out of his voice. "Okay. I'll let Dwayne know."

His mind raced in a hundred different directions. Adrenaline mixed with sweat as the questions started clamoring in his head. Whose blood was that? Who was in there with her? Why didn't she ask for help? Could this be a joke? Could this be a dream? What the hell should he do? Then his feet seemed to move on autopilot. They walked calmly and deliberately down the hall, then up the stairs, and into the office. When he sat down behind the desk he had to concentrate on breathing for a few seconds before he could do anything else.

He flipped open the lid to the cigar box on the desk. Uncle Quent's gun felt heavy as he gripped the handle. He held it up in front of his face. The simple weapon suddenly seemed impossibly complex. He pulled and twisted different parts until the cylinder suddenly clicked out to one side. It was empty.

He grabbed the phone and dialed three digits.

"Pick up. Pick up. Pick up. Pick up."

The voice on the other end of the line seemed too far away to be of any help. "9-1-1, please state your emergency."

Matt blurted it all out. "The guy! The killer guy! I think he's here! He killed something! There's blood! He has Christy!"

"Is this a medical emergency? Is somebody injured?"

They weren't getting it. Not fast enough.

"Sergeant Dwayne Murdock! Get him! Tell him Christy's in trouble!"

"Are you calling from a safe location? Are you in immediate danger?"

"No. Yes. Also, I have a gun. But no bullets." Matt looked inside the cigar box again. No bullets in there. "Where can I get some bullets?"

"The police department has been notified."

If Uncle Quent had a gun, there had to be bullets somewhere. "Bullets . . ."

"Units are on their way."

Matt grabbed the handle to the top draw of the desk. Pencils, pens, and ancient pink erasers jumped as he yanked it open. "Bullets . . ."

"Please try to remain calm."

He opened another drawer. All of his new paperwork, but no bullets. "No. Not there . . ."

"Please stay on the line, sir."

He opened up the bottom drawer. It looked empty, but he thought he heard something rattle when it slid open. "Where would I be if I was a bullet?"

The voice on the line was starting to lose its cool. "And please don't do anything with that gun."

Matt felt something hard and round hidden in the corner of the drawer. He held up the bullet in triumph.

"Found one!"

35

Adam stood with his back to the X-shaped thing in the center of the room. It looked like something you might tie somebody up to before you started torturing them. This whole room looked like a torture chamber. Adam didn't get it. He knew people paid to come in here and be tied up. It had something to do with sex. But sex was supposed to make you feel good. He knew that much. He even knew what it looked like when people had sex. He figured he'd be nervous enough just kissing a girl. If one had a whip, he'd probably run away. Maybe that's why they tied you up first.

"Here. Hold this." The guy with the knife handed him a book.

Adam looked at it. It looked like a fairy tale book for kids. There was a big tree on the cover with a sleepy-looking owl perched up in the branches. The tree was in a garden full of flowers, fruits, and vegetables. A woman was smiling at a flower she had just planted. It looked a little bit like the woman Adam had seen earlier when the walls started vibrating.

"What is it?" he asked.

"It's the thing you have to hold so I don't hurt you," said

Foster.

Adam's mom was on the leather bench in front of him. She was lying on her back, naked. She had one leg pressed over the other and her arms crossed over her breasts. The eye makeup she was wearing streaked back toward her ears. She wasn't really crying, but every few seconds a tear would roll out from the corner of one of her eyes and trace a path to the floor. From this angle she had to tilt her head back to look at Adam.

"Honey, please just do what he says," she said.

"Listen to your mother," said Foster, who arranged the book so it was lying flat in Adam's arms. Then he opened it up to a page in the middle. A scene sprang to life as pop-up paper trees and flowers lifted up from the pages. The tree that rose up from the center had a rope swing dangling from one of its branches. A woman in a white dress sat in the swing, and when the tree popped up into place, it set the swing in motion.

Foster looked at the book in Adam's arms and held up his thumbs and pointer fingers like he was framing a picture. He nodded and turned back toward Adam's mom.

As Foster walked away, Adam said, "I don't think he really wants to hurt anybody."

Foster paused halfway to the bench. He turned back to look at Adam and then pointed with his knife to the dead man on the ground. "That's not true. I wanted to hurt *him*."

Adam tried to keep his eyes on the floor, but he still had to say something. If he didn't, Foster would just do what he'd come here to do.

"I guess so," he said. "But the woman you speak to. The one in the garden. She's the one who wants you to hurt these women."

Foster continued to walk to the foot of the bench. "She

doesn't want to hurt them. She wants to help them. But she can't, so she needs me."

"She's using you," said Adam. "I told you. She only cares about what you can give her."

Foster seemed to ignore that. He looked down at Adam's mom and frowned. Then he gently pushed her leg to the side so that they were no longer crossed. He did the same with her arms. He didn't stare at her breasts or even between her legs. He just kind of tilted his head from side to side like he was looking for something.

"Hmm . . ." Foster pulled a pen out of his back pocket. It was a big, fat, blue marker. He flicked the cap off with his thumb. The room almost immediately smelled like blueberries. He knelt beside the bench and leaned down to talk to Adam's mom.

"Now don't move," he said. "If you move it might mess up the line. If that happens I'll have to go find somebody else. But I would have to cut you both first. I can't have you messing this up. I already messed up once today."

Adam's mom swallowed and gave a slight nod of her head. She was shaking a little.

"Here," said Foster, "I'll help you."

Foster put down his pen and took her wrist. He bent it backward over her head where there was a strap waiting. She gripped a bar that looked like it was there just for that purpose, and Foster did up a buckle. He did the same with her other arm and then her ankles. Finally, he placed a strap with a rubber ball between her teeth and tightened it to the bench so her head couldn't move much. More makeup mixed with tears.

Adam felt himself shaking. He could try to run. *He* wasn't strapped to anything. But he probably wouldn't make it very far. He would have to get past Foster to the door. Foster had locked the door and turned on the do-not-disturb light. This side of the door didn't need a key—he would just have to turn the latch—but it would still slow him down. Adam didn't want to leave his mom, though. If he ran, she would die.

Foster knelt down again, this time by one of her ankles. He picked up his pen and looked like he was about ready to start drawing on her. Then he paused and looked up at Adam.

"You're wrong about her," he said. "That woman you saw? She's the only one who cares about me."

When the pen touched her toe, Adam's mom tightened her grip on the bar. She squeezed her eyes shut and let out a little sound around the ball in her mouth, but otherwise she didn't move.

"How can you tell?" asked Adam.

Foster kept his eyes on the line he was drawing. "Trust me, nobody's going to cry when I leave this place."

"I mean, how can you tell that she actually does care about you?"

"She saved me. She could have let me die. Instead, she showed me her home. She invited me to come join her. She wants me there."

"Why would she do that?" Adam asked. "She doesn't even know you."

"She's like me," said Foster. "She was rejected. By . . . by everybody who mattered. So she made a new home for herself. It's beautiful. It's a place where things live and grow. She needs people to help take care of it."

From where he was standing, Adam couldn't see all of the line Foster was drawing. He saw the line spiral around his mom's ankle and then snake up her calf. Foster slowed down when he got to her thigh to make a pattern. It was a new one to Adam. More complex than the patterns he drew on the wall of the clubhouse. He thought he shouldn't be watching this, not when his mom was naked, but his eyes kept getting pulled back to the line and the patterns.

"Are you sure any of this is real?" asked Adam.

"Of course it is," said Foster. "You saw it, too, right? You walked the forest path."

Adam's eyes kept losing focus when he stared at the patterns for too long. There was also a faint buzzing in his head. That was a sign that he should take one of his pills.

"Yeah," said Adam, "but I'm off my meds. I get tremors, and I say things that don't make sense. It doesn't mean I believe everything I see."

"Maybe you should," said Foster.

"I can see that my mom is scared. She doesn't want this. Were the other women scared, too?"

"Everybody is afraid of change. We're giving them a gift. They can start their lives over. Wash away all their regrets and bad decisions. Be with somebody who cares for them and gives them purpose. Once they get to the garden they aren't afraid anymore."

The buzzing got louder. Adam thought he could also hear birds chirping. The blueberry scent faded, and he smelled other things on a wispy breeze that almost wasn't there—flowers, water, and warm earth. He thought Foster could smell it, too. He looked toward Adam and the book. Foster could obviously see something that Adam couldn't. When Foster looked at it, he seemed nervous.

"You're scared, too," he said. "My mom never makes me feel afraid . . . on purpose."

His mom tilted her head a little and tried to look at him. Her eyes were wet. She tried to mouth something, but it was hard to make out what it might be. He thought it was *I love you.*

Foster looked up at her. Her chest was heaving in silent sobs. He used his free hand to steady his other. "Stop crying. You're gonna make me slip."

"She tries to make the world seem less scary," said Adam. "She wants to be with me."

Foster rubbed his eyes and then continued drawing. "Does she?"

Adam's own voice sounded like an echo. "She's given up everything for me. She doesn't ask me for anything."

Now he could see what Foster was looking at. Roots lifted the dirt underneath Adam's feet. He backed up a little and bumped into something rough. The large wooden cross was no longer behind him. Instead, a twisted tree trunk stretched up from the floor. Bark flaked off like dry, dead skin. Thick branches reached and spread out, hiding the ceiling. Hanging from one branch was a large swing the size of a love seat. The woman from the book was sitting in it. Next to her were two other women in white sundresses. They stared forward with milky-blue eyes.

She spoke to Foster. "Don't listen to him. He has always been with his mother. He takes her for granted."

Adam closed the book and turned to look at her. "No, I don't. At least, I try not to. She's all I've got."

The Woman in the Garden looked at him first out of the corner of her eye, and then she turned her head to stare straight at him. If she was surprised to see Adam, it didn't show. Foster *was* surprised. He stopped drawing, his line broken.

"Do you think her life is better for having you?" she asked Adam.

"I . . ." Adam wanted to say, *Yes, of course,* but he couldn't.

The Woman in the Garden stood up from her swing. As she stepped onto the ground, paper flowers unfolded around her feet. The other women stayed where they were. An owl landed on the branch supporting the swing, fluttering down from somewhere above.

"A hug good night doesn't make up for years of whoring yourself out. Do you really think this was her *plan*? That she wanted to live like this? She could have been anything she wanted, but she gave herself up for you."

Adam's voice cracked a little when he spoke. "I don't think you can plan on loving someone. You just love them."

"Enough," she said. "This place isn't for you. You don't belong here."

"Neither do they. Neither does he."

"Leave," she demanded. "Now."

The owl screeched and flew at Adam. His vision went red as its talons squeezed around his eye.

36

Matt heard Adam scream through the door of the VIP room. He raised the pistol up in front of him. Now it seemed like such a simple machine. One handle, one trigger, and only one way for the bullet to come out. He also only had one bullet. No room for error.

He took the house key out of his pocket. His thumb pulled back the hammer on the gun until it clicked into place. He took a deep breath. And then another. And another.

"Hey, Matt. What's going on?"

A jolt of panic and adrenaline shot through Matt. He turned to look behind him. It was Amber. She looked worried. He wondered how many people had heard Adam scream. He realized she was looking at the gun in his hand. Maybe that's what worried her.

"Get everyone out. Now," Matt hissed.

Amber stared for a second, then turned and ran for the parlor.

Adam started to scream again, but this time his own voice cut himself off. "Ahh! The-Lord-is-faithful-He-will-establish-you-and-guard-you-against-the-evil-one!"

Matt had to move. Now. He held the key up to the lock. He pushed but it wouldn't go in. He tried turning it upside down but it still wouldn't budge. The scratch of metal on metal sounded like fingernails on a chalkboard. He had to be doing something wrong. Then he remembered he had two keys. The big one was in his hand. The small one was still in his pocket.

His hands were shaking so hard, he almost dropped it as he fished it out. This time the key slid in, and when he turned it, he felt the bolt slide back. *Thunk*. Three quick breaths and he was in motion. He twisted the knob and threw the door open, pistol raised. He started to charge inside but had to stop short. There was a man standing right in front of him. The killer from the news.

"I heard the key in the lock," said the man. Matt remembered the name below the mug shot on TV—Foster.

Matt tried to take in more details of the room, but all he could see was the box cutter in Foster's hand. His finger slipped. The hammer fell on the pistol with a sharp metallic *click*. No *boom*.

Both men looked at the gun. Matt was confused. The simple machine was supposed to work. He'd put the bullet in the chamber directly in front of the hammer. *Oh shit*. The cylinder *turned* when the trigger was pulled. The bullet was in the wrong place.

Foster looked confused, too. "Did you just try to—"

Matt squeezed his eyes shut and pulled the trigger over and over again. He flinched with each click, expecting an explosion and a splatter of blood. *Click. Click. Click. Click.* Then *cloof*!

It was much quieter than he thought it would be. Matt opened his eyes. There was a cloud of dust billowing through the air. Foster wasn't covered in blood. He was covered in white powder.

Foster sniffed and then sneezed. *"Aaachoo!"*

Then he slashed at Matt with the blade.

Matt's arms were up in front of him, so the box cutter just cut his wrist. At first it stung, then a second later, it felt like it was on fire. He stumbled back a step, his foot landing on something soft and squishy. Vanilla shake splattered as Matt tumbled back onto the floor.

He looked up at Foster, who just stood in the doorway for a second.

"Weird," said Foster.

Then he took the key out of the lock and closed the door. There was another click as it locked from the other side.

37

"Police! Everybody get the fuck out of my way!"

Dwayne's boot splintered the frame of the front door as he kicked it open. The door was probably unlocked, but Dani wasn't going to fault him for that. She felt like kicking something too.

They got the call maybe five minutes ago and had driven through two separate front yards on their way over. They had already been in the sergeant's car, heading toward a high-rise condo complex near the Strip. They were supposed to be checking out a noise complaint, probably related to a fight. Most likely a halfhearted, drunken throwdown or maybe a domestic brawl, but after the failed operation at the orphanage, they were checking out anything that sounded potentially violent.

That had all been forgotten as soon as Dwayne heard the report from dispatch. His name was called out specifically. So was Christy's.

They were first on the scene. Nobody came to meet them in the foyer, even after Dwayne broke down the door. The lights were dim, and slow, sultry music played from the parlor. Dani remembered seeing a few of the girls out on the sidewalk by the house, as well as an older guy, who was clearly a customer. He had stared right at Dani as she'd run up the steps with Dwayne. It was odd. Maybe he forgot he was doing something illegal.

Dani checked her watch. "Backup is still at least two minutes out."

"Christy? Adam?" Dwayne yelled into the house.

Somebody answered from the hallway. "Down here!"

It was Matt. He was leaning up against the wall at the far end of the hall across from the VIP room. As Dani got closer, she realized he was covered in blood. He was clutching his wrist with the other hand, but it didn't seem to be doing any good. Blood still trickled down his arm and dripped from his elbow. Dani crouched next to him, but Dwayne went straight for the door.

"Wait!" said Matt.

Dwayne spun around to look at them, and it was clear he had no intention of waiting.

Matt saw that and blurted out, "He's got them both in there. Christy and Adam. And he already killed . . . what's his face. The guy who keeps punching me."

Dwayne slowly turned back to the door. Then he looked down. Dani followed his gaze and noticed the pool of blood he was standing in, along with some other kind of liquid. Dani took a second to look at Matt's arm. That pool of blood wasn't from him, but he *was* starting to make his own.

"You're bleeding pretty bad," she said.

"Yeah," he said, "everything's getting fuzzy."

"Here, let me see."

She moved his hand away from the wound. Warmth splattered across her face as blood shot out across the hallway. She clamped her own hand around his wrist and reached for her radio.

She pushed the button. "Code two-seventeen in progress. Requesting eleven-forty-one."

Matt shook his head. "Should I be worried? None of that made any sense."

"They're sending an ambulance," Dani explained.

She pulled a zip tie off her belt and looped it around Matt's arm. Matt looked like he was about to protest when Dani yanked the free end tight. One of Matt's eyes squeezed shut, and the other went wide with pain.

There was a series of rapid thumps behind her as Dwayne pounded on the door.

"Foster!" he said. "This is the police. We know you're in there. Drop you weapon and come out. Now!"

There was a pause, and then a faint voice said, "That would be dumb."

Dwayne stepped close to the door so that his head was almost resting against it. "Christy, are you in there?"

Foster answered for her. "She's tied up. I put one of those rubber balls in her mouth. She's fine, but I do have a knife pressed against her throat."

Dwayne's hand started to clench around his pistol. He stopped it when his finger touched the trigger. "Adam? Adam, are you all right?"

"He's here, too," said Foster. "He's shaking pretty bad. I didn't do anything to him, though. He did that on his own."

Dwayne held his pistol with both hands and pressed the top of it against his head. To Dani it looked like he was praying.

It wasn't a prayer, though. "Oh fuck. Oh fuck. Oh fuck."

He was breaking. He wasn't the sergeant anymore. He was a man trapped in a nightmare.

Matt's arm was starting to change color. It felt cool and clammy. Dani took Matt's free hand and placed it over the cut again. This time there was no shower of blood, which was good because Matt's grip didn't seem very tight. She couldn't worry about that right now.

"Hey, Foster? My name's Dani. We can work something out. Nobody else needs to get hurt. What do you want?"

Foster didn't answer for a long time. Finally, he said, "I don't know anymore. I think I'd have to start all over. I don't suppose you could send in another woman. Somebody broken? I'd do an even trade."

Dwayne's pistol hung at his side. He was whispering now, mainly to himself. "He's gonna kill them. He's just gonna kill them."

Dani stepped closer to the door. "Look, you know we can't do that."

"Yeah," said Foster, "I figured."

"That boy is in trouble," said Dani. "He has seizures. We know you don't hurt kids. You should let him go. We can take him to the hospital, and then we'll have more time to talk this through."

"I don't think she'll let me."

"Of course she will. She's his mother."

"No," said Foster. "I mean the Woman in the Garden. She won't let him leave. He's too dangerous."

Okay, how do you reason with that? Dani's heart sank. *You don't.*

Dwayne was looking down at the ground. "There's blood on the floor. He has a knife. He's crazy. He's gonna kill them."

Then she heard Adam's voice. It wasn't comforting at all.

"The-voice-of-the-LORD-strikes-with-flame-The-voice-of-the-LORD-twists-the-oaks-and-strips-the-forests-bare."

38

The boy stopped shaking. His lips parted, and blood ran down his chin. His hand fell away from his eye, and Foster could see red tears dripping down his cheek. He wasn't sure if Adam was still breathing.

The boy's mother twisted in her restraints, trying to get a better look at him. The strap over her mouth muffled her screams, but Foster could tell she was trying to yell his name over and over again.

Foster bent down to where Adam was leaning against the cross. The storybook was closed at his side. Foster grabbed it. Splatters of blood decorated its cover. He opened it back up to the page with the tree swing and laid it flat next to them. His fingers trembled as he touched them to the side of Adam's throat to feel for a pulse.

Blood sprayed across Foster's face as Adam coughed. He blinked away the red smears in his vision. He opened his eyes to look at the boy again, and another cough shot out more blood.

Adam's voice sounded thick. "It's gone."

He was looking around the room wide-eyed. One of his eyes was normal, the other was shot through with jagged, red lines. There were no cuts or scratches on his face.

"I can't see it anymore," said Adam. "It's just a room again. There's no tree."

Foster still saw the tree and the Woman in the Garden. Her owl had returned to her and sat perched on her shoulder. Her white dress was stained red by one of the clenching talons. She was standing over by the boy's mother now. She looked down at her like she was trying to find some kind of meaning on her face. It was clear that Christy couldn't see her at all. If she could, she wouldn't be straining forward so much.

"What did you do?" asked Foster.

"I reminded him where he belongs," said the Woman in the Garden. "And where he's not wanted."

Adam crawled over to his mother. "I tried, Mom. I tried."

He laid his head down on her stomach. She mumbled something soothing.

"Will he be all right?" Foster asked.

The Woman in the Garden shifted her gaze to the boy. "Kill him. Take your blade, slash his veins, and hang him from this cross. Drain his blood, and end his corruption. If you don't, he'll bring a blight to all that I've sown."

"How? He's just a boy."

"He walked the path and entered the garden unbidden."

"So he should die?"

Christy whipped her head back to look at him. Her eyes fluctuated between rage and pleading. She must have heard that. At least the part that Foster had said.

The women in the tree swing continued staring blankly ahead.

"You've killed others," said the Woman in the Garden. "You said it was getting easier. In your heart you were starting to enjoy it."

"That's what scares me," said Foster. "But I knew I was sending them to you, so you could help them."

The Woman in the Garden turned her head toward the corpse by the door. "Not him."

"He was going to ruin everything," said Foster.

"So is this boy."

"He's just scared. He got lost and found you."

"He was drawn to me. And something else came with him. He doesn't realize what's just under the surface of his skin. He's beyond saving. He should never have been born."

That sounded familiar. Children could be cruel, and orphans were easy targets. Being defined by something you didn't have, and would probably never have, changed the way you thought about yourself and your place in the world. Some kids hardened to it like a calloused fist; others drifted through life believing they should never have been born.

As Foster went to the bench, Christy pushed her head back into the leather cushion. He knelt down next to her on the side opposite Adam. Foster reached toward her face, and she squeezed her eyes shut. He unfastened a buckle and the strap over her mouth fell away.

"What are you doing?" asked the Woman in the Garden.

Foster kept his eyes on Christy.

"Let my son go and I'll stay," she said. "He needs a doctor. They won't care about us. You and I. They'll be too busy with him. They'll . . . they'll give you more time if you let him out." She looked down at the patterns on her chest. "You could start over."

"No," said Adam. But it was quiet and weak.

A door crashed open in some other part of the house. There was yelling and lots of boots stomping across the floor. The woman on the other side of the door was yelling out warnings: *Don't shoot. Don't engage. Don't open that door. He's got a knife. He's got hostages. He has a kid in there. He's dangerous.*

Foster wiped his nose with the back of his hand. As he did, he noticed he was still holding the box cutter. He quickly lowered it down by his side and looked at Christy.

"What would you do if you were my mother?" he asked.

It seemed like she didn't understand him at first. She just looked confused. Then her face softened and her chin shook. She blinked, and two fresh tears squeezed out from her eyes.

At first she spoke in a whisper. "I would cry." She took a shuttering breath and then spoke a little louder. "Because I would have failed you. I would tell you not to hurt anyone. And I would tell you that everything is going to be all right. I would hold you close and do everything I could to protect you."

She wouldn't, of course. He knew that. But it didn't matter.

When the Woman in the Garden spoke, it sounded like she was right behind him, whispering in his ear. "She's not your mother. She pities you. She just wants to keep living so she can continue to grind out her shadow of a life."

Foster started to look at her but then turned back to Christy. "Do you pity me?"

They both answered his question.

"No," said the Woman in the Garden. "Together we will build something divine."

"Yes," said Christy. "I'm sorry."

He could tell they were both telling the truth.

"The thing is," said Foster, "people feel pity because they care. It's humiliating. You realize you're at your worst, and you can see it reflected in their eyes. Even if it makes you feel less than human, when people pity you it's because they want you to be a better person. They think, *What if that were me?* They feel a little afraid and a little relieved."

The whisper in his ear said, "I'm giving you the chance to be above those people."

Christy just nodded.

Foster held up his blade again. He clicked the blade closed, then open. Closed, then open.

"Do exactly as I say and the boy will live."

39

Adam stood by the door. He had to be careful, though, because the pool of blood made it slick.

Through his right eye everything was covered in a cloud of hazy red. All he could see were silhouettes and shadows. His left eye was a little blurry, but otherwise he could see out of it just fine. He had to keep turning his head from side to side to take in what was around him. Things seemed flat, and it was hard to tell how close everything really was.

He flinched back as somebody pounded on the door from the other side.

It was a woman's voice. His dad's partner. "Foster! How is this gonna end?"

Adam wondered where his dad was. It sounded like there was a bunch of people outside now. He could hear low voices and radios crackling.

Foster placed a bundle into his hands. It was wrapped in his mom's shirt, and the smell of her perfume suddenly made his next task seem impossible. He looked back at her. She just smiled and gave a slow nod. She mouthed the words *I love you*. He nodded back and held the bundle tight.

Foster leaned close to the door. He wasn't wearing a shirt

anymore, and it made him look smaller. He still had the knife, though, and his knuckles were white as he gripped it in a tight fist.

"All right," said Foster. "The boy's coming out on his own. I'll have a knife pressed to his mother's neck. If this door opens after he leaves, I cut."

He looked down at Adam. "It will be over soon. Then everybody can go home."

Foster walked back to the bench. He carefully put his knife in place. Then he nodded.

Adam opened the door. The hallway was filled with police officers. Some were in uniforms, some weren't. All of them had guns out. Nobody said a word as he pulled the door shut again behind him. As soon as the door clicked into place, Dani reached out and pulled him to one side. She crouched down around him and practically carried him down the hall.

She yelled as they moved. "He's hurt! Where's that ambulance?"

Then he was in his father's arms. The bundle was crushed between them, and Adam was worried that something might break. When the hug loosened a little, Adam could tell that his dad was shaking. There were tears in his eyes as he kissed Adam on the forehead.

He yelled over Adam's shoulder toward the door. "Christy, he's safe! We'll get you out of there, too, baby!"

His father set him down against the wall. Adam could see him cringe when he looked at his eye. He let go of Adam, took a deep breath, and stood up.

"Stay here," he said. "There's a medic on the way. Whatever happens, stay low. I'm gonna get your mother out of there."

"She's going to be all right," said Adam.

His father nodded, but Adam didn't think he believed it.

He turned to somebody against the wall next to Adam. "Stay with him." It was Matt. He nodded, too. Then his father drew his gun and walked down the hall. All eyes were on him.

"You okay?" Matt whispered to Adam. "What happened?"

Adam turned his head. He had to turn it more when all he saw was a red-and-black blur.

"I tried to be a hero," said Adam.

Matt showed him his bloody arm. "Me too."

His father's voice boomed down the hall. "Foster, talk to me! What do you want?"

Adam put the bundle in his lap. He found an edge of the shirt and started unwrapping it. He uncovered the storybook. It looked pretty banged up. The corners were dented, and there were flecks of blood across the cover. The owl looked at him from the oak tree while the Woman in the Garden was frozen in a smile. The music box looked fine, though. Not even a scratch on it.

"What's that?" asked Matt.

"This is what he wants," said Adam.

"Christy?" yelled his father. "Can you talk? Are you all right?" He pounded on the door.

Matt leaned over to look at the box. "Why did he let you take it? What happened in there?"

"He made me draw."

Adam flipped the lid open. The music box began plunking out slow, metallic notes that rang down the hallway. When Adam looked up, everybody was staring his way.

Then there was a low, ripping sound from behind the door. It started slow and then became impossibly fast. It ended abruptly in an animal scream.

His father screamed, too. "Christy!"

Then the door crashed open as his shoulder laid into it like a battering ram. He raised his pistol and stood perfectly still. His arm wavered, and the pistol clattered to the floor. His father opened his arms as his mother rushed forward to meet him.

She was covered in blood, but Adam knew it wasn't hers. The lines he had drawn were on Foster.

40

"That looks pretty badass."

Matt was looking at Adam's eye patch. White gauze was taped over the boy's eye, but Adam had clearly decided to embrace his inner pirate and cover up the gauze with a proper black patch.

Matt pointed to the wrap around his own wrist. "All I got was this stupid bandage."

They were in the clubhouse, sitting at the table. Azrael had immediately come over to give Matt a head-butt when he came in, but now that he had his treat, the cat had returned to his blanket nest to resume napping.

Adam looked at Matt's arm. He gave a tight-lipped smile, apparently agreeing that the bandage was, indeed, stupid. "They said I should be able to see again. They don't know when, though."

"Did they say how it happened?" asked Matt.

"They think my tremors burst some blood vessels," said Adam. "They said it put pressure on the lens or something. I have to take eye drops now. *And* pills."

Matt leaned back in his chair and had to catch himself before he tipped backward. "Did they also say a sweet eye patch would get you tons of chicks?"

"No," said Adam. "Because I'm still nine."

Matt smiled. "Oh, right."

He was hoping that would lighten the mood a little, or at least keep the conversation going. Instead, Adam looked down at the table and the tiny room filled with awkward silence.

It had been a couple of weeks since the . . . What do you call it? Incident? Bloodbath? Nightmare? The house had been pretty quiet since then. Occasionally, the police would stomp through to take more pictures or fill out more paperwork. Christy spent most of the time in her room. She slept a lot and occasionally broke down into tears. Matt had tried to comfort her, but she just wanted to be left alone. Adam mainly hid away out here. He didn't want to talk much, either.

Matt tried again. "So, uh, did you want to talk about anything that happened? You know, *in there*."

"No," said Adam. "Not really."

Matt kept going anyway. "Because that was pretty messed up."

"Yeah, I know." Adam paused for a second and looked up at Matt. "You were going to shoot that guy."

That wasn't what Matt had been expecting. It hit him pretty hard. He hadn't thought about it much himself since he hadn't actually shot anybody. But he *had* pulled the trigger. Over and over again. The sergeant had kept that fact out of his report. He'd kept a lot out of his report.

"I think I just got him high, instead," said Matt. "That's probably why he made you . . . *you know*."

Adam looked at him, and Matt could tell the boy didn't believe that at all.

They were spared another awkward silence when the

door opened. Christy poked her head in. She was smiling, but Matt could tell she wasn't really committed to the smile.

"What are you boys talking about out here?" she asked.

They answered at the same time.

"Nothing," said Adam.

"Girls," said Matt.

Christy looked like she didn't believe either of them. "Uh-huh."

She came in and reached down to pet Azrael. The cat didn't open his eyes, but he did raise his chin to make it easier for her to scratch the right spot.

"Dani's here," she said. "I guess they have everything they need. Officially, they're listing it as a home invasion. No mention of the business. I guess we can reopen soon, but she did recommend lying low for a while."

"That should be easy," said Matt. "I don't imagine people will want to visit the VIP room anymore."

Christy sniffed and looked over at him. "Are you kidding? I bet we could charge double."

"How is she? Dani? She was pretty close to Erica, right?"

"She won't talk about it. She's taking it pretty hard. Me too . . . I don't know, maybe we should—"

"Take the weekend off?" Matt suggested.

"I was gonna say move out."

Adam looked up at that. "I don't want to move."

Christy bent down to his level. "Are you sure, honey? We'll be okay if we do. We can make it work."

"I fought through the tremors that night," Adam said. "You heard him. I saw what he saw."

Christy raised her eyebrows and spoke slowly. "He was crazy. And look what happened to your eye."

Adam met her gaze. "I'm getting better here. I had a tremor yesterday, and I was able to end it on my own. I just stepped back into myself, and it ended."

"Honey, you need to tell me when you have those. To me it sounds like they're happening more frequently, not less. And you say you're seeing stuff that's not there."

Adam shook his head. "It's just a way for me to control things."

"We'll see how it goes," she said.

"But Mom—"

"We'll see how it goes," she repeated. "We don't have time to argue about this. Dwayne's gonna be here soon."

Now it was Matt's turn to put on a fake smile. "What are you guys doing?"

Adam perked up. "Dad's taking us to dinner and a movie."

Matt liked Dwayne well enough, he just didn't want to see Adam get disappointed. Something had shaken loose in Dwayne that night, and he'd just frozen up. Matt couldn't blame him; he'd felt pretty useless himself. And Dwayne did seem to rally once Adam was safe. It was clear that he cared about Christy and Adam. Matt just didn't know if Dwayne knew *how* to care for them.

"Cool," said Matt, "what are you going to see?"

"The one with all the explosions," said Adam.

Matt's smile was real now. "All of them?"

"A comedy," said Christy.

This was news to Adam. "But—"

"You're saying that a lot today," said Christy. "Don't make me take us to a *romantic* comedy. I'll do it."

Matt followed them back inside. The police tape had been removed from the VIP room door. He didn't open it. He wasn't ready to face that mess just yet. Ice cream and blood still stained the carpet out front, and he had enough trouble with just that.

He hid in his office until they had gone. Dwayne hadn't come upstairs; he just waited for them down in the foyer. Adam sounded excited, and Matt had heard him rush down, taking the stairs two at a time from the sound of it. Christy had come down a few minutes later. Matt hadn't heard any arguing or yelling, so it seemed like movie night was off to a good start.

Matt thought about going to a movie himself. He didn't want to think about what he should do next. He spun around in his chair to face the window. His bandage was itchy. He peeled it off slowly, which he knew was the exact wrong way to do it. The stitches in his wrist looked strange, almost fake. He touched them experimentally, and they felt real enough. The cut was still sore, but everything looked clean and the pain meds were pretty good. Maybe he would take a couple of those pills and sit in front of the TV instead of going out.

The cut wasn't very long, but it had gone deep. It had severed an artery, but Dani's zip tie had slowed the bleeding enough to keep most of his blood inside his body. They said it would scar. And the scar would go right through the brand on his wrist.

"That's not gonna get me any chicks," he whispered to himself.

He jerked his head up when somebody answered.

"Probably not." It was a woman's voice.

Matt spun his chair around again and saw a woman sitting across the desk from him. She was full figured and wearing some kind of uniform. She looked like she might be a cleaning lady. She also looked kind of familiar.

"Whoa!" said Matt. "How did you get in here?"

She seemed kind of bored with his reaction. "The front door was open."

"It was? Well, unfortunately we're closed, so . . ." Matt started to stand. He was going to show her the way out, but of course, she already knew the way out. "I'm not sure when we're going to open again."

The woman didn't take the cue and remained firmly in her chair. "I do."

"What?"

"I know when you're going to reopen. And it's going to be soon."

Matt sat back down. "Are you here to clean up the crime scene? I didn't call anybody."

"I can help with that. But that's not why I came. My name's Bethel. I knew Quentin. We went way back."

"I'm sorry, but he passed away."

"Yep. I helped with that, too."

"The clean up?" asked Matt.

"Sure," said Bethel. She looked at the stitches on his wrist. "I understand you've had a pretty rough time since he left. I want to help get things up and running again."

"Why would you want to do that?"

"You could say I have an investment in this place."

"Uncle Quent didn't mention that."

"How could he? He's dead."

This seemed like a scam. If she were a telemarketer he would have hung up on her already. Best just to hear her pitch and get her out of there as soon as possible.

"What kind of investment?" asked Matt.

"We can talk more about that later," she said. "First you're going to need to deal with them."

She pointed at the phone on his desk.

"The phone company?" asked Matt.

The phone rang.

At first he was startled, but then he realized this was all

part of the show. She probably sent a text to her partner to give him a call. Matt decided to play along.

He hit the speakerphone button and answered. "Hello? This is the Golden Delicious. I'm sorry but all of our sex workers are currently on vacation. Can I take a message?"

"Cute," said the voice on the phone.

Matt recognized the voice instantly. "Aunt Rose?"

"Hello, Matthew," she said.

Happiness and terror jockeyed for position under Matt's skin. The result was a long pause.

"How did you get this number?" he finally asked.

"It's on your tawdry website."

"I have a website?"

"Your brothel does."

Matt looked at Bethel who was just quietly listening. She shrugged and nodded her head.

"Do they know where I am?" he asked.

"Of course they know," said Aunt Rose. "They heard all about it. They're coming."

Fight-or-flight was kicking in again. This was definitely going to be flight. "I'm not going back with them."

"They're coming for the boy."

Epilogue

Adam and the Music Box

This is the story of Adam, the boy who could see between walls, and his journey along the forest path. If you would like to follow along on his adventures, please turn the page when you hear the cat say, *Meow meow.*

■ ■ ■

The day Adam first listened to the music box was the worst day of his life. He was only nine years old so he didn't have a lot of days to compare it with, but based on the amount of blood on the floor, this was definitely the worst so far.

The music box was made of wood. It didn't have much decoration on it, and it seemed pretty old. When Adam lifted the lid of the box it played an old tune. He didn't know all the words to the song, but he knew it was about longing for home and simpler days.

There was nothing simple about Adam's home.

Meow meow.

■ ■ ■

Adam's best friend was a cat. His name was Azrael, which was also the name given to the Angel of Death by some sects of Islam. In the Jewish Zohar, Azrael was called Azriel, instead. He commanded legions of heavenly angels. Christians tended to ignore Azrael, and that was just fine by him. Adam's Azrael was actually named after a cartoon cat that terrorized tiny, blue, Belgian creatures. But he didn't command, or battle, or preside over death. He mainly just napped and followed Adam around.

One day, Azrael followed Adam between the walls of their clubhouse. Adam was listening to his music box when all of a sudden, everything began to shake. Including Adam! He shook, and his eyes fluttered open and closed. He said things that didn't make sense. When Azrael rubbed up against Adam to see what was wrong, they both slipped between the walls.

Meow meow.

■ ■ ■

Adam was ready though. He had walked between the walls before. The first time it had been by accident, but this time he was *trying* to walk between them. He wanted to see if he could find his way back to the forest path that lead to a magical garden. He had seen the garden and the path in his dreams, but he figured out that when he had those dreams, he was actually awake. So this time, he thought about the path and he thought about the garden as he drew on the wall.

The pattern he drew was a new one. He had learned it from the man who had given him the music box. That man had gone to the magic garden, and Adam wanted to see if he could find it, too. But he didn't want to hurt anybody to get there. He just wanted to walk. So he let the music box play, and when the patterns on his wall looked like the stars in the sky, he started walking.

Meow meow.

■ ■ ■

Adam was a little afraid when he saw the forest path again. The last time he had stood on the trail, he had been frozen in place, and when he tried to talk, somebody else used his mouth to make words. This time he could walk, and touch the trees, and use his own mouth.

The first thing he said was, "Azrael! You came with me!"

"*Meow,*" said Azrael. He didn't really know what else to say.

"I'm glad you did," Adam admitted. "This forest can be scary, and I'm not really sure where I'm going."

"*Meow,*" said Azrael again. He was only a cat after all.

Adam's clubhouse looked different. The roof was covered with moss, and instead of being lit up with Christmas lights, it was surrounded by a swarm of fireflies winking in and out of existence. Outside the door a trail stretched off through the forest in two different directions.

He tried to remember what the garden had looked like. He remembered parts of it had looked pretend and parts of it had looked real. Sometimes, the real things would start to look pretend, and the pretend things would start to look real. The big tree in the center always looked real to him. So did the owl perched up in its branches.

As Adam thought about the owl, he heard a screech far off in the forest. It sounded more like an echo that had forgotten to fade away. He decided to follow the path toward the sound.

Meow meow.

■ ■ ■

The forest was dense and dark. Sometimes Adam thought he saw shadows moving among the trees. They reminded him of fables and fairy tales. In those stories, it was never safe to leave the forest path so Adam watched his feet carefully and made sure Azrael never wandered off too far.

Once he thought he heard a baby crying far off in the woods. And once he thought he saw his father waving to him and smiling. Adam knew these weren't real, though, and tried his best to ignore them as he hurried along.

The forest ended suddenly. He followed the path around a tree as large as his clubhouse. As he turned the corner, the trail opened up to a large clearing. Adam picked up Azrael and stood at the edge. All the trees bent back from the clearing as if they were trying get away.

They had found the magic garden, but the garden was dying.

Meow meow.

■ ■ ■

No owl greeted them as they stepped into the clearing.

The plants and trees that looked real were wilting. All their color was draining out of them, and their leaves littered the yellow grass below. The plants and trees that looked pretend were curled up on the ground like forgotten paper. They looked brittle and faded.

There was a dry stream winding through the garden that looked like a patchwork of cracked mud. A small pond still had some water left in it, but it smelled foul, like a dog that had just come in from the rain. There were no birds chirping or butterflies flitting about. Instead, there was a faint, continual sound of crunching and clicking. To Adam it sounded like bugs crawling and eating their way through a compost heap.

Even the great twisted oak tree looked like it was sagging under its own weight.

Meow meow.

■ ■ ■

Something moved under the oak tree. Adam was expecting the Woman in the Garden to step forward with her daughters. To call out a warning or a curse. To unleash her owl and try to take his other eye.

But there was no woman, and there was no owl.

Instead, a man was sitting under the tree, leaning back against it. He lifted his head. He looked old, but then most people looked old to Adam. The man also looked tired, as though he had been awake for a year. Adam's eyes widened. It was the man with the blade who could draw lines and patterns like he could. It was Foster.

When he spoke, his words didn't match his smile. "Have you come to destroy me?"

"No," said Adam. "I came to see if I could help the women you brought here. I came to take them home. Or at least away from this."

Meow meow.

■ ■ ■

Foster stood but was still using the tree for support. Adam set down Azrael. The cat's back was arched, and his tail looked like a bottle cleaner. He growled a low warning to Foster, but that hadn't helped a whole lot last time.

Foster smiled at the cat but made no move toward him. "They left with *her*," he said. "She took an acorn from the tree and left this place behind."

"Why?" asked Adam.

"She knew you would come," said Foster, "and that you would bring the Other."

"What other?" asked Adam. "My cat?"

Foster's smile faded, and he looked closely at Adam. "The one inside you who leaks out when you lose control. The one with wings and horns. She called it your familiar."

"If it exists, it hasn't helped me before," said Adam.

"You could have lost more than your eye that night," said Foster. "It pulled you away, out of the garden. Now I see it staring at me through that same eye."

Meow meow.

■ ■ ■

Adam looked at himself in the pond by the tree. The surface was still and reflected the angry-looking clouds in the sky. The Adam in the reflection wasn't wearing an eye patch. He looked back with two eyes. One was hazel, the same eye that stared back at him when he watched himself brush his teeth in the bathroom mirror. The other eye was milky-white but also seemed to glow with a faint blue light.

When Adam looked into that eye, he heard words echoing through his head. Some were in a language he understood and some sounded like Latin prayers. None of them were *his* words, and the words didn't make him feel safe.

Meow meow.

■ ■ ■

Adam turned back to the oak tree. A dry leaf fluttered to the ground and landed on a yellowed picture of a rose bush. Azrael swatted at the leaf, and it crumbled to dust. Foster was sitting under the tree again, his head bowed.

"Why don't you leave?" asked Adam.

Foster kept his head down. "Where would I go?"

"Someplace new," said Adam.

"I'm tired of walking the path," said Foster. "I think I'll stay here. Maybe I'll learn to grow things. Plant a garden of my own."

Adam turned to go, but then he stopped. "Maybe this will help." He held out the old wooden music box to Foster.

As Adam left the magic garden behind, he heard the old tune one last time. He knew he wasn't done walking the forest path.